THE LAST SCOOP

Also By R. G. Belsky

THE LAST SCOOP

A CLARE CARLSON MYSTERY

R.G. BELSKY

OCEANVIEW (PUBLISHING

SARASOTA, FLORIDA

ISBN 978-1-60809-357-1

Published in the United States of America by Oceanview Publishing

Sarasota, Florida

www.oceanviewpub.com

10 9 8 7 6 5 4 3 2 1

PRINTED IN THE UNITED STATES OF AMERICA

*"Murder is not about lust, and it's not about violence.
It's about possession. When you feel the last breath
of life coming out of the woman, you look into her eyes.
At that point, it's being God."*

—Serial killer Ted Bundy

"I know it's true . . . I saw it on TV."   —John Fogarty

For Laura Morgan

THE LAST SCOOP

PROLOGUE

The young woman on the bed saw only blackness. At first, she thought he must have blindfolded her. She could feel the ropes on her arms and legs that he'd used to restrain her to the bed. But she realized there was no blindfold. As her eyes adjusted to the lack of light in the room, she was able to make out a shadowy figure in there with her.

It was him.

He was watching her.

How long had he been there?

How long had she been there?

The figure moved quietly to the side of the bed now, took out a large knife, and placed the knife against the woman's throat.

She began to sob.

He took the knife away from her throat then and—for just a few seconds—it almost seemed like this was part of some kind of sex game. He stroked her hair and the side of her face gently. He leaned down and kissed her.

Then he raised the knife back in the air—and plunged it into the woman's chest.

Again . . . and again . . . and again . . . and again.

OPENING CREDITS

THE RULES ACCORDING TO CLARE

I AM A woman who deals in lies for a living.

There are all sorts of lies. Big lies. Little lies. The lies that people tell casually every day with little thought or remorse: fibbing about sticking to a diet, calling in sick for work to go to a ballgame, or fudging a few numbers on an income tax return. The bigger lies that politicians and real estate brokers and used car salesmen tell to get us to buy whatever they're selling. And then there are the lies so breathtaking in their scope and audaciousness that most of us could never fathom resorting to them no matter how desperate we were.

My job at Channel 10 News—the TV station where I work as the news director—is to catch people in their lies and expose these lies to the world. Of course, I make a lot of enemies that way. But I tell them, "Hey, if you don't want to see yourself on the evening news, then don't do it."

I've been thinking a lot about this topic these days. Lying, that is. It was Adolf Hitler who once famously said that the bigger the lie, the easier it was to tell. "People will believe a big lie sooner than a little one," Hitler boasted. I'm not sure I agree though. I believe it is sometimes the little lie, the insidious lie we might not even be aware of until it's too late, that can be the most dangerous and damaging and disturbing. Not only because it is so difficult to detect. But because once you find out a person has lied—no matter how small that lie is—you immediately begin to wonder what else they're not telling you the truth about. I mean, if someone lies about one thing that you know about, the odds are pretty good he or she is also lying about a lot of other stuff that you don't know. And so—before we even realize it—we find ourselves caught up in an endless cycle of dishonesty and deception.

A lie is a little bit like murder, I suppose. They say killing someone for the first time is extremely difficult because of all the moral and ethical and religious taboos that have been ingrained in us throughout our lives. The second time you kill is supposed to be easier. And then after that . . . well, murdering another human being becomes almost as casual as swatting a fly.

I guess that's the point I'm trying to make here.

About lying.

And about murder.

They both get easier the more you do them.

Not that I would have any firsthand knowledge of either one, of course. I've never murdered anyone. And I never lie. Maybe that's a residual effect of my work, being around people who lie so much. Maybe it's the moral values I grew up with and have held onto all of my life. Or maybe it's because I've seen up close all the damage and heartbreak and tragedy that lies—even the seemingly innocuous ones—can bring about in this world.

But the bottom line that you need to understand about me is I am all about the truth. I believe in the truth. I tell the truth myself at all times. I expose anyone who doesn't tell the truth. Yep, it's the truth, the whole truth and nothing but the truth for me. That's the credo I follow in my career as a journalist—and in my life, too—above everything else.

Clare Carlson has a lot of faults—believe me, you'll find that out about me soon enough—but lying is not one of them.

* * *

Now see what I just did there. I lied to you.

Because everyone lies. Including me. Nothing is what it seems to be in this life. And no one is either.

Well, almost no one.

There's only one person I've ever met who always told the truth—the hard, cold, absolute truth—no matter what the circumstances.

As far as I know, the man never told a lie in his entire life.

And yet, I didn't believe him the last time we talked.

Just before he died.

PART I

FAKE NEWS

CHAPTER 1

I WAS SITTING in my office at Channel 10 News, drinking black coffee and skimming through the morning papers when I saw the article about Marty Barlow.

It was a brief item about the murder of a man on an East Side New York City street. It identified the victim as Martin Barlow. It also said that Barlow was a retired journalist. It did not say Barlow was the first—and probably the best—newspaper editor I ever had.

The police reported that he'd died from a blow to the head. Apparently, from a solid object, although the object itself was never found. Cops first assumed it had been a mugging, but later backed off that a bit because his wallet wasn't taken. Instead, it just seemed—at least on the face of it—to be one of those crazy, senseless crimes that happen too often in New York City.

The article never mentioned Marty's age—he refused to ever tell it to anyone—but I figured he must be well up in his sixties by now. He was a frail-looking man. He had disheveled white hair, pasty-looking skin, and he couldn't have weighed more than 150 pounds. He always wore the same old wrinkled suit that looked like it had last been cleaned during the Reagan administration.

But more than twenty years ago, when I was starting out at a newspaper in New Jersey, Marty Barlow had helped me become the journalist that I am today. He was my editor, my mentor, and my friend.

Barlow was a grizzled old veteran even back then, and I soaked up every bit of knowledge and wisdom I could from him. He taught me how to cover police stories, political scandals, and human-interest features. "Never turn down an animal story," was one of his mantras. "People love animal stories!" But mostly, he taught me what a noble calling it was to be a newspaper reporter—and about all the integrity and responsibility that went with it. His favorite quotation was from an old Humphrey Bogart movie where Bogey played a managing editor talking about the job of being a newspaper reporter: "It may not be the oldest profession, but it's the best."

I moved on eventually to a bigger newspaper job in New York City where I had a career filled with pretty spectacular moments. I won a Pulitzer Prize by the time I was thirty, I scored a lot of other big exclusives and front-page stories for the paper, and became a big media star because of all that. Then the newspaper I worked for went out of business, and I moved into TV. After a few false starts there—mostly finding out that I wasn't very good as an on-air TV reporter—I wound up on the executive side of the business. First as a segment producer, then as an assignment editor, and now as news director of the whole Channel 10 operation. Along the way, I found the time to get married—and divorced—three different times, too.

Marty had helped me get through the highs and lows in my life—both professional and personal—over the years. He was always there for me. He always supported me and took my side in everything. Well, almost everything. Everything except the marriage stuff. Marty could never understand why I couldn't make my marriages work. "Why don't you find one man, the right man, and settle down with him for the rest of your life?" That's what Marty said he had done with his wife. "It's not that easy," I told him. "Sure it is," he said. "You make sure your marriage is as important to you as your job in the newsroom. Then the rest will take care of itself." It was good advice from Marty, even though I didn't always follow it.

Marty stayed on as editor of the same New Jersey paper where we'd met, doing the job he loved, until he was pushed into retirement a few years ago. At some point after that his wife died, and he came to live with his daughter in Manhattan. Even after he retired though, Marty became very active in local political and community events. He started a website that skewered local politicians and demanded more accountability/public disclosure in New York City government. Then he became a kind of local gadfly—showing up at town hall and council meetings to demand answers from politicians. That was Marty. Still looking for his next big scoop even after he retired.

We'd kept in touch and he was always asking me to meet him for coffee, but I hardly ever got around to it. Or to checking out any of the various news tips and leads he kept sending me. I never could find time for Marty Barlow anymore.

Until that last day when he showed up in my office.

* * *

"Hello, Marty, how are you doing?" I said. "Sorry I never got back to you on your calls and emails before. I've been busy covering a bunch of stuff."

"Yeah, probably a big, breaking Justin Bieber news story, huh?" Barlow said, without even attempting to hide the contempt in his voice.

I sighed. Marty Barlow was an old-fashioned journalist who believed the news media should cover serious topics like politics, schools, and government waste the way newspapers had traditionally done in the past. But now newspapers were dying off as people turned to the internet to give them instant news. And TV newscasts, including Channel 10 where I worked, focused even more these days on glitzy celebrity news, viral videos, and all the rest of the gimmicks known online as "traffic bait" in order to increase our all-important ratings and sales. Marty hated that. I wasn't wild about it either, but I had no choice in the rapidly changing journalistic landscape.

"This time the big story was Kim Kardashian," I said.

"You're kidding, right?"

"I'm kidding."

"Good."

"Actually, it was Khloe."

"My God, what happened to you, Clarissa? The Clarissa Carlson I remember cared passionately about the stories she covered. She wanted to make a difference in the world with her journalism. I miss that woman."

Fake news is what Marty called it. Yes, I know that term has a whole different meaning in today's political world. But Marty had been using it long before that. For Marty, *fake news* encompassed pretty much everything on TV news or in newspapers or on news websites today. He didn't just mean the celebrity news, either. He was contemptuous of the constant traffic reports, weather updates, lottery news, and all the rest of the things I did for a living. He complained that there was hardly any real journalism now. He was right. But the journalistic world had changed dramatically in recent years, even if Marty refused to change with it.

He sat down in a chair in front of my desk.

"So, Clarissa . . ."

"Clare."

"What?"

"My name is Clare, not Clarissa."

This was a ritual we had played out many times over the years. Yes, my full name is Clarissa Carlson, but I always use Clare. Have ever since I was a kid and decided how much I hated being called Clarissa. Everyone knew that. Friends, family, coworkers, even my ex-husbands never called me anything but Clare. Except for Marty. He insisted on calling me Clarissa. I never understood exactly why, but it had gone on for so long between us that it didn't seem worth bothering to ask anymore.

I figured he wasn't here for a social visit. That he came because he needed my help. Some big scoop he thought he was going to break, even though his days of breaking big scoops had long past. Marty always got very intense when he was working on a story, and this time he seemed even more intense than usual. I asked him what was going on.

"I'm working on a big story," he said. "The biggest story of my life. And it's all because I started taking a good look at one person."

I nodded and tried to think of an appropriate response.

"Who?" I asked.

It was the best I could come up with.

"Terri Hartwell."

"Hartwell?"

"Yes, the Manhattan district attorney."

I nodded again. Terri Hartwell was the darling of the New York City media and political world at the moment. She'd been a top-rated radio talk show host in New York for a number of years before she ran for the district attorney's job—and surprised political experts by unseating the incumbent. Since then, she'd aggressively gone after crime, corruption, and all sorts of entrenched special interests in the city. Which made her a lot of enemies, but also made her popular with the voters. She was even being touted now as a potential candidate for mayor.

"I started out thinking this was a story about building corruption. Illegal payoffs to politicians and authorities by wealthy New York City landlords. But now it's bigger than that. Much bigger. There's murder involved, too."

"Murder?"

"More than one murder. Maybe lots of them."

I nodded again. Pretty soon I was going to have to stop nodding and ask more than one-word questions.

"Who is being murdered? And what does any of this have to do with Terri Hartwell?"

Now I was rolling.

"I can't tell you any more details. Not yet. I'm still trying to figure it all out myself. But this is a sensational story. More sensational than any story I've ever covered. And I have to stop whatever is happening before it's too late!"

Marty was getting really agitated now, pounding on my desk for emphasis.

A lock of white hair had fallen over his forehead and his eyes were blazing. He frankly looked insane.

"Who's your source on all this, Marty?" I asked.

"I can't tell you my source, Clarissa. You know that."

"Is it a good source?"

"All of my sources are good!" he thundered at me.

He was right about that. All of Marty's sources were good. Or at least they always had been in the past. But I wasn't so sure how much I could trust them—or Marty himself—at this point. I didn't think he was lying. Not intentionally anyway. Marty never lied to anyone, most of all to me. But I did suspect his desperation to get back into journalism in some meaningful way—to prove he wasn't finished in the news business, no matter how much it had passed him by in recent years—had distorted his judgement and his connections with . . . well, reality.

"Will you help me? Give me a few days to get all the details together, and then I'll tell you everything. You're the head of a big news operation now. You have resources I don't at your disposal. Maybe we could work on this story together. You and me, Clarissa. Just like the old days."

Mostly because I didn't know what else to do, I told Marty I'd get back to him about it. I told him we'd get together for coffee—like he'd asked me to do so many times—to go over the details of his story and maybe reminisce a bit about old times, too. I told Marty I'd call him the next week and we'd meet up at the Sunrise Coffee Shop on the Upper East Side, which was his favorite place.

Except I never did meet Marty Barlow at the Sunrise Coffee Shop the next week.

Or any time after that.

I never got around to calling him back.

I thought about all that again now as I read the article about Marty Barlow's death. "Maybe we could work on this story together," Marty had said. "You and me, Clarissa. Just like the old days." I didn't have the heart to tell Marty those days were long over.

* * *

My boss was Jack Faron, the executive producer for the Channel 10 News. I went to see him now.

"Problem?" he asked when I walked in the door of his office.

"What makes you think I have a problem?"

"Because you never come to see me this early in the morning unless it's about a problem."

"My God, whatever happened to the simple courtesy of saying good morning to the people you work with? What is wrong with us as a society, Jack? Have we lost all civility in this day and age? Why can't you greet me one time with a cheerful: 'Good morning, Clare. How are you today?'"

"Good morning, Clare," Faron said. "How are you today?"

"Actually, I have a problem."

I showed him the short newspaper article about the death of Marty Barlow and told him about my relationship with Barlow.

"What do you think about us doing something on the news tonight about his murder?" I asked. "I feel like I owe him at least that much."

Faron made a face. "Not our kind of story, Clare. There's no celebrity or sensational angle, no pizzazz, no ratings of any kind there for us. I'm sorry your friend got killed. I understand he meant a lot to you. But that doesn't meet the criteria for getting a story about him on our newscast. You already knew that before you even came in here, didn't you?"

I did. I was feeling guilty because I'd let Marty down at the end. And I didn't need another thing to feel guilty about right now. Marty was like family to me. And I had no other family. Well, I did, but that was the other thing I was feeling so guilty about. I've screwed up a lot of things in my life.

"Kind of ironic, isn't it?" I said. "A guy like Marty devotes his life to the news business. And now, when he dies, he doesn't even rate a meaningful goodbye in what the news business has become today. It makes me sad. And yes, guilty, too, that I couldn't do more for him, after everything he did for me."

"He was an old man," Faron said. "He died. There's no story there."

CHAPTER 2

MARTY BARLOW HAD been found dead on the street by a dog walker on East 68th, between Park and Lexington—outside the address where he had been living with his daughter, Connie, and her family.

Earlier that day, he'd attended a local community board meeting. People at the meeting said he'd infuriated a lot of the attendees by making inflammatory accusations of malfeasance and corruption against several board officials. He'd also delivered a powerful diatribe about greedy landlords being protected by powerful political figures, some of the same things he'd been talking to me about in my office that day when he brought up the name of District Attorney Terri Hartwell. And he'd had several angry confrontations with people at the meeting. Cops questioned everyone there that day to see if one of those things might have led to the later violence against him. But that fizzled out along with other possible leads they pursued.

"This appears to be a mugging gone bad," a homicide investigator wrote in the police report I managed to get on the case. "There's been a number of muggings recently in that area. Barlow probably resisted so the mugger killed him. Then the mugger panicked—or maybe saw the dog walker approaching down the street—and fled without taking time to grab Barlow's wallet or any other possessions."

There were a few more details, but nothing that helped me understand what had happened. Of course, not all details of a murder are always included in a police report. To get every bit of information about a case like this, I needed to talk to the homicide investigator who wrote the report. Which was a problem for me.

The police report on Marty Barlow was written by my exhusband—well, one of my ex-husbands—Sam Markham. We'd had a bad encounter the last time I ran into him at a party. He'd drunkenly suggested we have sex together again. I pointed out to him that was not a good idea because 1) he was married to someone else now, 2) he had a new baby at home, and 3) I wasn't interested in having sex with him anymore. These seemed like compelling arguments to me, but he took the rejection badly and hadn't spoken to me since. This all happened quite a while ago. I wondered if he was still mad at me.

I looked out the window of my office. This was early June, and summer was only a few weeks away. But there was no sun out there today. It was raining. Raining hard, turning the intersections into big puddles. My umbrella was home in my closet. If I went out now, I'd get drenched. It would be easier to call Sam to ask for more information. But I knew I had a better chance of getting what I needed if I did it in person. I sighed and made my way over to the precinct where he worked.

By the time I got there, my hair was matted down from the rain, and I was dripping all over his desk.

"My God, just what I don't need in my life today," Sam said. "My batshit-crazy ex-wife showing up to make my life a complete nightmare again. What the hell do you want, Clare? And by the way, you look terrible. Like a wet rat or something."

Yep, he was still mad at me.

"It's raining out," I said, "and I forget my umbrella. Listen, I came over here to help you on a crime."

Sam leaned back in his chair and looked over at a detective sitting at the next desk.

"Jeez, isn't that lucky for us? I was saying to Larry here how I wished some hotshot TV journalist would come by and help us out today. Someone really smart. Someone like my ex-wife. Wasn't I saying that, Larry?"

The other detective smiled.

"She doesn't look so smart to me," he said. "She's not even smart enough to come in out of the rain."

They both laughed loudly.

I ignored that and asked him about the police report he'd filed on Marty's murder.

"Like I said in the report, I figure it was a robbery that went wrong."

"What about the murder weapon—whatever the killer used to hit him with—the blow to the head?"

"Never been found."

"I wonder why not?"

"The weapon could have been something small the mugger kept in his pocket for attacking people. Or even a rock or a tree branch. Maybe he took it with him when he fled, maybe he dumped it somewhere along the way. But we can't find it."

"What else?"

"Nothing else. Hopefully, we catch this guy mugging someone else and we're able to link him with Barlow's murder."

"So that's all there is to the investigation?"

"It's a pretty simple random murder case, Clare. Not a lot of options to pursue."

I told him how Marty had said he was pursuing a big story about city corruption and possibly even murder before he died. Sam rolled his eyes. Not a surprise—I had no real details.

"And you figure maybe someone killed him to shut him up?"

"It's a possibility."

Sam shook his head no. "We get a lot of people—especially crazy old people like Barlow—who come in here with some secret lead or conspiracy information about something they've solved. A few months ago, a guy claimed he knew who killed Jimmy Hoffa and that he could lead us to where the body was buried in New Jersey. We trekked out there with some Jersey troopers to dig up the area. Needless to say, the Jimmy Hoffa case remains unsolved and the whereabouts of the body unknown. Oh, the guy later insisted the New Jersey authorities must have been in on the cover-up and moved the body. These people see secrets and conspiracies everywhere. From what I can tell, Martin Barlow was a lot like that. Sad to see, but people like Barlow get confused and irrational and disoriented when they get old."

"He was still in his sixties," I pointed out. "Not that old."

"I don't mean just his age."

"What then?"

"The dementia."

"Marty Barlow suffered from dementia?"

"From what I understand. That explains a lot about his behavior. Maybe that even played some role in putting him into the circumstances where he wound up getting murdered. I had a grandfather with dementia. It's a nasty business to watch somebody falling apart mentally like that."

"Who told you he had dementia?"

"His family. Have you talked to them?"

"I'm going there next."

*   *   *

"Dad came to live with us here after my mom passed away," Marty's daughter, Connie, told me. "He couldn't live alone in that house in New Jersey anymore. And he refused to go into any kind of assisted living facility. We—well, I—didn't know what else to do."

She sat next to her husband on a couch in the living room of the brownstone they owned on East 68th Street. Their daughter—who looked to be in her early twenties—was there, too. Connie thanked me—without much apparent emotion, almost mechanically—for stopping by and talked about the last few years of her father's life.

"I'd warned him about the dangers of a man his age being out alone on the street at night. But you know my dad . . . he was stubborn."

"Bull-headed was more like it," her husband said. "He shouldn't have been living here. I told him he belonged down in Florida in one of those retirement places. I even told him I'd pay whatever it took to get him a place there. But he said he wasn't going to sit around playing shuffleboard and checkers. So he wound up getting himself killed."

The husband's name was Thomas Wincott, and he said he was the CEO of some big company based in Manhattan. He must have been pretty successful at it. They owned the entire townhouse where we were sitting in a historic Upper East Side neighborhood.

Wincott acted more annoyed by the inconvenience of Marty's death than upset about it. His wife seemed almost as stoic. She never cried or showed any emotion about losing her father. The young woman—the daughter, whose name was Michelle—

fidgeted as they talked, looking down at her watch several times. I had a feeling she wasn't comfortable in the house and was only here now because of her grandfather's murder.

"I understand Marty had been diagnosed with dementia," I said.

"Yeah, yeah," Thomas Wincott muttered, "he had dementia."

"When did the doctor tell him—or you—about his dementia?"

"He was never actually diagnosed with it," Connie said. "Dad hated to go to doctors. You probably knew that, Ms. Carlson. We tried to convince him to see someone, but he refused. He said he was okay. That there was nothing wrong with his mind."

"You don't know for certain that he had dementia?"

"Well, he was acting crazy all the time," her husband said. "So he must have had dementia or something like it."

I thought about my last meeting with Marty. I didn't see any signs of dementia or other mental deterioration. Oh, he was acting crazy—maybe crazier than normal for him—but he'd always acted crazy. Even back in the days when we were working together at the New Jersey paper. Crazy was part of the package you got with Marty. But it was always a good kind of crazy. Of course, I hadn't seen him in a long time except for that one meeting—and these people lived with him every day. So maybe they knew more than I did about his mental state at the end.

"I'm sorry the old man died," Thomas Wincott was saying now. "But, like I told my wife, you have losses and profits in life, the same as in business. You absorb the losses and move on to make more profits. You don't waste time crying about the things you lost. I mean the man was almost seventy . . ."

Michelle Wincott stood up at this point and excused herself, saying she needed to get a glass of water. I said that I was thirsty, too, and followed her into the kitchen.

"I'm sorry about your grandfather," I told her when we were alone.

"He was a good man," she said. "I'm going to miss him. But, to hear my father talk, it's like a damn spreadsheet problem instead of losing a member of the family."

I nodded. "What do you do?" I asked.

"I'm an actress."

"No kidding? Anything I might know?"

"Probably not. I'm making some headway though. A few off-off-off Broadway plays. I'm auditioning for a lot of movie roles and TV commercials, too."

"Sounds like interesting work."

"Try telling that to my father."

"He doesn't approve?"

"He wants me to get an MBA and go into the business world. So I can make a lot of money. Like him. He says I'm wasting my life away trying to be something so impractical as an actress. Me and my father, we haven't gotten along well since I told him I wasn't going to follow in his tradition of chasing the almighty dollar."

"What about Marty?" I asked. "How did he feel about you trying to make it in show business?"

She smiled.

"He encouraged me. He was the only one here who did. He told me I should follow my dream. He said that's what he'd done his whole life—and was still doing. Being a newspaperman. Because that's what he loved."

"That sounds like Marty. He always talked about being a journalist like it was a noble profession. He instilled that in me, too. He taught me so much. He meant an awful lot to me and my career."

"You know, he talked to me about you," she said. "He told me about giving you your first job at a newspaper. He was proud of you."

That made me feel good, but sad, too. Sad that I was never able to find the time for him later.

"My father doesn't understand me," Michelle Wincott said. "And my mother listens to everything my father says. To hell with both of them. I don't care what they think. They're waiting for me to fail. Everyone's waiting for me to fail. No one has ever supported me in this dream."

"Except your grandfather."

"Yes, he was okay." Her eyes glistened with tears. "Christ, I'll miss him."

It was the first real emotion I'd seen from anyone in that house.

Before I left, I asked Marty's daughter, Connie, if I could see the room there where he lived. She led me to one of the upstairs bedrooms. I wasn't sure why I went there or what I hoped to find. But I looked around anyway.

Marty always took a lot of notes for his stories. When I knew him back in New Jersey, he kept them all—pages after pages—in a voluminous notebook. I saw some notebooks in a drawer. There was also a big filing cabinet with a lot of papers and newspaper clippings he'd collected. But Marty had apparently kept up with the journalistic times. His daughter told me that he typed a lot of his things into a laptop computer. I asked her if I could take Marty's computer with me back to the Channel 10 office to look through his files. I was curious. I figured whatever Marty was working on those last few days would most likely be on his computer. She shrugged and said sure. I don't think she cared one way or another.

When we got back to the living room, Thomas Wincott was on the phone. He was talking animatedly about making a campaign finance donation. He was clearly in full business mode. I guess Wincott's mourning process for his dead father-in-law was now officially over.

"Goddammit!" he muttered when he finally hung up the phone. "I hate politics!"

"Politics?" I asked.

"Yes, I'm involved in this big political negotiation right now. It's been so stressful and time-consuming and aggravating."

"I guess Marty's death happened at an awfully inconvenient time for you, huh?"

"It sure did."

If Wincott had any idea at all how insensitive that sounded, he didn't show it.

"I don't quite understand though," I said, simply trying to make conversation before I said my goodbyes to Marty 's family. "Why are you involved in politics? I thought you said you were the CEO of a company. What does that have to do with politics anyway?"

A lot of times a journalist gets a break on a big story because he or she cleverly figures out a brilliant question to ask.

But other times, it' s dumb luck to ask the right question.

That's what happened to me this time.

"Everything. I own and manage a lot of buildings around town. The best way to get anything done in New York City real estate is to have politicians on your side. The higher the better. They grease the wheels of the bureaucracy for you. The only thing is—to get them to do that—you have to grease them, too." He laughed. "Which means contributing to their campaign fund. But what the hell, if things work out right, this will all be worth it."

"Who's the politician?"

"Terri Hartwell," he said. "She's going to run for mayor, you know. And I'm jumping on her bandwagon big-time."

CHAPTER 3

I WAS STILL trying to sort everything out when I met my friend Janet Wood for drinks that night. About Marty. But about something else going on in my life right now, too. I had a lot on my mind at the moment.

"Let me ask you a hypothetical question," I said to Janet.

"Sure."

"What kind of a mother do you think I'd make?"

She stared at me.

"Are you pregnant, Clare?"

"God, no."

"Thinking about adopting?"

"Not really."

"Then why ask me a question like that?"

"It's a perfectly reasonable question. You're a mother. You're raising two beautiful daughters. You have a successful career as a lawyer. And, as far as I can tell, you have a happy marriage, too. I'm asking if you think I could ever balance my career and motherhood the way you do. Would I be a good or rotten mother, Janet?"

"But you don't have a child and, from what you say, no plans to do so."

"Hence, my use of the word *hypothetical* to describe the question."

Janet and I were sitting at the outside bar of a restaurant on East 29th Street, above the East River Drive and the East River running alongside that. It was a beautiful summer night, and we could see all the cars on the highway along with boats making their way up and down the river. Across the water on the other side were the lights of Brooklyn and Queens; north and south was the splendor of Manhattan.

Janet was drinking a daiquiri, which she always did when we went out. She was drinking it very slowly the way she always did. Janet always drank two daiquiris. Never more, never less. She was a very precise person. I couldn't imagine her ever being drunk or out of control in any way.

Me, I was starting on my third Corona of the night. I did think about ordering something a bit more exotic or special to go with the terrific view. I'd even asked our waiter for the special drink menu to peruse. But, in the end, I went for the beer. I like beer. I took a slice of lime off the top of the bottle, squeezed it into the beer, and took a big gulp.

"What's going on with you anyway?" Janet asked me now.

"What do you mean?"

"You seem different lately."

"Different how?"

"I don't know, different. Quieter. More subdued. Not so many wisecracks as usual from you tonight."

"Sorry to disappoint you, but I am working on some new material."

"It's like you're preoccupied with something. And now you hit me out of the blue with this motherhood stuff."

"I simply asked you a question about being a mother, Janet. That's all. Don't make a big deal out of it.

Janet sighed and took a drink of her daiquiri. She knew me well enough to know that I wasn't telling her everything. But she also knew me well enough to know not to push me for more at that moment. We'd been friends for a long time, me and Janet. It's hard to fool people like that.

"Look, Clare, you've never lived successfully with anyone else in your life. You've been married three times, but none of them lasted long. You've always been totally preoccupied with your job to the exclusion of nearly everything else in your life. You're kind of selfish, I suppose, never caring about anyone but you and your own life. As for a child, I've never seen you relate outwardly to children or show any apparent interest in ever raising one."

"I get it. You think I'd make a lousy mother."

"Not so fast. No one is truly qualified to be a mother, no one knows how it's going to turn out. Not at the beginning anyway. I certainly didn't with Karen and Kim. You learn about yourself along the way in motherhood. It just happens. That's what would happen to you, if you ever take that step. You're a good person, Clare. You'd make a good mother in the end, no matter what you think. If that's what you ever decide you want to do. Did I answer your question?"

I finished my Corona and ordered another. Then I looked out at the boats passing by us on the East River. I thought about how nice it would be to be on one of them right now. Maybe sailing out of New York Harbor all the way up the New England coast. Cape Cod. Maine. Maybe all the way to Canada. Some place where I could forget about everything for a while. It was a nice dream. But that's all it was, a dream. I'd probably get seasick out there.

I told Janet at some point about Marty Barlow. About the questions I had over his death. About the strange connection between Terri Hartwell and his son-in-law. About how he'd come to me for help on a story he was working on and I never got back to him. About how badly I felt about that.

"I remember you telling me about him," Janet said. "He was important in helping you start your career."

"Maybe the most important influence I ever had as a young journalist. I owed everything to him."

"So it makes sense that his murder would shake you up so badly."

"I suppose."

"Maybe that's why you've seemed so different, so preoccupied. It's because of Marty Barlow's death. It was such a shock—and you have so many regrets about that last meeting you had with him—that it's on your mind all the time."

Except it wasn't Marty Barlow I was thinking about right now.

It was the conversation we'd just had about motherhood.

That was the most important thing on my mind—even more than Marty Barlow. You see, I'd been a mother once, a long time ago. I had a beautiful daughter. Then I lost her. Now I'd found her again. I even met her. So I have a daughter, but I don't have a daughter. I realize that probably doesn't make sense to anyone, but then, it doesn't make much sense to me, either.

Which is why I couldn't tell the truth about my daughter to anyone—even my best friend, Janet.

"You're right, it's Marty Barlow's death," I told Janet. "That's what's been bothering me so much."

CHAPTER 4

ONE OF THE first rules of journalism Marty ever taught me was that every news story should answer the five Ws—who, what, where, when, and why. I knew the answers to the first four about Marty's death—but not the "why"? What if it wasn't a random mugging, as the police believed? That meant he was killed for another reason.

What was it? Well, Marty had come to me and said he was working on a story about Terri Hartwell. He said it had started out about building corruption and illegal payoffs, but might also involve murder.

Now I find out that Thomas Wincott, his son-in-law, is a major building owner in New York City.

And also, a key campaign money supporter of Hartwell's upcoming bid to be mayor.

Was all that a coincidence?

I was still thinking about the best way to pursue all this the next day at the Channel 10 news meeting. We held two of them a day. One in the morning, then again in the afternoon a little before the 6 p.m. newscast. I ran both meetings, and they were my favorite part of the day. I got to forget about advertising campaigns, marketing ideas, ratings books, and all the other annoying parts of my job, and instead, concentrate on the one thing I care about the most—the news.

Basically, the meeting consisted of everyone talking about a lot of stories happening that day and then us—well, mostly me—narrowing it down to the handful that would make it on the air. There's never a shortage of news stories to choose from, not in New York City. A lot of stuff is always happening here.

The big story today was about a call-girl ring that had been found operating a block away from police headquarters. One of the girls had come forward to claim they had "serviced" many police brass in return for being allowed to operate freely in downtown Manhattan. The police commissioner called a press conference to say he had known nothing about the rampant prostitution happening right next door to him. Which either made him a liar or a very stupid police commissioner. It was a helluva story that had exploded in the tabloid papers, on TV news, and all over the internet.

"Someone's already posted a video that went viral with a GIF of the police commissioner with hands over his eyes, ears, and mouth, saying, 'Hear no evil, see no evil, speak no evil,'" Maggie Lang, my assignment editor and top deputy, said.

"I'll bet he's hoping there's a 'happy ending' to this," quipped Brett Wolff, one of the Channel 10 co-anchors. "One way or another . . ."

"Yep, he's going to have to 'beat off' the critics over this scandal," chimed in Dani Blaine, the other co-anchor.

"Oh, my God, this is all so 'whore-iffic,'" someone said with a laugh.

"Okay," I told everyone, "we'll go big with it all at the top of the newscast. Excerpts from the commissioner's press conference. Clips of the interview with the call girl. Reaction from city leaders. Flashbacks to other big sex scandals. But no jokes. No bad puns on this. Let's play it straight. The story is funny enough on its own without any of that."

The rest of the news was the usual stuff. A train derailment that had snarled morning traffic, even though no one was badly hurt. A confrontation between the Board of Education and the teachers' union over a possible school strike. Some crime stories. There was an early summer heat wave headed for the city. And the Yankees were eyeing a trade for another big slugger to add to their lineup. I looked through all of the options, ran through the order we'd put them on air, and added a few comments about other stuff we should be following.

At the end of the meeting, I finally brought up the thing that had been on my mind.

"I'd like to find out more about Terri Hartwell, our district attorney and potential future mayor," I said. "Also, a man named Thomas Wincott, who owns a lot of real estate around town. I want to know about the relationship—or any connection—the two of them have together. Let's check it out—public records, sources, whatever you can find."

"Why?" Maggie asked, as I knew she would.

"I have this thirst for knowledge, Maggie."

"Seriously, why do you suddenly care about Terri Hartwell and this Wincott guy?"

"I think there might be a story there."

"What kind of story?"

"I'm not sure yet. That's what I'm trying to find out."

After the meeting was over, I had another big issue to deal with. Brett Wolff and Dani Blaine, our co-anchors. They both wanted to talk to me in my office privately. I wasn't sure why, but I figured the conversation would not go well. I was right.

"Brett and I want to be totally transparent—completely up front with everyone—about our personal relationship," Dani said once we closed the door.

"You have a personal relationship?" I asked.

"I'm in love with Brett," she said.

"And I'm in love with Dani," Brett said.

They smiled at each other, reached over, and held hands. It was a very touching moment. Except for one thing. They'd been having this on-again, off-again personal relationship in the office for quite a while now. I was having trouble keeping up with it all.

"Didn't you want to file a sexual harassment charge against Brett the last time we talked about this, Dani?" I asked. "And, Brett, you accused Dani of stalking and harassing you."

"That was before," they both said, almost in unison.

"Before what?"

"Before Brett left his wife for me," Dani said.

"You left your wife?" I asked Brett.

"Yes, I plan to tell my wife I'm leaving her for Dani."

Okay, I thought to myself. This might work out well for us at the station. Sure, there'd be a lot of sensational publicity about the sexual relationship between these two on-air news stars. But publicity is good for ratings. Everyone's going to want to tune in to see them interacting together on the air. I remembered when the co-anchors on MSNBC's morning show, Joe Scarborough and Mika Brzezinski, had formally announced they were a couple. Hell, you couldn't buy that kind of free publicity. But then, even before I could get too excited about all this, it began to fall apart.

"What do you mean you're *planning* to tell your wife that you're leaving her?" Dani asked Brett.

"I told you that I would," he said.

"No, you said that you had told your wife."

"Don't make a big thing about the wording."

"Have you told her yet?"

"I'm going to, Dani. I have to wait for the right moment."

"And when would that be? Sometime before we get married, I hope? Or am I going to look over in bed on our wedding night and see her sleeping there with us?"

It very quickly turned into a screaming match between the two of them.

I put my fingers in my ears and waited until they finally stopped.

"Just let me know the sleeping arrangements as soon as you figure them out," I said.

*　　*　　*

The information I got back about Terri Hartwell was pretty much what I expected.

She was forty-six years old, married to a pharmaceutical executive, and had two children—a boy, fourteen, and a girl, twelve. She'd started out her career as a consumer lawyer, representing customers against big corporations employing questionable business practices. That had gotten her a lot of media attention. She was attractive, personable, and smart—so she soon began making appearances on TV news shows as a guest commentator.

At some point, she got herself a talk radio show, which she did as a part-time gig in addition to her work as a consumer attorney. But pretty soon the radio show became a full-time job. Hartwell was outspoken, opinionated, and—most importantly of all—extremely popular with the listeners. Her ratings soared until she became one of the most popular New York political voices around.

A few years ago, she decided to go into politics by running for—and winning—the district attorney's job. Since then, she'd put a lot of people in jail. Many of them violent street felons, but also white-collar criminals, big mob bosses, and other powerful forces in the city who had never been touched by law enforcement in the past. She sure seemed like someone who was on the right side of the war against corruption. But was she really? Or had Marty found out something about her that might torpedo her rising political career?

There wasn't nearly as much about Wincott, but some of it was intriguing. His company owned a number of commercial and residential buildings in the city, and he had become extremely wealthy as a landlord. Along the way though, there'd been a controversy. He was one of several business real estate owners accused in the past of using strong-arm tactics to force out longtime residents in order to get higher rents. There were also questions about whether he'd received preferential treatment in his dealings with city officials, unions, and political leaders for his buildings. No one specifically mentioned payoffs, but that was the implication. And many of his commercial tenants had unsavory underworld reputations, which had put them in trouble with the law before. All in all, it seemed like Thomas Wincott—like many rich real estate people in New York City—sure had things to hide.

I'd left Marty's laptop computer in a drawer of my desk, but I hadn't had time to check through it yet. I opened the computer now and began reading through Marty's files. Marty had been interested in a lot of stories. Neighborhood crime. Community board rezoning. Political corruption. Police malfeasance. He'd even managed to get the city to fix a broken traffic light where schoolkids crossed.

There was a link to Marty's website where he had written news stories about a lot of these things. I read through some of the stories. They were crisp, well written, and hard hitting. Whether or not he was suffering from dementia, Marty hadn't lost any of his journalistic skills. There was also a link to another website, but I couldn't access that one. It was password protected. And there was no option to try to set up a password of my own. The subject line for the file simply said: "The Wanderer." I wondered what that was all about.

But the most recent file did seem relevant. It was a list of building addresses. Eight locations scattered throughout Manhattan. Marty had added notes along with each building—detailing various illegal activities like prostitution, gambling, drug dealing, extortion, and rent gouging that he apparently believed were happening at these spots. I looked up all the addresses of the buildings online, but couldn't find out anything about who owned them. Except I knew his son-in-law, Thomas Wincott, did own a lot of real estate in the city.

I searched through the rest of the stuff I could find on Marty's computer. Much of it was more of the same kinds of things he'd been writing about since moving to New York—schools, government corruption, zoning laws. But then I found something different. A recent story he'd saved. Not a story he'd worked on—or even about New York. It was from a newspaper in Indiana, the *Fort Wayne Journal Gazette*, and it had been published a few months earlier. I read it:

30 YEARS LATER, THE MURDER OF BECKY BLUSO REMAINS A BAFFLING MYSTERY TO POLICE

By Eileen Nagle
Journal Gazette Crime Reporter

On a warm summer day in 1990, a pretty high school cheerleader, Becky Bluso, was found brutally stabbed to death in the bedroom of her own home in the quiet town of Eckersville, Indiana.

Today police are no closer than they were back then to solving the baffling crime.

"We've had leads, we've had new evidence emerge, we've had some suspects show up on the radar," Eckersville Police Chief Jeff Parkman told the *Journal Gazette*. "But none of it has panned out. We're not giving up though.

"I realize it happened a long time ago, but this is a crime that still doesn't make sense. A teenaged girl is horribly murdered in her bedroom in the middle of the day in a quiet, crime-free neighborhood. I want to find out who killed her and why and how.

"Somebody out there knows something. We need them to come forward and help us with information. We need to find out who stole this young girl's life away from her before she even had a chance to live it. If anyone knows anything about the murder of Becky Bluso after all these years, please come forward now and contact us in the Eckersville Police Department."

The article then went on with details on the long-ago crime itself. It was all interesting enough. But I had no idea why Marty would care about a murder that happened six hundred miles away after all these years.

There was nothing I could find on his computer about Terri Hartwell or the DA's office or Thomas Wincott. Maybe Marty was afraid his son-in-law would look at the computer. Maybe that information was in the password-protected file. Or maybe he just ran out of time.

In the end, the only thing that seemed important here was the list of eight building addresses.

Did these eight buildings belong to Thomas Wincott?

Was Marty investigating his own son-in-law's business?

From what I knew about Thomas Wincott—and the relationship between the two of them—there would have been something especially satisfying for Marty in that.

CHAPTER 5

I'm a reporter at heart. Always have been, always will be. So, instead of waiting until the next day and assigning someone to check out the buildings on Marty's list, I decided to do it myself that night after I left work. I talked to tenants and business owners and other people at each spot. Many of them remembered Marty being there. An elderly man writing down notes. Asking a lot of questions about the buildings and the businesses.

The first spot I went to was a tenement on the Lower East Side. The building was very run down, but all the ones around it were new and fancy. It was a part of the city where a lot of expensive co-ops had been built for wealthy New Yorkers in recent years. The people who lived there told me a young child had died not long ago after falling down an elevator shaft. The elevator had been broken for months. But no one ever responded to their pleas to fix it—even though it was considered dangerous. The boy's death hadn't changed that. Everyone believed the owners of the building were trying to force them all out in order to raze the place and build expensive new apartments.

They said Marty had talked to a lot of people there about the boy's death and the unsafe condition of the abandoned elevator, promising he would get action by the city to help them.

The next place I went to was in Chelsea. This one housed a thriving pizza parlor with long lines and cars double-parked on the street outside. Neighbors said that the reason it was so popular was because it was run by the mob—who had forced all of the small pizza places in the area out of business to reduce competition. Complaints about the double-parked cars on the streets went unheeded, too, they said. The authorities were looking the other way and letting the mob pizza business run without interference.

Another building housed what was supposed to be a plumbing contractor business. Except the company never actually seemed to do any plumbing. Instead, people in the neighborhood said it was a front for an illegal gambling operation where big-money bets were placed on horse races, football games, boxing matches, and all sorts of other events.

The last spot I went to—a warehouse-type building on East 23rd—had a kinky house of prostitution, masquerading as a massage and therapy center, located on the ground floor. Except it wasn't offering sex. At least not in the traditional way. This was a sex dungeon that provided bondage, spanking, and other such activities for their clients.

"We get lots of old guys here," said Rebecca Crawley, the woman who ran the place. "Men who still want to live out their fantasies like this with young girls even though they're pretty well up in years. So, we provide them with . . . well, our unique services . . . for relaxation and enjoyment."

I wondered for a second if Marty had turned into a dirty old man in his senior years. I should have known better. With Marty, it was always about business. The business of getting a story.

"He wasn't interested in any of that," Crawley said. "He wanted to ask me questions about how long we'd been here, if we had any troubles with the landlord or city officials or the police. Said he was a journalist covering stories in the neighborhood. Truth is, he was kind of endearing. So intense and so determined with his questions. I don't know if I helped him much. But I liked him."

"When was he here?" I asked.

"The first time was several weeks ago."

"First time?"

"Yes. Then he showed up again. The second time was not that long ago . . . last Monday night, I think."

That was the same night Marty was murdered.

"Do you remember anything unusual about that last night he was here?"

"As a matter of fact, he did seem strange. The first time he was very businesslike, as I said. I mean, we specialize in all kinds of kinky stuff here. There're guys who want to be spanked, tied up, or dressed like French maids or babies and the like. In addition, there's all sorts of bondage and torture devices lying around here. None of that bothered him. He asked his questions and left. But the second time he seemed . . . well, rattled or upset. Like something was wrong."

"What do you think was wrong?"

"I have no idea."

*   *   *

There were two men waiting for me when I came out of the building. One of them was a building security guard. The other one was dressed in street clothes. He was a big guy; he seemed to be the one in charge.

"What were you doing in there?" he asked in a gravelly voice, pointing to the place I'd just left.

I froze in my tracks. I didn't like this. It was late, it was dark, and I was alone, confronted by two strange men. Sure, I was scared. Damn scared. But I didn't want to let these two know that. I tried to cover up my fear with bravado and said, "Just looking for a way to augment my income with a little wholesome work in the sex industry."

"Aren't you kind of old to work in a place like this?"

"I'd probably look a lot better to you once I was dressed in leather and spike-heeled boots."

"C'mon, all those women are barely twenty-one up there."

"Haven't you heard? Forty is the new twenty."

Nobody laughed. Nobody even smiled.

"You've been asking questions there and at a bunch of other buildings around town," the big guy with the gravelly voice said. "Why?"

I decided to forgo the bravado and get the hell out of there. I started to try to walk away. The security guy grabbed my arm and stopped me. I saw now he was carrying a gun in a holster on his side. He had one hand on my arm and his other hand on the gun. He looked at the big guy and waited for his next order. This was escalating quickly. I decided there was no reason not to tell them the truth at this point—or at least part of the truth.

"My name is Clare Carlson, and I'm a journalist for Channel 10 News. That's why I've been asking questions."

"What kind of questions?"

"Did you ever hear of a man named Martin Barlow?"

"Who's Martin Harlow?"

"It's Barlow."

"Okay, whatever . . ."

"Martin Barlow was murdered a few nights ago. He visited this building beforehand. I'm trying to find out if that might be connected in any way to his death. So I'm simply exercising my First Amendment rights as a reporter to acquire information. I'm sure you understand."

The security man looked over again at the big guy. The big guy shrugged. Then they both glared at me.

I was pretty sure they didn't understand.

"Look," the big guy said to me, "no one here knows anything about this Martin . . . what was his name again?"

"Barlow."

It didn't seem like that hard a name to remember.

"No one knows anything about him here. Or any murder. Or anything else. So the best idea is for you to get out of here now and never come back. That would be a very wise course of action."

"I was thinking the same thing myself."

"There's no story here for you."

"None whatsoever," I agreed.

*   *   *

I went back to the Channel 10 offices and thought about what had happened. I still didn't know exactly what Marty was working on before he died, but I'd sure upset somebody when I went to those buildings asking questions. What did they have to do with Marty's death?

I checked the city building records and still couldn't find a direct connection between Wincott and any of the eight buildings, which surprised me. But then I hadn't figured out who actually owned them. All of the buildings were listed as being managed by a company called Big M Realty Corp. The only address I could find for them was a post office box where the rent checks were mailed. No one I talked to knew anything about Big M Realty Corp. or who they were or where they were located. Or, if they did, they weren't telling me.

I had no idea how any of the facts I'd uncovered fit together. But that's what I did as a journalist. I gathered facts and followed those facts wherever they led me. I'd done that on every story I'd ever worked on. Marty taught me how to do that a long time ago. It was the least I could do now for Marty on his own story.

CHAPTER 6

"I HAVE AN announcement to make about myself," I said at the morning news meeting.

"You're getting married again?" one editor said.

I sighed.

"No, I'm not getting married."

"Are you getting divorced again then?" another editor asked.

"How can she get divorced before she gets married?"

"Well, her marriages are so short maybe she decided to skip that in-between step and go right to the divorce."

Everyone laughed. My marital status—or lack of it, at the moment—was a constant source of amusement in the newsroom.

"I'm going back on the air to personally cover a story," I told them.

"My God, that sounds like a bigger disaster than any of your marriages," someone said.

More laughter.

"What's the story?" asked Maggie, always the pragmatist.

"The murder of an elderly man named Martin Barlow on the streets of New York a few nights ago. The police think it was a random robbery that went bad. But Barlow was an old friend of mine, and so I want to look into it further. I think there's more to this story than a simple robbery. A lot more."

"Like what?" one of the people in the room said.

"I'm not sure yet."

I believed there was a big story here—though I wasn't sure what it was yet. I also believed that going public with what I did know might break more information open. And I knew, too, that Jack Faron—who I'm pretty sure wouldn't have allowed me to do this—was away at a business meeting on the West Coast. These factors were not necessarily listed in their order of importance.

When the meeting was over, Maggie asked if she could talk to me alone. We went into my office.

"You disapprove of me going on air myself to do this story?" I asked.

"Not at all."

"Really?"

"Why would I disapprove?"

"I don't know . . . this kinda seems like a disapproval situation. How come you're on board with it?"

"Do you remember Dora Gayle?"

I sure did remember Dora Gayle. The previous year, a homeless woman was found dead in a seemingly meaningless murder that no one else in the media was interested in covering. But Maggie convinced me that we should do it. "You never know where a story is going to lead—any story no matter how insignificant it appears at first" was her quote to me at the time. Well, actually, it was my quote. One I'd used in the newsroom many times. But Maggie threw it back at me to convince me to cover the Dora Gayle murder, which turned out to be a sensational story involving a number of prominent New Yorkers before it was over.

"There's only one problem with you doing this, Clare."

"Okay, what's your problem?"

"It's not my problem. It's your problem. Jack Faron."

She was right. I knew Faron would go ballistic when he found out I was doing this without telling him. But I had a plan to handle that. Well, sort of a plan. I'd break the story wide open before Faron got back. He'd find out I pulled off this big exclusive, he'd praise me for my initiative and give me a big raise. Or maybe not.

I explained this game plan to Maggie. She looked dubious.

"Faron's going to find out before he gets back here, Clare."

"Who's going to tell him?"

"You're going on the air with it tonight, remember?"

"Oh, right."

I had to admit it wasn't a perfect plan.

I told Maggie to cancel all my appointments for the rest of the day so I could concentrate on getting the Martin Barlow story ready to put on the air for the 6 p.m. newscast.

"Including Gary Weddle?" she asked.

"Who's Gary Weddle?"

"Uh, that big media consultant. Faron arranged a meeting for you with him this afternoon."

The station had hired a media consulting firm to analyze our newscasts and come up with ideas for improving ratings. This was supposed to be my first meeting with the hotshot media guy that would be handling it all. Faron had told me it was a top priority before he left for LA.

"Call Weddle and tell him I can't make it today. Say there's a big breaking news story or whatever else halfway believable reason you can come up with."

"Jack Faron's not going to be happy with you," she said.

"He rarely is."

*   *   *

That night I went on the air with what I knew about Marty Barlow and his death. Well, not all of it. I couldn't confirm a lot of things about illegal activities at the individual buildings or any possible involvement by Terri Hartwell or Thomas Wincott. Not yet anyway. But I talked in general about Marty's investigation before he died into corrupt housing practices in New York City. About the holes in the police version that Marty's murder was just a random robbery. About the possibility that his murder could have been related to what he was working on as a reporter. And, I talked about my long, personal relationship with him, too, and what a terrific journalist he'd been for his entire life. That may not have been totally professional, but it was pretty damn poignant—if I do say so myself.

I knew there would be reprisals. And they came quickly. When I got back to my office after the newscast, I found a series of voice-mail messages.

The first one was from my ex-husband Sam Markham. He was even angrier at me than the last time I'd talked to him. He accused me of attacking his integrity—and that of the entire police department—by implying they didn't do a proper investigation of Martin Barlow's murder. He questioned my ethics as a journalist. He also made several comments about my sexual performance in the past with him that weren't . . . well, let's say they weren't complimentary. The word "bitch" was used several times in his phone diatribe.

The second angry call—which I expected—came from Thomas Wincott. He didn't specifically mention my reference to Marty's investigation of housing owners in New York City, but I'm pretty sure that's what set him off. He said I should let his father-in-law rest in peace and not use his death as a cheap ratings ploy.

The next call was a surprise—and a disturbing one. The caller did not identify himself but left a message in a gravelly voice saying: "You were warned about this story, Carlson. This is your last warning." That was it. I couldn't say for sure that the caller was the same big guy I'd met outside one of the buildings Marty was investigating, but it seemed like a pretty good bet.

Then I heard from Gary Weddle, the hotshot media consultant I'd blown off that afternoon. He wasn't happy, either. He said we had critical business to discuss and we had to reschedule immediately—and implied, without actually saying it—that I damn well better show up this time.

Finally, there was the message from Jack Faron in LA. "What the hell are you doing, Clare? You cancel the important meeting I set up for you with Gary Weddle without any notice or explanation. And you go on the air yourself, without my permission, to do a story that I specifically told you we shouldn't be doing. When I leave the office, I put you in charge to deal with problems. But you're not dealing with a problem there for me, you *are* the problem. Just do your job!"

Damn. I sure had gotten a lot of people mad at me today. Not that there was anything new about that. I'm very good at getting people mad at me. It's a special talent of mine. But then, making people mad meant you were asking the right questions as a journalist. That you were opening the right doors. I sure hoped so. Because I'd just opened the first door on this story, and now there was no turning back.

CHAPTER 7

THE MARTY BARLOW story wasn't the only worry on my mind though. Working on a big story usually made me forget about the other problems in my life. But even a big story like this couldn't stop me from still thinking about the motherhood stuff I'd tried to talk to my friend Janet about the other night. Of course, I couldn't tell Janet the truth about why I was asking her those questions about whether or not I'd make a good mother. I'd never told anyone the truth about that.

It's really ironic, I suppose. I mean, I fight against lies every day of my life as a journalist. I expose lies to the viewers of Channel 10 News. I use the power of the media to force people to pay the price for their lies.

And yet, I am living this life of lies of my own right now.

So what does that say about me?

A long time ago, when I was young and wild—well, wilder than I am now—and in college, I had a baby. An unintended pregnancy, the outcome of a drunken one-night stand with a guy I never saw again. I gave up the baby for adoption as soon as she was born. It messed up my college experience, damaged irreparably my relationship with my parents, and convinced me to be more careful about my drinking. But, in reality, having a baby didn't seem to be that momentous an event in my life. Not for a long time anyway.

But later—through a complicated set of circumstances, some of which were my own doing—I tracked down the location of my child and met her and her adopted family. Her name was Lucy Devlin, and she was eleven years old then. She had no idea that I was her biological mother, and I never told anyone else either. Not even after Lucy disappeared off the streets of New York and became one of the most famous missing child cases ever. Instead, I covered the story as a journalist and even won a Pulitzer Prize for my work—without ever revealing my secret.

That all happened more than fifteen years ago.

I recently found out Lucy was alive somewhere. I compromised my journalistic integrity to cover up a damaging story about a powerful politician—who had played a role in Lucy's disappearance—in an effort to find her. Eventually, I tracked Lucy to an address in Winchester, Virginia, and, after a lot of thought and trepidation, I finally went to see her.

Her name was Linda Nesbitt now, and she was twenty-seven years old. She had a husband and an eight-year-old daughter of her own. My granddaughter. I found this all out as I sat drinking coffee with her in her living room. After all this time, I'd finally found her. A real mother and daughter moment at last, huh?

Except for one thing.

She still didn't know I was her biological mother.

I'd introduced myself to her as just Clare Carlson, the journalist who'd won a Pulitzer Prize covering her long-ago disappearance. I told her I was looking for closure to the story, not about the true emotional closure that I was seeking. I also told her that I would not reveal her secret past—I gave her my solemn promise as a journalist on this—to anyone else until she agreed to go that public route.

Why did I do it this way?

I guess it's because I've always felt more comfortable dealing with my emotions as a journalist, instead of as an actual person. As a journalist, I can be objective and separate myself from the emotions of the story. Which is what I did with Lucy Devlin, now Linda Nesbitt. I tried to convince myself she was just another story.

Except it didn't work.

Seeing my daughter—and then meeting her—that first day as a grown-up woman had unleashed a lot of powerful emotions in me. Emotions I'd kept bottled up inside me for years. Ever since the day I gave her up for adoption in a hospital back when I was a college freshman.

God knows how, but I held it all together when I introduced myself to her as Clare Carlson, TV reporter—and gave her my cover story about being there as a curious journalist who was only looking for answers.

But, once I left and got back in my car, I began to cry.

I cried for Lucy.

I cried for myself.

And, I guess most of all, I cried because I so badly wanted to set things right with my daughter after all these years and all this pain—but I didn't know how to do that.

Which is why I brought up the question of motherhood with my friend Janet.

What kind of a mother did Janet think I would make?

"No one knows what kind of a mother they will be," she had told me. "No one is qualified to be a mother; no one knows how it's going to turn out. Not at the beginning anyway. I certainly didn't with Karen and Kim. You learn about yourself along the way in motherhood. It just happens. That's what would happen to you if ever take that step. You're a good person, Clare. You'd make a good mother in the end, no matter what you think. If that's what you ever decide you want to do."

Except I might never know the answer to that question for sure.

Because I was a prisoner of my own lies.

I lied back at the beginning when I covered the Lucy Devlin disappearance as a reporter without ever telling anyone about my real relationship with her.

I'd lied again a few years ago when I covered up the story of the politician's role in what happened to Lucy in order in obtain information about where she was.

And I'm lying now when I tell my daughter that I'm interested in her as a journalist, nothing more than that.

That's the trouble with lies.

The more you lie, the worse it gets.

Then one lie piles on top of another until one day you're buried in all the damned lies!

"There is no trap so deadly as the trap that you set for yourself," Raymond Chandler once wrote.

And that's the truth.

CHAPTER 8

MARTY BARLOW WAS investigating eight buildings where he thought corruption was flourishing. I visited the same eight places and saw what appeared to be questionable and illegal activities going on in them. All eight companies were owned by a company called Big M Realty Corp. Obviously, I needed to track down information about Big M Realty.

But I had had no better luck at that than the people in the building with the broken elevator or any of the other tenants had had. There was no phone or email listing, no website, no information of any kind about Big M Realty. Their business operation seemed one directional: You send in your checks, and we don't want to hear any more from you. Very effective way to do business, if you could pull that off.

But someone had to be running Big M Realty Corp.

They existed somewhere. I just had no idea how to find them.

I knew someone who might.

His name was Todd Schacter and he was a computer expert. Actually, Schacter was a computer hacking expert. Janet had once represented him in court and gotten him acquitted of charges of breaking into companies' computer files for personal information about their top officers. I'd used him, too, a year ago when I was looking for my daughter, Lucy. What he did wasn't exactly legal. Let's face it, what Schacter did wasn't legal at all. But it wasn't like he was stealing money or anything from these people. Only information. I was willing to bend the rules to get what I needed.

I told him about Big M Realty Corp. and all the dead ends I'd run into.

"I can think of two ways right off to get what you're looking for," he said. "It should be easy."

"What are they?"

"First, there has to be a link to whatever financial institution Big M Realty uses. These tenants sent checks to them, you say. The cancelled checks they get back from their bank will have the bank that cashed them for Big M. Then all I have to do is get the details about Big M out of that bank's files."

"How can you get into the bank's files?"

"You don't want to know."

Schacter was right. I didn't.

"What's the other way?" I asked.

"A phone number. They must use some kind of phone. No business could operate without using a phone."

"But I couldn't find any indication of a phone number anywhere."

"Maybe you're looking in the wrong places," he said.

Sure enough, the next morning he gave me a phone number that he said belonged to Big M Realty.

All right, that was easy.

Except it wasn't.

When I called the number, I got a voice message that said: "You have reached Moreland Enterprises. This is an automated message. If you have a question, leave it here along with your contact information. Don't waste our time with frivolous queries. If we feel it is necessary, we will contact you." This was followed by a beep to leave a message. I hung up. I didn't want to waste their time. Besides, I preferred they didn't know I was calling them yet.

But at least I now knew they existed under the name of Moreland Enterprises.

When I googled Moreland Enterprises, I found out more. For one thing, it was spelled "More-Land." Clever. The company had been in the news a few years ago when the district attorney announced an investigation of their real estate practices. Not Terri Hartwell. The district attorney before her. There was no indication that investigation ever went anywhere though.

Even more interesting was the owner of More-Land Enterprises— Victor Morelli. Which is where the "More" in "More-Land" must have come from. Victor Morelli, I knew quite a bit about. He'd been one of the top mob bosses in New York City in recent years. Supposedly, he had his hand in a lot of illegal operations, but he'd never been convicted of anything. He seemed to be a Teflon Don—no one in law enforcement could touch him—in the same way John Gotti had once been.

That sure explained some of the things I'd seen at the buildings where I'd gone. The gambling operations, pizza extortion rackets, sex businesses, etcetera. Was Wincott—and maybe Terri Hartwell, too—working with a mob boss like Victor Morelli? Had Marty found that out? Was that why Marty was killed?

Well, I couldn't get any answers from Big M Realty Corp./ More-Land Enterprises because they apparently wouldn't talk to anyone.

Or from Thomas Wincott, who was mad at me.

Or from Victor Morelli.

And Marty Barlow was dead, so he couldn't talk to me anymore.

But there was one person who might be able to tell me something. One person I still hadn't talked to yet. A person who had been a part of this story right from the beginning, even though I wasn't exactly sure how.

Terri Hartwell.

*   *   *

"Good luck with that," Dani Blaine said to me when I told her what I was trying to do.

I'd gone to Dani because she'd been a guest on Terri Hartwell's radio show a few times when Hartwell was on the air, talking about New York City crime stories we'd covered on Channel 10. It was a high-profile way to promote our station and newscasters on a popular radio show. I figured I'd find out from Dani the best way to approach Terri Hartwell and then subtly segue from that into the status of Dani's relationship with co-anchor Brett Wolff.

"She's got this annoying guy named Chad Enright who works for her and won't let anyone talk or see Terri without going through him," Dani said. "He's a total pain in the ass. Thinks he's a big shot, thinks he's really important, brags about how no one gets to Terri Hartwell without his approval. Jeez. Like I said, a pain in the ass. Watch out for him."

She gave me Enright's contact information.

"How's everything going between you and Brett these days?" I asked her then.

"What do you mean *how is it going*?"

"I mean are you two . . . uh, well, pursuing a relationship outside the office?"

"In other words, you want to know if we're still screwing?"

"Okay, are you and Brett still screwing?"

So much for the subtle segue.

"Yes and no."

"That doesn't answer my question."

"Brett and I are still together as a couple. But we've decided to step back from an intense personal relationship for now until he resolves some issues in his life, like the situation with his wife. Brett and I talked about this all, and we're fine. This seemed like the mature, logical way to deal with this."

She was right. It was the mature, logical approach. Unfortunately, it also was doomed to failure. I'd been through this kind of thing before in my own personal life and I knew it would all explode and get ugly again at some point in the future unless he actually divorced his wife.

But I couldn't worry about that now.

"Exactly how big a pain in the ass is this Enright guy?" I asked her before she left my office.

"The worst."

"I've met some pretty big pain in the asses in my life."

"Not like this one."

CHAPTER 9

JACK FARON WAS back from Los Angeles. There was a message waiting for me when I got to work the next morning. He wanted to see me in his office immediately.

"What do you think he wants to talk to me about?" I asked Maggie after I showed it to her.

"Gee, what do you think?"

"Well, there are several possibilities. 1) He wants to give me a pat on the back—and maybe even a big raise—for the great job I've been doing, 2) he's going to promote me, or 3) he's still mad about me going on the air with the Marty Barlow story while he was out of town. I'm betting its either 1 or 2."

"Really?"

"I'm a glass-half-full kind of gal."

"This isn't going to be pretty, Clare. I'm glad I'm not in your shoes right now."

She was probably right. I decided to put it off as long as possible. Before I went in to see Faron, I asked Maggie to run down for me all the top stories she was working on for the news meeting later that day. Then I called Terri Hartwell's office and got an appointment to see the Chad Enright guy Dani had told me about. I also called the media consultant, Gary Weddle, and rescheduled our meeting that I'd blown off the other day. After that, I went downstairs and bought myself a big cup of coffee and a poppyseed bagel with cream cheese. I ate the bagel and drank the coffee at my desk. Finally, when I couldn't think of any other way to delay the inevitable, I went to see Faron.

Trying to maintain my positive attitude, I greeted him with a big smile and a cheery, "Welcome back, Jack. How was your trip to LA?"

"How was my trip to LA? Well, let me try to answer that question for you. We didn't get any of the new advertising accounts we wanted. It rained the whole time I was there. The airline lost my luggage on the trip home. And, worst of all, the woman I left in charge of the station here ignored my instructions and went out on the air with something that I didn't want—and that is now causing me and the station all sorts of repercussions. That's how my trip to LA went."

"I have an explanation," I told him when he was finished ranting at me.

"I certainly hope so."

"I don't believe Martin Barlow died in a random mugging. I found out some new information about Barlow and what he was doing before he was murdered. I think there's a good story here."

I went through everything I'd found out so far. About the connection between Marty's son-in-law and Terri Hartwell. About the buildings that Marty seemed to be investigating. About how Marty had talked about murder—maybe lots of murders—being involved in this. And about the big guy that warned me off the story after I went to visit one of the places.

"But what is the story?" he asked after I finished. "There is no story. Just a series of individual pieces of information and events that might or might not be related. Murder, corruption, illegal payoffs, Terri Hartwell, this Thomas Wincott guy . . . you have no evidence, no hard proof of any kind to put on the air."

"How about the guy who told me to stay away from the building—or else? Why would he not want me around unless he had something to hide?"

"Maybe he just didn't like you."

"How could anyone not like me?"

"Hard to believe, I know."

He then talked about the meeting with the media consultant that I'd missed. He explained again how important it was for the station and our ratings and our ad sales to incorporate the consultant's ideas in our planning going forward. He said the order to hire the consultant had come from Brendan Kaiser himself, the owner of Channel 10 and a lot of other media properties.

"This media consultant has an excellent reputation," Faron said. "He's one of the best in the business."

"Well, you know what I always say about consultants," I said. "Those who can, do. Those who can't, teach. And those who can't do either become consultants."

I've never had much use for consultants of any kind, particularly media consultants. I don't understand the logic of paying someone who doesn't work at a TV station a lot of money to tell the people who do work at a TV station what they should be doing. And their ideas never seem to be any good.

Faron repeated to me again how important this meeting was for the station. He said that I needed to show up for the meeting this time. And he said I should keep an open mind and not display any kind of negative attitude to the consultant.

"Be nice, Clare."

"I'm always nice."

"Yeah, right . . ."

"Don't worry, Jack, I'll try to work with the guy."

"Thank you."

"No matter how big a jerk he is."

Before I left Faron's office, I asked him again about the Marty Barlow story.

"There is no Marty Barlow story."

"I'm supposed to have an interview with Terri Hartwell's top aide, a guy named Chad Enright. Hopefully, he'll let me talk to her directly. I might find out something good."

"Okay, go ahead with the Enright meeting. If you find out something good from him or Hartwell, we'll put it on the air. In the meantime, forget about the damn Barlow story and concentrate on spending time with the media consultant."

CHAPTER 10

CHAD ENRIGHT TURNED out to be everything I expected him to be, and more.

Enright was in his thirties, with blond hair and good looking in a pretty-boy kind of way. He was wearing a blue pinstriped suit, pink shirt, and blue tie with speckles of pink in it. Perfectly color-coordinated. His hair hung down a bit over his ears—not too short and not too long. Like he went to a stylist every week so it looked like he never needed a haircut. I figured him for the kind of guy who spent a lot of time checking himself out in the mirror before he left the house.

There was an array of pictures on his desk and more photos on the wall behind him. All of them were pictures of Chad Enright. With Terri Hartwell. Hanging out with other important political officials and celebrities. Behind the wheel of a fancy sports car. On a sailboat in the Hamptons. And, in more than a few of them, there was a pretty woman with him. The message he was sending seemed clear: "I'm Chad Enright, and you're not!" I could see already why Dani had used "pain in the ass" to describe this guy.

And that was before he even started talking.

"We're going to lay out the ground rules before we start," Enright said to me when I sat down in his office. "You follow the ground rules, we'll get along fine. If you don't, you and I won't get along. It's important that you understand that from the start, Ms. Carlson. Okay?"

I said okay.

"First, any access you have to Terri Hartwell goes through me. No one else. Not anyone else on the staff here. Not a public relations person. No friends of hers or any other connections you think you might have. Just me. I'm the gatekeeper. I'm the only way you get to talk to Terri Hartwell at any time. No exceptions. Everything—and I mean everything—goes through me. Okay?"

I said okay again.

"Next, you be straight with me, and I'll be straight with you. That's the kind of person I am. But you lie to me or mislead me or be less than forthcoming to me in any way—and I will cut off your access to me and Terri Hartwell in an instant. Terri is one of the hottest political names around at this moment. You can be a friend; or you can be an enemy. I'd prefer you be our friend. But that's up to you. Okay?"

I just nodded this time. I was getting bored of saying okay.

"Now what is it we can do for you, Ms. Carlson?"

I took out a sheet of paper that I'd printed out with addresses of the eight buildings I'd found in Marty's files and I had visited. I showed the list to Enright. I also showed him a picture of Victor Morelli and one of Thomas Wincott.

"Do you know of any connection Terri Hartwell might have with these buildings—or either of these men?" I asked.

"What is this?"

"You're answering a question with a question, Mr. Enright."

"How does any of this have anything to do with Terri?"

"You're doing it again."

I told him I'd been alerted by someone that the buildings' owners were breaking laws and housing questionable enterprises, apparently under the protection of the Morelli crime family. How the same person who told me this was a relative of Thomas Wincott, another major real estate owner of buildings in the city. How I'd learned that Wincott was also a campaign contributor to Terri Hartwell.

"Ergo," I said, "I'd like to find out what Ms. Hartwell knows about all this. When can I see her?"

"What do you mean?"

Another question answered with a question.

"Ergo is a term that means 'therefore,' Mr. Enright. Or 'consequently,' 'thus,' 'accordingly' . . ."

"I know what ergo means," he said impatiently. "Is this coming from that crazy old guy? He came here a while back ranting on about corrupt building owners and a lot of this same stuff. He had no proof, no hard evidence. To be honest, he looked like he was a nut job. I told Terri about it, but we never found anything that backed up his claims. Is he still pushing all this nonsense? Is he the one behind all this?"

"Uh, no . . . not anymore . . . he's dead."

"Dead?"

"Yes, he was killed recently."

"How?"

Clearly, he was not a regular viewer of the Channel 10 News or he would know all this from the story I did on air.

"Murdered on a Manhattan street. Police are calling it a robbery. I'm not so sure. I think his death might have been connected to this information about corruption at these buildings. I think it possibly could all be related, but I don't know how yet."

Enright looked startled. I could tell I'd thrown him for a bit of a loop, knocked him off his usual game.

"You think Barlow might have been murdered to keep him quiet about something he knew?"

"Yes."

"Have you talked to the police?"

"I have."

"And what is their response?"

"They are dubious."

"Well, so am I."

He looked down at the list of buildings one more time.

"I don't know anything more to tell you about these buildings," he said finally. "But our office will be in touch if that changes."

"I'd like to talk to Ms. Hartwell about them myself," I repeated.

"I said I'd handle it. If she decides to talk to you at any point in the future, I will be in touch. But you will not talk to her directly. Like I told you in the beginning, I'm the gatekeeper. I'm the door you need to go through to have any contact with Terri Hartwell. Don't forget that. Okay?"

"No, that's not good enough," I said.

"Now wait a minute—"

"You wait a minute, Enright. I want to talk to Terri Hartwell about this. Not just you. Now get me in to see her."

He stood up. He was pretty imposing when he did that. Maybe about 6 foot 3, and he looked to be in good physical condition. Probably worked out every day at the health club. Yep, Chad Enright was a helluva impressive-looking guy. And, if you didn't believe that, all you had to do was ask him.

"I think we're done here," he said. "You can see your way out."

"I don't think we're done at all . . ."

"Do you want me to call security and have them escort you out of the building?"

"No, I don't."

"Then goodbye, Ms. Carlson."

I left. But instead of going down on the elevator, I wandered around the floor. I'd seen a sign in the lobby indicating that I was on the same floor as Terri Hartwell's office. I thought there might be more security, but there wasn't. I found her door, knocked on it loudly, and yelled her name.

The door opened, and Terri Hartwell was standing there.

"I'm Clare Carlson from Channel 10 News, Ms. Hartwell. I'd like to talk to you."

Before she could answer, I heard a commotion behind me. It was Chad Enright who had heard us and come running out of his office. He looked furious. He was screaming at me and calling for someone to call security.

"I'm sorry, Ms. Hartwell," Enright said. "I'll make sure she doesn't cause you any more trouble. I told her she couldn't see you. She's . . ."

"I know who she is, Chad."

"How?"

"She just told me."

"But she can't simply walk in here and talk to you. There are procedures we need to follow . . ."

"Oh, give it a rest, Chad," Hartwell said, then turned back to me. "Come on inside and tell me why you're here."

I followed Terri Hartwell into her office.

Before I did though, I turned around and flashed a big grin at Chad Enright.

He looked furious.

He started to say something to me, then stopped and stormed off down the hall toward his own office.

I had a feeling I wasn't okay with him anymore.

CHAPTER 11

TERRI HARTWELL LOOKED even better in person than I remembered from her pictures or during media appearances. I was
kind of a fan of hers. I used to listen to her radio show regularly
when it was on. I loved the way she yelled at people who argued
with her and shouted down the idiots. Okay, sometimes she went
a bit too far. But I liked that, too. Now she was using that same
forceful personality in the DA's office. She was definitely a hot
commodity at the moment.

I knew Hartwell was in her mid-forties, about the same age as
me. But she sure could have passed for younger. She had long red
hair, piercing blue eyes, a flawless-looking, yet expression-filled
face and she was wearing a classy business outfit that showed off
the trim figure of a fashion model. Her voice was strong and loud,
but not shrill. The most impressive thing about her though was
her magnetic personality, which I felt from the first moment I
walked into her office. It seemed to fill the room.

"Wow, that was some scene out there!" Hartwell laughed. "I've
never seen anyone take on Chad the way you did. He's pretty intimidating. But I guess you're pretty intimidating yourself. You're
a tough lady, right? I can relate to that because I'm a tough lady,
too. We're a couple of tough ladies."

Hartwell offered me some coffee, which I took. Then she poured herself some, sat back down at her desk, and leaned back causally in her chair. There wasn't a lot of pretense about her; she seemed very real. Terri Hartwell was sort of like the anti–Chad Enright. I pointed that out to her.

"You don't like Chad, right?"

"I think his people skills need work."

"Lots of people don't like Chad."

"Why do you keep him around?"

"That's a good question. Chad is my guard dog. I guess that's the best answer I can give you. It's a bit like a bad cop, good cop routine. I'm the good cop. You hate Chad, then meet me and find me likable. It works pretty well, huh? It sure did with you. After meeting Chad, I'll bet you find me a breath of fresh air."

She laughed at that.

She was right though

I did like this woman.

"Let me say up front that if you're here to ask about any future political aspirations I have—for the mayor's office or anywhere else—I have absolutely no comment for you on the record. My on-the-record comment about this is 'no-comment.' Off the record? Of course I'm running for mayor. And I'm going to win. I'll be in City Hall and living in Gracie Mansion by this time next year."

"That's all very interesting," I said. "But it's not why I came here to see you."

I handed her the list of eight buildings and repeated the details of my conversation with Enright.

"Do any of these buildings—or these addresses—mean any-thing to you?"

She looked through the list, then handed it back to me. "No, should they?"

"I believe all of them are being run by a corrupt landlord company. A front for the Morelli crime family. A man named Marty Barlow came to your office to tell you about the corruption at these buildings a few weeks ago. Do you remember him?"

"No."

"Do you know Thomas Wincott?" I asked.

"Doesn't ring a bell either. Who is he?"

"Wincott is a real estate developer in Manhattan."

"Okay."

"He's also trying to donate campaign funds to your mayoral campaign."

"Lots of people want to jump into my campaign because they think I can win. But I don't deal with the direct fund-raising from people like that. You'd have to talk to Chad about this person to see what he's given—or at least pledged to give—for my campaign. I'm sure you'll love talking to Chad again!"

I rolled my eyes, and she laughed.

"Look," she said to me," I'll look into this business about the eight buildings and what you say is going on there. I'll get back to you with whatever I find out. I promise that. I do appreciate you bringing this to my attention and—"

A phone on her desk rang, interrupting her. She picked it up.

"Russell Danziger?" she said. "Where is he?"

She nodded and hung up.

"I'm afraid I have to see someone else right now. Thanks again for coming to me with this."

"Thank you," I said to her.

But she was already going to the door to let this Russell Danziger in. He burst into the office with an angry look on his face and brushed past me—as I was making my way out—like I wasn't even there. He was older than Enright, with short-cropped gray hair—but just as stylish. He was wearing a dark black suit, white shirt, and red tie, and everything was crisp, neat, and clean. I kept walking past him until I was out in the hall. Then I heard him slam the door of Terri Hartwell's office behind me.

I wasn't sure who Russell Danziger was.

But he sure must be important.

He didn't even have to go through Chad Enright to see her.

*　*　*

I had some unanswered questions after I left Terri Hartwell's office.

One of them—even though I wasn't sure what it meant—was about the man who had barged into her office so authoritatively as I was leaving.

It didn't take me long to find out about Russell Danziger when I googled him after going back to Channel 10. He wasn't a political superstar well known to the public like Hartwell; he tended to fly under the media radar most of the time. Which was probably why I didn't know him. But he was a real mover and shaker in the back rooms of New York politics.

Danziger had helped elect countless candidates to office in recent years. Some of them were smaller jobs, like councilmen or judges or state assemblymen. But he'd been involved, too, in congressional, senate, and gubernatorial campaigns, almost always on the side of the winner. He'd even worked with one of the presidential candidates in the New York State primary last time the White House was up for election. His candidate didn't make it to 1600 Pennsylvania Avenue, but he did win the state primary. All in all, it was a helluva impressive record for Russell Danziger.

Danziger didn't have an official title in any of the campaigns; he always seemed to be a shadowy figure in the background. But his influence was said to be enormous. And not only in political circles. His reach extended into big business, union organizing, and even—according to some reports—connections with mob leaders that helped him get things accomplished.

Even though Danziger didn't do many interviews, he had said something interesting once to a reporter who'd confronted him about the rumors of his connections with possible illegal union activities and even involvement with mob bosses and other underworld figures. Amazingly enough, he didn't deny it. He said, "This isn't a Sunday school softball game we're playing here," Danziger said. "Politics is a tough, no-holds-barred game. That's how it works. You can believe in standing on idealistic principles and integrity and all those things people claim they believe politics should be. But the only way to get things accomplished is by using every tool available. Making deals with politicians you don't agree with sometimes. Making deals with unions who run so much of this city. And, yes, maybe even making deals with people you need who might be associated with organized crime. If you don't do this, you won't be a winner. And I'm a winner."

I suspect that Danziger regretted being so candid with the reporter once he saw the rare quotes from him in print. But did that mean he—and by extension Hartwell—might have secret dealings with a mobster like Victor Morelli?

Then there were the questions I had about what Terri Hartwell told me—or, in some cases, hadn't told me—during our abbreviated conversation in her office.

First off, she said she didn't know Thomas Wincott. But Wincott clearly knew her. I'd heard him talking about making a big contribution to her mayoral campaign. And, because he'd told me he was trying to gain political influence if she got elected mayor, I had to assume the contribution represented a significant amount of money.

Would Hartwell not be aware of a potential political contribution of that size? Possible, but seemed unlikely to me. I found a list of guests/contributors at a big political fund-raising event a few months earlier. Both Hartwell and Wincott were listed as attending. It was a long list, and maybe she didn't meet everyone there that night. But it did show they moved in the same political circles.

Did Terri Hartwell really not know Wincott?

Did she forget his name?

Or was she lying to me for some reason about Thomas Wincott?

*　　*　　*

The eight buildings on the list from Marty—the ones owned by Morelli's company—continued to be a problem for me, too.

Hartwell said she didn't recognize any of them. But several stories appeared in newspapers or aired on TV news about a crackdown by the city on buildings housing criminal activities like prostitution and gambling—which involved numerous law enforcement agencies, including the district attorney's office.

Wouldn't these buildings be part of this investigation?

Also, I had trouble getting past the question of why she didn't know about Marty raising questions about building corruption in the city. Enright said he had told her about Marty's visit, but they didn't find any evidence to back up his claims. It only took me one visit to figure out about all the bad stuff going on at those eight locations. So why didn't Hartwell and her office know about it?

Was she lying again?

If she was lying, there might be a perfectly reasonable explanation of why she would lie. It didn't necessarily mean there was any significance to it in terms of Marty's death—or anything else. And maybe she didn't even realize it was a lie. Maybe she thought she was . . . well, just shading the truth when she talked to me about all this. Not really lying.

Yep, there are all sorts of lies.

Big ones.

Little ones.

And a lot in between that.

But, in the end, they are all still lies.

No matter how much we try to rationalize them.

No one knew that better than me.

CHAPTER 12

"CAN WE TALK about the day you disappeared?" I asked Linda Nesbitt, who a long time ago, used to be Lucy Devlin.

"What is there to talk about?"

"All of it. Did you get on the school bus with the other kids that day? Did you make it to the school? When exactly was it that they took you? What happened after that? Anything and everything."

"I told you . . . I can't remember."

"Can't or won't."

She shrugged. "Maybe a bit of both. I've read up on this kind of stuff recently. Especially since I started talking to you and you started asking me all these questions. They say a person sometimes buries a traumatic incident like this in their subconscious so they don't have to confront the reality of it. Maybe that's what I've done. Or maybe it's because I was only eleven years old when it happened. That's a long time ago. Even the things I do remember as a child from back then aren't necessarily accurate—they've gotten distorted in my memory over the years. How much do you remember about the time you were eleven?"

We were sitting in the living room of Linda Nesbitt's house in Winchester, Virginia.

I can't even begin to describe how bizarre it all seemed to be sitting in my grown-up daughter's home with her and listening to all this.

Pretending the whole time I was nothing more than an objective journalist.

When in reality, I was overwhelmed by my feelings of guilt and regret and sadness over everything that had happened between Lucy and me since I walked away from her so casually on that long-ago day.

Linda Nesbitt had light brown hair, like me. She had brown eyes, like me. She had a face that resembled mine when I was her age, or at least I thought it did. Even the way she talked reminded me of a young Clare Carlson. I could see myself in her. And why not? I was her biological mother. Even though no else knew that, including Linda Nesbitt.

Nearly three decades after giving birth to her—and years after meeting her for the first time, just before she became one of the most famous missing-child cases ever—I'd tracked her down under this different name and to this house in Virginia where she had a husband and a daughter of her own.

But here I was still using my desperate cover story of being there as a journalist—the journalist who won a Pulitzer Prize reporting on the story of her disappearance a long time ago—and not revealing I was her biological mother. I kept telling her I was there because I needed some kind of closure as a reporter; I said I needed answers for her story. That was why I wanted her to talk to me about her past as Lucy Devlin, I told her. Nothing more than that.

I wanted to blurt out the truth to her.

I wanted to tell her about everything I'd done.

I wanted to tell her how much I loved her.

But I didn't do any of those things.

Instead, I just kept taking notes like a journalist working on a story—not the mother she'd never known.

Because being a journalist was what I was good at.

"Let's move on to something else besides the actual day of the kidnapping," I said. "What about before you disappeared? Do you remember anything in New York City?"

"Some things. Mostly fragments. I remember growing up there when I was still Lucy Devlin. I remember my bedroom. I remember the video games I played in that room. I remember a dog next door that I loved to pet. I remember a few of my friends at school. I remember having some good times back then until it all . . . well, until it wasn't so good."

That last line was a helluva understatement. She'd been horribly abused—both physically and emotionally—as a little girl. Things had gotten so bad for her in that house that a self-styled vigilante had snatched her on her way to school that last day in an effort to save her.

The man who did it was now a U.S. senator. Elliott Grayson, a very powerful man in Washington. Grayson was the one I'd made a deal with to bury the story of his involvement in Lucy's abduction in hopes he'd help me track her down and find her alive the way I had now. It wasn't an arrangement I was proud of. But he also agreed not to reveal what I was trying to cover up—that I'd hidden the fact Lucy Devlin was my own biological daughter while I was winning a Pulitzer for covering the story of her disappearance. We both desperately wanted to hold on to our secrets.

"Didn't your new parents—the ones you were placed with— ever tell you anything about how they got you?" I asked. "About your past? About how you had been Lucy Devlin and how your pictures were on milk cartons and you were written about so extensively in the media during those days afterward when the whole world was searching for you?"

"No, they never said anything about it. And I didn't ask a lot of questions. I loved my new life and I wanted to grow up pretending that I was a normal teenager, I guess. It wasn't until later, much later, that I began putting the pieces together. And at first those pieces didn't add up. They didn't make sense to me. But, when they finally did, I realized that I was Lucy Devlin. The little girl who vanished and all the rest. That's when I decided to do something about it."

"You sent an email to your mother, Anne Devlin, two years ago that set everything in motion. Why did you do that?"

"I'm not sure. I suppose I wanted to see what happened. I suppose maybe I wanted some closure, too, just like you. I was right."

"You didn't want to be forgotten," I said, echoing the thought I'd had, which helped me track her down as the writer of the email.

"Something like that."

It was that event which had eventually led me to find her living in this house in Virginia, all grown up and with a family of her own.

I pointed that out to her.

"There's one thing I still don't understand about you doing this," she said. "Why do you care so much?"

"You were the biggest story of my life," I said, repeating the story I'd told her that first day one more time. "Whether or not I ever air any of this now, I need to know the real story."

"I don't know," she said. "It seems to me like you have more at stake here than just a big story."

"Like what?"

"I'm not sure."

"But you trust me?"

"I do."

"Why?"

"Because you seem like a nice person, Clare."

A nice person? Hell, I was a lot more than that to this woman. She called me "Clare" like I was her friend. I wanted to tell her to call me "Mom." Maybe one day she will. Maybe one day she'll finally know the truth about me. Maybe.

This was my third trip to see her. I'd taken the Acela train down to Washington. It was only a three-hour trip from New York so I could go and come back all in the same day. From Washington, I'd rent a car to make the drive to Winchester.

I'd lied to Jack Faron and said that I had a sick family member down here that I had to deal with in order to explain my absence from the offices.

I'd lied to the media consultant, too, when I canceled another one of our meetings with the same excuse—even though I knew I was going to have to deal with him sooner or later.

And now I was lying to my own daughter.

"Are you sure there's nothing more to this for you?" she asked.

"That's all."

"It's simply a journalistic obsession for you?"

"All about being a reporter."

Jeez, for a woman who claimed she hated lying, I sure did a lot of it.

CHAPTER 13

I was supposed to meet Gary Weddle, the media consultant, for lunch. The idea—Faron's idea—was that we meet for a friendly lunch and get to know each other a bit before diving into the specifics about any changes for the Channel 10 newscast.

Faron left it to me to pick the lunch spot. I chose the cafeteria on the first floor of our building. Not because of the food, which was mediocre on its best days. But because we could eat quickly there and I could get this out of the way without wasting a lot of my time. I had no desire to get to know Gary Weddle.

I reluctantly made my way down to the cafeteria for the meeting now. I didn't see anyone that might be him inside. So I stood in line myself—surveying the assortment of Jell-O, salads, and sandwiches on display.

"You got anything hot?" I asked the guy behind the counter. He nodded.

"Perhaps some *Poulet roti au citron*," I suggested. "Or maybe a *Foie gras en brioche*?"

"Nah," he said, "we don't have anything like that."

"What are my culinary options?"

"Well," he said slowly, "you can have the tuna casserole or . . . you can have the tuna casserole."

I pondered that briefly. "I think I'll take the tuna casserole."

"Good choice."

I put a plate of the stuff on my tray, walked over to the cashier, and paid for it. Suddenly, from behind me, I heard a voice say: "You should have held out for the *Poulet*."

I turned around. There was a very ordinary guy standing there, probably in his mid-thirties—but hard to tell, wearing glasses and a pair of baggy khakis with an open-collared green sports shirt that didn't match the pants.

"I didn't want to cause a problem." I smiled. "I'm afraid I complain a bit too much sometimes."

He smiled back.

"From what I've heard about you, that's sort of like saying the *Titanic* sometimes takes on a bit too much water." He picked up his tray of food. "Can I join you? I believe we were supposed to have lunch together."

"You're Gary Weddle?"

"I'm Gary Weddle."

We sat down at a table in the corner.

"Not exactly the kind of place where I'd expect to eat lunch with a big New York City TV news executive like you, Ms. Carlson."

"I figured this would be best for both of us. You know, more convenient and . . ."

"Quicker? So you don't have to spend any more time than necessary with me today?"

"Uh, yes . . . there was that, too."

I tried some of my casserole. It had noodles, tuna, cream sauce, peas, and some kind of black stuff throughout that looked like pepper. Not bad. I kind of liked it. If I could figure out what the black stuff was, I'd like it even better.

"I understand right now that you think I'm your enemy," Weddle said. "But I'm not. I'm here to help you. I mean that. I don't want your job. I have my own job. I want us to work together, not at odds with each other. What do you say?"

Weddle had ordered a hamburger and fries. Seemed like a safe choice. He took a big bite of the burger and smiled again. I smiled back. I didn't want to, but it happened before I realized I was doing it.

"Have you ever really worked at a TV station?" I asked him.

"No, I haven't. But I've worked with a lot of TV stations."

"Then what makes you think you can do my job better than I'm already doing it?"

"I don't want to do your job. You know a lot more about that than I do. But I know about some things that you don't know about."

"What kind of things?"

"Let me sum up my idea for what your station's newscast could be in four words: 'The News Never Stops.'"

"The News Never Stops?"

He nodded.

"That's the slogan we use to promote it. In this case, it refers to a mind-set that sets your newscast apart from all the others on the air. Everything is live, everything is immediate. When there's a fire, a press conference, a traffic jam, Channel 10 News is reporting from the scene as it's happening. You don't watch Channel 10 News to find out what has happened during the day, you watch Channel 10 to see what's happening right now."

"We only have a couple of newscasts a day. Mainly at 6 and 11 p.m. A lot of news is going to happen when we're not on the air to broadcast it."

"That's yesterday's journalism," he said. "I want Channel 10 to be at the forefront of today's journalism. Do you know how most people—especially younger people—get their news these days?

Not from traditional newscasts. From their smartphones, tablets, and other mobile devices. They want to know what's happening immediately, not wait until 6 or 11. We can give them that opportunity on Channel 10. We can use the Channel 10 website to livestream, tweet, and everything else from the scene of the news all day. Then we can use the best of all that to feature on the actual newscasts at 6 and 11. You get viewers while the news is happening, then you get them again later. It's a win-win situation."

"That sounds like a lot of work," I said.

"It doesn't have to be. I think it could make your job easier and more fun for everyone, too. Do you want to hear more?"

"I'm still listening."

He went through more details of how it would work. A lot of them made sense. I was impressed by Gary Weddle's knowledge of a TV news operation. And, the more he talked, the more impressed I got with Gary Weddle himself.

At one point, he got a big dab of catsup from the burger on his cheek and some more on the front of his shirt. I reached over with a napkin and wiped it all off. From his face and his shirt. The guy was kind of a klutz, but I somehow found that endearing. Weddle thanked me sheepishly after I finished my cleanup job on his face with the napkin.

"I would have probably gone out of here with that stuff still on my face. And my shirt, too. Me, I'm the kind of guy that can walk around all day like that and not even realize it."

"What would your wife say when you got home tonight?" I smiled.

I threw that question out there just to see where it went.

"Oh, there is no Mrs. Weddle."

"You're not married."

"No, how about you?"

"Not at the moment," I said.

We talked for quite a long time then, much longer than I assumed we would when I'd made the appointment to meet with him.

"You're not at all what I expected," I told him when we got ready to leave.

"What did you expect?"

"I expected that you'd be a jerk."

"Why?"

"I assumed that all media consultants were jerks."

"Well, I guess you were misinformed." He smiled.

We picked up our plates and dumped them on a tray by the cashier. As I walked past the food counter, the guy behind it asked: "What's the verdict on the tuna casserole?"

I made a circle with my thumb and forefinger and held it up in the air for him to see.

"Nothing but compliments," I said. "By the way, what was that black stuff in it?"

"Beats me." He shrugged. "You got any idea?"

"I was afraid you'd say that," I told him.

I heard him laughing as Weddle and I headed for the door. Weddle was laughing, too.

"Everyone's a comedian," I said, shaking my head.

"I'll talk to you soon," Weddle told me.

CHAPTER 14

"I SORTA LIKE this consultant guy the station hired to work with us on the newscasts," I told Janet.

"Do you mean you 'like' him in terms of a professional who will do a good job at promoting the newscast and making the station more money and helping you do your job easier?"

"Yeah, well . . . that, too."

"Oh, God, you don't have the hots for this guy, do you, Clare?"

"I'm saying that I felt a certain chemistry there between us that could be developed."

"A sexual chemistry?"

"Is there any other kind?"

We were sitting in Janet's office, which was on Park Avenue in the East 40s with a view of the Manhattan skyline and even all the way over to the East River. Much nicer and much bigger than my office. It bothered me that Janet had a better office than I did. Of course, I never would tell her that. Well, I have, but she never pays any attention to me when I do.

"I suppose he's good-looking, slick, super-macho, and he's got a great come-on approach that he's already tried on you—which you fell for completely."

"No, he's not like that at all. He's not that great-looking, he's kinda shy, and he's a bit nerdy, I suppose. Smart, but definitely not slick or macho."

"He doesn't sound like your type, Clare."

"I don't have a type."

"Sure you do, and he's not it."

I sighed. She was right.

"Anyway, it's tricky to have a relationship with someone you work with professionally these days," Janet said. "The whole political climate about sex in the office has changed, you know that. I'm involved in a few cases on this topic right now. The #metoo movement has accomplished plenty of worthwhile things, stopping a lot of sexual harassment that had been going on against women for years. But it does make it difficult to carry on an office relationship, even one when both sides are consenting. For women as well as men. Especially a woman like you who is in a prominent executive position. You could jeopardize your career."

"Ah, what the hell. Like you said, he's not my type anyway. It was just a thought. Maybe I'm getting desperate in my old age. Closing in on fifty and all that. I haven't been with anyone seriously since the Scott Manning debacle last year."

Scott Manning was a police officer I'd met while covering a story the previous year. I fell in love with Manning and I slept with him. He was smart, he was charming, he was good-looking—and he was also married. Separated from his wife at the time, but still married. Eventually, he went back to his wife, which pretty much determined that he and I weren't going to live happily ever after.

I decided it was time to change the topic. I told Janet about my meeting with Terri Hartwell. I also told her about my unpleasant encounter with Chad Enright before I saw Hartwell.

"I've heard about Enright," Janet said. "He's supposed to be a real jerk."

"That seems to be the consensus opinion."

"I wonder why Hartwell keeps him around."

"What do you know about her?"

Janet shrugged. "Not much. I've never met her and I haven't dealt much with her office. I used to listen to her radio show before she became DA. Plenty of people think she could be our next mayor. How do you figure she fits into this story you're working on?"

"I don't know who fits in yet or why or how. There are a lot of moving parts to this right now, and I can't figure out what they all mean. I think my friend Marty Barlow had some of the answers, but now it's too late to ask him. I'm out there on my own."

I ran through everything I knew again with Janet.

"Is that even a story?" she asked when I was finished.

"That's what my boss at the station asked, too."

"You have to admit there's not much substantial proof there, Clare. Only suspicions and speculation on your part. What did Hartwell say about it all when you told her this?"

"She said she didn't know about any of it. But I didn't get a chance to question her for long. We were interrupted by Russell Danziger."

"You met Russell Danziger?"

"We passed each other coming and going."

"Wow, you and the colonel together. That could have been a scene."

"The *colonel*?"

"That's what people call Danziger."

"Why?"

"Because he used to be a colonel. He was in the Army for like twenty years before he went into private business. Still acts like he's in the military though. Very intense, very precise, very regimented, expects everyone to jump to attention every time he issues an order. That's why people still call him the colonel."

That sure sounded like the no-nonsense guy who barged into Terri Hartwell's office, brushing past me as if I weren't even there. I described that to Janet now. "I guess I should have saluted him," I said.

"Hartwell must be serious about the mayor thing. Danziger's a real political heavyweight, the top power broker in the city. The guy is connected to everyone."

"Maybe I should try to talk to him."

"Good luck with that. He's notorious for avoiding the media."

"I can be very persuasive," I said.

Before I left, Janet asked me again what I was planning to do about Gary Weddle, the media consultant.

"Follow my instincts, I guess."

"In other words, you'll probably screw it up."

"C'mon, I've had good relationships in the past."

"Name one."

I thought about my three marriages. About my affair with the married Scott Manning. About all the other men who had come and gone in my life over the years.

"Let me get back to you on that," I said.

CHAPTER 15

I NEEDED MORE information about what Marty Barlow was working on. All I had from his computer were bits and pieces, like the list of eight buildings I'd visited. But not a lot of details.

I'd seen notebooks and papers in his room at the East 68th Street townhouse where he'd lived with his daughter and her husband while I was there. I didn't have any reason to look at them then because I didn't know yet about the specific buildings Marty was investigating or about the connection between Terri Hartwell and his son-in-law. But maybe I could find something in them to give me a better idea what he was doing those last days of his life. It was worth a try.

Connie Wincott, Marty's daughter, was not happy to see me when I knocked on the door of the townhouse. She told me her husband was angry because I had dragged his business into the investigation of her father's death. She said he told me I was no longer welcome in their house. She told me a lot more things like that, but didn't really do anything about them.

And she did let me in.

I think she knew how much her father cared about me and that I was only trying to do the right thing for him. I also think she wasn't a strong-willed woman. She allowed herself to be bullied—

mostly by her husband. But I eventually convinced her to let me look around Marty's room again. I was afraid they might have already gotten rid of Marty's stuff, but she said it was all still there.

On my way up the stairs to Marty's old room, I passed by the bedroom that must have belonged to Michelle, the daughter. There were pictures on the walls of actors and pop stars; a banner from Stuyvesant High School in Manhattan; and a lot of other stuff that marked it as a young woman's room. But the room also looked like it had been unused for a while, which made me more certain that Michelle didn't spend much time in the house anymore.

Marty's room looked pretty much the same as it had the last time I'd been here, except for the laptop computer I'd taken with me. I went through a big filing cabinet that held all sorts of papers and records—mostly notes and newspaper article clippings. Many of them were quite old. From stories Marty had covered over the years, mostly from the New Jersey paper.

Some of the newspaper clippings were yellow and tattered with age. I read through them anyway. All about people who had lived and died that Marty had covered as a journalist for so long. It all seemed important at the time, but not anymore. That's the thing about news. It's got a short life span before we move on to the next big story.

But none of this helped me find the answers I was looking for. Marty's daughter had said he now used the computer to keep all his current journalistic notes. If there was anything connected to his death, that's where I would have to look for it. But I'd already gone through those computer files, which was why I was here. At least, I'd gone through the ones I could read.

There was still that mysterious one with a subject line of "The Wanderer" that was password-protected. I had no idea what that meant, but maybe there was a clue there. Except, I'd tried a lot of passwords to get onto the site. Hoping I'd get lucky with one of them. Marty's name. His dead wife's name. His daughter. His granddaughter. His son-in-law. But all of them gave me a message back that said: "Incorrect Password—Access Denied."

If Marty had gone to all those lengths to hide this information, it stood to reason that this mysterious file called The Wanderer might be relevant. Only that didn't help me if I couldn't figure out what it was. Where did that leave me?

I'd have to try the computer again later when I got back to the office. See if there was any way I could break in and read it. Maybe some of the tech people at the station could help me figure out how to do that. Or I could go back to Todd Schacter, I realized. I figured Schacter would be able to break into the secret file. Except I was reluctant to use someone like Schacter again unless it was absolutely necessary.

Meanwhile, I kept going through the rest of the stuff here in Marty's room until I found something interesting. Didn't seem like much to me at first. Just a collection of bills and receipts Marty had paid in the preceding weeks and months.

I paged through them casually, not sure what I was looking for. Most of it was ordinary payments and financial stuff. Bank statements. Medicare and other health bills. Credit card receipts. I found out that Marty had a substantial amount of IRA money put away for his retirement. That he took a series of medicines for high blood pressure, gout, and a few other ailments. And that he still maintained subscriptions to the *New York Times*, *Wall Street Journal*, and other major publications. None of it seemed important to me.

Until I got to the travel stuff.

Marty had taken a trip recently—several of them over the past few months—to Fort Wayne, Indiana. There were receipts from plane tickets there and back—plus records of hotels and restaurants in Indiana. What in the hell was Marty doing going back and forth to Fort Wayne, Indiana?

I went back downstairs and asked his daughter if she knew anything about trips he'd taken.

"Oh, yes. He was traveling a lot at the end. That was unusual for my father. He always hated traveling when I was growing up. We hardly ever went away on a vacation. Which is why I was so surprised when he started going away so much now."

"Do you know why he was traveling?"

She shrugged. "No, Dad never told us. To be honest, we didn't communicate a lot at the end. He and my husband . . . well, they didn't get along. That affected my relationship with my father, too. My husband, he didn't want me encouraging my father in what he called his crazy foolishness. I tried to stay quiet and out of everyone's way. The times my father was traveling were peaceful for me here because I didn't have to deal with the battles between him and my husband."

"Any idea where he went on these trips?"

Another shrug.

"Was one of the places Fort Wayne, Indiana?"

"I suppose it could be."

"Why would Marty go to Indiana?"

"Well, you know . . . because of his background there."

"What background?"

"That's where he came from. Indiana. He was born and raised there. And his first job in journalism was as a reporter for the *Fort Wayne Journal Gazette*. He later became city editor there. That's where we lived when I was growing up. In Indiana."

Damn. I never even considered anything like that. I assumed Marty had started life as a fifty-year-old crusty editor at a newspaper in New Jersey. But he had a past. He'd come from somewhere. That somewhere was Indiana.

He'd had a newspaper article from Indiana, too. The one I'd found the first time I looked through his computer files. About the murder of a teenaged girl named Becky Bluso in Eckersville, Indiana, back in 1990. That newspaper article—and long-ago murder—didn't mean anything to me at the time. But now I wondered if there was a connection between it and Marty's recent trips back to Indiana.

But why?

Why would Marty still care about a thirty-year-old murder case in Indiana?

CHAPTER 16

WHEN I GOT back to the office, I googled Becky Bluso. Even though the Bluso murder had happened thirty years ago, there were still a number of stories about it on the web. It had been one of the most sensational murder cases ever in Indiana and that area of the country.

Becky Bluso was a high school student in Eckersville, Indiana, a small city located between Fort Wayne and Indianapolis. Eckersville was—by all accounts—an All-American town and the Blusos were an All-American family. Becky's father, Robert, sold insurance, her mother, Elizabeth, was a nurse, and Becky was a cheerleader and an honor student at the local high school. She had two sisters, one named Betty who'd gone away to school in Maine, and another named Bonnie a year behind Becky in high school.

They lived in a quiet, bucolic neighborhood where crime was a rarity, not a part of everyday life as it was in New York. There had only been a handful of murders in Eckersville over the years, and none of them even remotely as horrific or unexplained as the death of Becky Bluso.

She was killed in her home in broad daylight on a hot summer day in August of 1990. School was about to resume in the fall, and

Becky and her younger sister, Bonnie, had gone out that morning to shop for clothes. Her sister then headed to a swimming class at the local YWCA, while Becky said she was going home to try on some of her new clothes. Their parents were at work and her older sister was already away at college, so Becky was there alone in the middle of the day. But she had told her sister she expected to meet a friend at the house later.

It was the friend—a neighborhood girl named Teresa Lofton who lived on the same street—that found her when she arrived later that afternoon. The front door was open, the Lofton girl went in and discovered Becky Bluso's bloodied body lying on the bed. She ran screaming from the house and police soon arrived onto a horrifying scene. Becky had been stabbed a dozen times. She'd been tied to the bed by rope and her clothes were mostly off, but there was no evidence of sexual assault. The ME's office later placed the time of death at around 1:30 p.m., an hour after she'd gotten back from shopping with her sister.

The investigation was exhaustive. Hundreds of people were interviewed—friends at school, neighbors, local store owners of places Becky visited—looking for a suspect or reason for the shocking murder.

At first, police thought she might have surprised a burglar who panicked and killed her. But it was later determined that nothing had been taken from the house. Also, the brutality of the murder—the fact that Becky was stabbed a dozen times—indicated it was a crime of passion, not someone out for monetary gain.

All of her boyfriends and potential boyfriends and pretty much any other man in her life was questioned extensively. As a cute cheerleader, Becky was popular with the boys. She'd been dating one boy, recently broken off a relationship with another, and had a lot of potential suitors, too.

A few of them emerged as potential suspects for the police at first. One of them, a seventeen-year-old at her high school, had become so obsessed with her that he besieged her with phone calls and notes professing his love. A female student who was secretly a lesbian—this was long before people felt comfortable coming out publicly as gay—had come on to Becky in a school shower after gym class, but was rebuffed.

But no hard evidence was ever found to link either of these two—or anyone else—to the murder. The operative police theory though was still a stalker of some sort had gotten into the house, she'd confronted him, and the encounter turned violent. Except the police never could say who that person might be. And now, thirty years later, they still had no idea.

They also re-traced Becky's steps in the hours and days leading up to the murder. The shopping trip with her sister. What she'd talked about with her mother and father that morning before they left for work. All the other recent things she'd done.

On the night before her murder, there had been a barbecue in the Bluso family's backyard with several neighborhood families attending. One of the neighbors who was there—a man named Ed Weiland, who lived next door to the Bluso family—said Becky seemed distracted and quiet during the barbecue. "Like she had something on her mind" was the way he put it. But whatever that was, she never said anything about it before she was killed.

I found out all this by reading through articles at the time of the crime. It had been a big story, especially in the Indianapolis/Ft. Wayne area. There had probably been a lot of local TV news coverage, too, but back then most of that would be on videotapes stored away in a library at the station—not available on YouTube like now.

I did manage to find one video from a local station at the time online, though. In it, Becky's mother and father are interviewed

on camera talking about the death of their daughter. It was difficult to watch and brought back memories of many times I'd interviewed the family members of a murder victim or tragedy. They
were crying on camera as they tried to deal with the enormity of
their loss—the shocking murder of their beautiful and smart and
popular seventeen-year-old daughter. My God, I thought to myself as I watched it now, Becky Bluso would be older than I was
today if she'd lived.

"I know we can't bring Becky back," the mother sobbed on the
screen. "All we can hope for at this point are some answers.
Answers to how something like this could have happened. And in
our own home. We want the answers to those questions so that we
can allow Becky to rest in peace."

Except the answers never came.

There was a picture of Becky Bluso on the video. She was dressed
in her cheerleader outfit. A pretty, smiling teenage girl, with her
whole life seemingly ahead of her and no hint of the horrible end
she would soon meet at the hands of a brutal killer.

* * *

My assumption was that Marty had covered the Becky Bluso
murder story while he was at the Fort Wayne paper—and had
gone back after all this time looking for answers to the unsolved
murder.

I was able to confirm the first part of this quickly with a phone
call to the Fort Wayne paper. Marty had been the city editor at
the time of the Bluso girl's murder, and he led the coverage of
the story so well that the paper won numerous awards for it. All
this acclaim led to a bigger job offer from a paper on the East
Coast. He moved there several months after the Bluso murder,

eventually winding up as editor of the paper where I met him years later.

The Becky Bluso story had catapulted Marty's career. I thought of how similar that was to me and the Lucy Devlin story, which won me a Pulitzer as a young reporter and made me a media star. I had never been able to rest until I got all the answers about Lucy Devlin a long time later.

I wondered if that was what Marty had been doing with Becky Bluso—going back to get answers to questions he still had about what was probably the biggest unsolved crime story he'd ever covered.

In fact, the more I thought about it, I was pretty sure that must have been what Marty was doing.

Except one thing didn't make sense.

Marty had been obsessed with a story about New York City building corruption and about Terri Hartwell and presumably about his son-in-law's business/political campaign dealings with her.

Was there some connection that I was missing?

No, Marty probably just got curious about what happened with the old murder, that long-ago big story he covered back in Indiana. He started looking at it again at the same time he was investigating the corruption stuff here. One thing obviously had nothing to do with the other.

But I was curious, too.

That's the thing about being a journalist—you get curious.

Sometimes that curiosity takes you places you wouldn't normally go.

CHAPTER 17

I TOOK OUT Marty's computer again and began going through his files one more time, looking for some kind of lead. In the end, I kept coming back to the file I couldn't open. I looked at the file name again—"The Wanderer." What the hell did "The Wanderer" mean? There must be answers in there. All I had to do was figure out how to read it.

I tried new passwords. The name of Marty's dog that he loved so much for years when I used to work with him. The name of the paper where he was an editor for his whole career. Humphrey Bogart who was his favorite actor. Bob Woodward and Carl Bernstein who were always his journalistic heroes. Hell, I even tried my own name. Clare first. Then Carlson. Finally, both of them together.

Nothing worked until I thought of another thing.

Marty didn't call me Clare.

He called me Clarissa.

I punched in the name "Clarissa" as my password, and suddenly I was on the site. The entire website—Marty's secret, password-protected website—opened up in front of me.

At first, I couldn't believe what I was seeing.

There was a big picture of Ted Bundy at the top of the page. Yes, that Ted Bundy. America's most prolific serial killer who had murdered at least thirty women—maybe even as many as fifty—back in the seventies and eighties before eventually being executed in Florida. Handsome, suave, charming—he lured his female victims to their deaths by convincing them that he was a nice guy. Until it was too late for them.

There were also pictures and drawings of David Berkowitz aka Son of Sam; The Zodiac Killer; Richard Ramirez, known as The Night Stalker; The Hillside Stranger; and many more. America's most famous—or infamous, I guess—serial killers.

But why had Marty been so interested in all these serial killers from the past, many of them dead now?

The answer—at least as much as an answer as I could figure out—came in the next section.

There was an article there that Marty had posted to the site. Presumably meant for publication by him at some point. But, for now, it was only on this personal and password-protected website of his.

The headline was:

THE SECRET SERIAL KILLER

Scarier Than Ted Bundy or Any of the Others
By Marty Barlow

There is a misconception by the public about the serial killer phenomenon—a mistaken belief that a serial killer always seeks media attention. This is fueled by all the movies, all the TV shows, and all the thriller novels about serial killers.

This is true for many serial killers. Like Son of Sam or the Zodiac Killer and others who taunted the police and public with messages boasting about their rising body count and threats of future victims. Yes, they did crave the public spotlight.

But there is an even more dangerous kind of serial killer. The serial killer we don't know about until it is too late.

I believe there is someone out there like that now.

Carrying out murder after murder quietly—over a period of years and in many states and cities and locations around the country—without anyone noticing the connections between all these killings.

I'm calling him "The Wanderer" . . .

I read through the entire article. There was a series of pictures with it. All of these were head shots of young women. I counted twenty. They were all attractive women. I presumed that all of them were dead. I was right.

But it was the first picture on this list that interested me the most.

A picture of Becky Bluso.

I sat there in stunned silence in the newsroom. A TV played in the background, but I'd turned the sound down to concentrate on Marty's notes. The only sound I could hear now was my own rapid breathing as I tried to grasp the enormity of all this.

Damn, Marty wasn't just investigating a buildings corruption scandal when he died.

He wasn't only trying to dig up political dirt on his son-in-law.

Marty Barlow believed he was on the trail of a serial killer.

CHAPTER 18

MARTY HAD BEEN working on two different stories at the same time.

He'd started out investigating the building corruption story in New York. But then, for some reason, he'd become interested in the old Becky Bluso murder case from when he was a young journalist in Indiana. Whatever he uncovered led him to the serial killer idea. This was the only scenario that made sense.

Except it didn't really make sense.

First off, Marty had violated a basic rule of journalism, one he taught me and other young reporters. That rule was: "Work on one story at a time. Finish that story before you start another one. Otherwise, you'll do a half-ass job on each one and wind up with no story at all." I can't count how many times Marty lectured me about that, both while I was working for him and even afterward. And yet, in the middle of working the New York City corruption scandal story, Marty switched gears and began chasing a serial killer story.

Also, how had Marty found out about all these murders? He was an old retired—or almost retired—newspaperman living in New York City. Okay, he probably stumbled onto the corruption scandal because of his son-in-law's presumed involvement in whatever was going on with Terri Hartwell's office and all the rest. And then began looking into the long-ago Becky Bluso murder because of his past newspaper connection covering it. But the rest of the murders were in totally different locations and no one had ever put the pieces together the way he was doing over a thirty-year-period. Why Marty? And why now?

Were these two stories—the city building corruption and the murder victims—somehow connected in a way I couldn't see? Was it possible Marty thought his son-in-law, Thomas Wincott, was the serial killer he called The Wanderer? That seemed unlikely to me. What about someone else in the corruption story? Chad Enright? No, Enright was only in his thirties. He'd have been like five years old when the killings on that list started. Was there something—or someone—else in the picture that I was missing?

Then there was the biggest question of all.

Was any of this serial killer stuff even true?

Or was Marty just a crazy old man at the end?

So desperate to prove he still mattered in today's fast-changing world of journalism that he created an imaginary serial killer?

I returned to the pictures of the twenty women murder victims on the computer screen in front of me.

The picture of Becky Bluso was at the top. It was larger than the pictures of the other women. Maybe that's because Bluso meant more to Marty because she had been his first big crime story. Or maybe because he believed she was the first victim. Or maybe some combination of the two.

Underneath the pictures of each victim were their name, the date and place they were killed, and some details about the murder.

I read through the information about all of the murders, looking for an obvious pattern. I found none. The murder sites jumped back and forth all over the country. The method of murder was not consistent. Many victims had been stabbed. But a few had died after being been strangled or from a blow to the head. The killer never used a gun, but that was the only thing exactly the same in all of the murders.

Even the physical characteristics of the victims varied. Some were brunette, some blond, one was a redhead—and their ages varied from seventeen—Becky Bluso—to the twenties and late thirties. Most serial killers have a "type" of woman they target. But apparently not this one.

There was another problem, too.

I picked up the phone and made a few calls to local media and law enforcement agencies and discovered that several of the murders on the list had already been solved or were close to being solved. Which meant they weren't the work of a serial killer, just individual murders committed randomly by different suspects in various locations over the years.

If they didn't fit the pattern, why had Marty put them on his list?

I went back to Marty's files again. In them, he had included a lot of other material about serial killers.

There was a series of quotes from Ted Bundy, collected over the years. I read some of them now: "I'm the most cold-hearted son of a bitch you'll ever meet"; "We serial killers are your sons, we are your husbands, we are everywhere"; "What's one less person on the face of the earth anyway?" and—perhaps his most chilling quote of all—"Murder is not about lust and it's not about violence. It's about possession. When you feel the last breath of life coming out of the woman, you look into her eyes. At that point, it's being God."

There were more quotes collected from other infamous serial killers over the years. From Son of Sam: "I am a monster. I am the Son of Sam. I didn't want to hurt them, I just wanted to kill them."

From Richard Ramirez, the Night Stalker: "I love to kill people . . . love all that blood." From the Zodiac Killer: "I like killing people because it is so much fun. It is much more fun than hunting wild game in the forest."

Scary stuff all right.

Marty also explained a bit more about why he had come up with the name "The Wanderer" for the serial killer he believed was out there. He wrote:

"This man has been carrying out murder after murder quietly—over a period of years and in many states and cities and locations around the country—without anyone noticing the connections between all these killings. I don't know this person's identity yet. But, when I was a young man, I always remember that song from Dion called 'The Wanderer.' All about someone chasing pretty girls all over the country, never staying long in one place—but moving on after each girl. 'I roam around, around, around . . .' the refrain goes. It seems particularly appropriate now."

I looked back at the pictures of the twenty young women again. Victims—or possible victims—of "The Wanderer."

Was a single person responsible for all these deaths?

Or even some of them?

And was The Wanderer—if he even existed—still out there targeting more women for death?

I didn't have the answers to these questions.

But I knew what I had to do to go looking for them.

Follow another important rule Marty taught me a long time ago about how to cover a complex or confusing story.

Start at the beginning.

The beginning of this story was Becky Bluso.

CHAPTER 19

I'D NEVER BEEN to Indiana. But I found out I could get there in under two hours by flying directly to Indianapolis, then renting a car for the forty-five-minute drive to Eckersville, the town where Becky Bluso had been murdered. I figured I could do it all in a day, in and out without staying the night.

I wasn't exactly sure why I was going—or what I was looking for. I'd already googled a lot of material about the Becky Bluso murder and read the recent article in the Fort Wayne paper. But I've always found as a journalist that it's better to see things first-hand on a story you're covering. I wanted to do that now with Becky Bluso. Maybe it would help me get some answers.

Between this and my trips to Virginia to see Lucy, I was piling up the days out of the office. Sooner or later, Faron was going to call me on that. But I'd worry about that when it happened. Because that's the way I've always operated. Did everything I had to do to get the story, then worried about the other stuff afterward.

The first place I went when I got to Eckersville was the house where Becky Bluso had lived—and was killed. A simple white house with blue shutters and trim about halfway down the block on a street called Oak Park Drive. Surrounded by other houses that looked almost identical, right down to the blue shutters and trim on many of them. It all seemed so ordinary and so peaceful and so safe as I stood there on the street and tried to envision the terror that had taken place there on that long-ago day.

There was no one on the street at this time of morning, and no sign of anyone inside the house where Becky Bluso once lived. Whoever lived there now was probably at work or at school or whatever they did. No one was thinking about the brutal murder that took place here a long time ago except me.

I thought about walking up to the house and peering in one of the windows, but decided that might draw unwanted attention from the neighbors. I might have done that in New York City, where no one paid any notice to anyone else. But not in Eckersville, Indiana. I just sat in my car and stared at the house.

I tried to envision what it must have been like here back on that August afternoon in 1990. The girlfriend from down the street coming over to meet Becky. Finding her bloody body dead inside the house. Police cars and ambulances converging on Oak Park Drive for the biggest crime Eckersville ever experienced. But now Oak Park Drive was a quiet small-town street again.

I got back in my rental car and drove next to the high school Becky Bluso had attended. This time I did get out and walk around the school area a bit. In the back was a football field and a grandstand and a scoreboard that said "Go Bulldogs!" I thought about how Becky Bluso must have stood on this spot and led "Go Bulldogs" cheers as a teenaged cheerleader for Eckersville High.

On the other hand, the school behind me looked new. Maybe the high school had been somewhere else when Becky Bluso went there. It was all a moot point anyway. I didn't expect to find the killer still lurking under the grandstand. I just wanted to get a feel of the life Becky Bluso would have led before someone took it all away from her so violently and senselessly at the age of seventeen.

*   *   *

The police department in Eckersville was housed in a modern brick building in the center of town, next to the city hall and a library and a recreation center. I introduced myself to the police chief, a man named Jeff Parkman, and told him what I was there for. Parkman didn't seem surprised.

"You're the third reporter to come here asking questions about the Bluso murder," he said when I asked him about it.

"Who were the other two?" I asked, even though I already knew the answer.

"Eileen Nagle, works for the Fort Wayne paper. And some old guy who said he came here from New York City to find out more about the case. Just like you."

"Marty Barlow?"

"Yeah, that was him. Weird old guy. I mean I liked him, but he seemed seriously intense about Bluso's death. What's all the interest in it now with you people after all this time anyway?"

Parkman looked to be in his forties, a decent-looking guy in a crisp blue uniform who seemed affable enough and willing to talk to another reporter. I saw only one other police officer in the station. Of course, the rest of them could be out chasing ax murderers, but I got the feeling crime was not an overwhelming problem in Eckersville.

I told him my station was doing a roundup of some of the most violent unsolved murder cases around the country. It seemed like the best way to go. Another lie. But just a little one this time. I was lying to everyone these days. My boss, my daughter—and now this guy. The lying got easier the more I did it.

"It's the biggest crime case we ever had around here," Parkman said, pretty much stating the obvious. "I was around back then, so I remember it well. It changed this town. It changed me, too. I'll never forget it as long as I live."

"Were you on the force when she was murdered?"

"No, I was too young. But I knew her. Becky, that is. I mean, I knew who she was. I went to high school with her. I was a freshman at Eckersville High that year. I still remember the memorial service they held in the school auditorium here. People crying and praying . . . it was awful. Tough to relate to something like that when you're a kid. Hell, it still is."

He took me through the facts of the case. A lot of them I already knew, but there were new details. Including what happened to the family afterward. The younger sister, Bonnie—the one who had gone shopping with Becky that day—died of leukemia six years later. She was only twenty-two. The father later died of a heart attack, and the older sister, Betty, never came back to Eckersville after college, apparently because of all the tragedy. That left the mother all alone, so it was no surprise when she died, too, a few years later. "They said it was cancer," Parkman told me, "but everyone has always believed she died of a broken heart. She never got over losing Becky like that, followed by all the rest."

I asked him if there were ever any real suspects in the Bluso murder.

"If we're talking on the record here, the answer is no."

"How about off the record?"

"You promise you won't put any of this on the air or report on it in any way?"

"I'm just looking into the Becky Bluso story at this point to see if it's even worth covering for us. I don't even have a video crew here with me. Anything you say to me is between us. I wouldn't go public with it before checking with you first. You have my word as a journalist on that, Chief Parkman. And I take my word as a journalist seriously."

He nodded.

"After I became chief here, I started looking into the case whenever I could. Like I said, I had a personal interest because I knew Becky. At first, I'd suspected the neighbor. Ed Weiland, the one who was at a barbecue with the family the night before the murder happened. He had a lot of guns and knives in his house. No one ever directly linked him to the murder, but I always wondered about Weiland.

"Then there was his son. Seth. He went to school with Becky and supposedly had a big crush on her. People said he was always hanging around the Bluso house, and someone once caught him trying to peep into the window there. He was a strange kid. I liked him even better for it than the father. But it was too late to question him by then. Seth Weiland was killed in a car crash about fifteen years ago. The father is gone, too, now."

I asked if there had been any other suspects.

"Oh, lots of suspects. Hell, Becky had a lot of admirers—and a few that even seemed obsessed with her. And why not? I mean, she was this pretty, popular cheerleader who seemed almost perfect. Pretty much everyone at Eckersville High back then had a thing for Becky Bluso."

"How about you?" I asked.

"How about me what?"

"You said you went to high school with her. Did you ever go out with her?"

Parkman laughed. "Jeez, I was a freshman, and she was the star cheerleader. She barely knew I existed. I used to see her in the halls and cheering at the games, but I never got a chance to know her. I was too young. And then she was gone."

Parkman had several pictures displayed prominently on his desk. Pictures of himself with his family. A pretty wife and three kids, two girls and a boy. The pictures had been taken over a period of years, showing the children at different ages as they grew up. Parkman looked over at the pictures now.

"I've had a good life so far," he said, talking almost more to himself than me. "Good job, good family. Every once in a while, I look at my own children and think about Becky Bluso. My oldest daughter is a teenager now. In a couple of years, she'll be the same age as the Bluso girl when her life was cut so short. It still all seems so unbelievable. How Becky Bluso never had a chance to live a life like I did. Like my own kids hopefully will do. Someone took all that away from Becky. Her death was a terrible tragedy."

I tried to couch the next question as carefully as I could.

"Was there ever any indication that Becky Bluso's death could have been connected to any other murders?"

"You mean like a serial killer?"

I was surprised at how quickly he suggested the serial killer theory.

"You don't seem surprised by the question," I said.

"That's because the other reporter from New York already asked me about it."

Of course. Marty.

"What did you tell him?"

"Same thing I'll tell you. We never had any leads on anything like that. Of course, anything is possible. Maybe it was a serial killer who came through Eckersville a long time ago and murdered Becky Bluso as one of his victims. We haven't been able to figure anything else out about the murder. Why not a serial killer?

We still don't know anything about what happened to Becky Bluso that day, Ms. Carlson. Hopefully, one day we will."

*   *   *

Before I went back to New York, I stopped in at the Fort Wayne newspaper to meet Eileen Nagle, the woman who had written the recent story about the Bluso murder. Nagle was in her mid-twenties, seemed ambitious and impressed that a TV journalist from New York was interested in her story. She confirmed the basic facts I already knew from that story and from my interview with Parkman, but couldn't add many more details.

She did say that Marty Barlow had been to see her. That he told her he'd once covered the Becky Bluso story, too, when he worked at the newspaper. She said she was sorry to hear he had died.

"But why do you care so much about the Becky Bluso story?" Nagle asked.

"Marty was my friend, and he asked me to help work with him on a big story before he died."

"And you figure you'll solve this case now for him in his memory?"

"Something like that."

"And exactly how do you plan to do that?"

"Beats me," I said.

CHAPTER 20

THERE'S AN OLD newsroom adage that says the best way to be a good reporter is to have a good editor. Which is true a lot of the time. I think about Bob Woodward and Carl Bernstein, the two most famous reporters in journalistic history. Without Ben Bradlee, another editor might have relegated Watergate to the unimportant police robbery story that everyone else thought it was at the beginning. We never would have heard about stuff like "Deep Throat" and "follow the money" without Ben Bradlee.

Of course, not all editors are Ben Bradlees. There's a million jokes reporters tell about editors who do too little—or too much—to ruin a good story.

Like the joke about the reporter and the editor walking through the desert. The sun is beating down, and they're thirsty beyond belief. Suddenly, they see an oasis ahead with water. The reporter runs to it and begins drinking the water. Then he hears a splashing sound next to him. The editor is peeing in the water. "What are you doing?" the reporter asks. "Making it better," the editor replies.

Or there's another one that goes:

Q: "How many editors does it take to screw in a light bulb?"

A: "Just one, but first he has to rewire the building."

I don't really have an editor these days for my job in TV news, but I do have a boss. Jack Faron. I put him closer to Ben Bradlee—well, a bit closer—than to the majority of other editors journalists have to deal with out there. But I knew I was still going to have a rough time convincing him that all of the material I'd accumulated since Marty's death was a story for us to put on the air.

"A serial killer?" he said now, as I sat in his office going through everything I'd found out over the past few days.

"A potential serial killer."

"Who might have been killing people for decades without anyone ever figuring out the connection between any of the murders. Except you don't have any actual evidence for this."

"Not at the moment, no."

"This is all based on some rambling notes you found from this crazy old guy?"

"Marty wasn't crazy."

"You said he had dementia."

"Possible dementia."

"Whatever . . . there's still nothing here about serial killers or decades-old murders that we can put on air."

"I know that. I just wanted you to know about it all."

"Then that means now you can go back to being news director again, right?" Faron said.

"Well, there is a story I got from Marty's stuff that I do think we can do. The one I started talking about that first day I went on the air when you were out of town and got so mad at me."

"Jeez, Clare, you're not going to start up with that again . . ."

"Jack, hear me out on this." I told him more about the buildings I had visited. The ones from Marty's list that seemed to be run by underworld and corrupt owners. About tenants being forced out of their apartments to make room for sex industry spots, gambling operations, mob-run pizza places, and other businesses that were much more profitable. About the connection to a shady shadow company that seemed to exist only as a front for mob boss Victor Morelli. I'd thought about this a lot since coming back from Indiana. No, I didn't have a story about any serial killer. Certainly nothing I could put on the air. But I still believed there was a story I could put on the air about corrupt building owners. Including Victor Morelli.

"I go back to these places now with a camera crew," I told Faron. "I get people talking on air about what's been happening there. I look deeper into the ownership issues and the mob connections to these buildings. Then we demand to know from city officials what they're going to do about it. Especially Terri Hartwell, the DA who wants to be mayor by being a champion in the fight against city corruption. This is real journalism. Something we don't do enough of these days. It's a good story, Jack."

"And you'd do the story yourself on air?"

"Yes."

"At the same time you're working as my news director?"

"That's right."

"But at least you're not working any more on this crazy serial killer thing, right?"

"I still do want to make a few checks on that . . ."

Faron groaned.

"What about being news director?"

"I'll do my job as news director, too."

"How can you possibly do all those things at once, Clare?"

"I don't sleep, eat, or have sex anymore, Jack. Trust me. I can handle it all."

In the end, he agreed. I'd assign video teams and other reporters to go back to all the buildings to gather enough material for the segment, but I would be the one to report it on air. Before I left the office, Faron asked me again about the serial killer stuff.

"On the remote possibility that there might be some truth to what the old guy was saying—an until-now unknown connection between a series of murders over the years in a lot of different places—how could you go about confirming something like that? Do you know any law enforcement investigative sources that could help you?"

"I do know one person. At least, he could probably point me in the right direction. But there's a problem with me reaching out to this guy."

"Who is it?"

"Scott Manning."

"Isn't he the NYPD homicide cop you worked with last year on that Dora Gayle/Grace Mancuso murder business?"

"That's right. Only he's not with the NYPD anymore. He left the force a few months later to join the FBI. He's with the FBI Behavioral Sciences Unit, the one that tracks and chases after serial killers. He's a good investigator, too. He'd be perfect for me to go to with all this serial killer stuff."

"So what's the problem?"

"I slept with him."

"And?"

"I'm not sleeping with him anymore."

"What exactly is your relationship with this guy right now?"

"Not sure, but I guess I'm about to find out."

CHAPTER 21

THE LAST TWO times I'd seen Scott Manning had gone very differently.

The first time, I'd slept with him. We had just finished working together on a case in which a man was shot to death a few feet away from us. It had been a very traumatic experience for me, and I asked Manning afterward to come over to my apartment to comfort me. He did that, and a whole lot more. We'd shared at the time what I thought was a pretty tender, meaningful—and damn exciting—sexual experience.

The second time, it got very ugly between us. I met him in a coffee shop a few days later. He told me he was going back to his wife and wanted to try to make their marriage work. I did not take this news well, and we hadn't spoken since.

I sure liked that time in my apartment a lot more.

Manning was a homicide detective back then, but he'd been put on limited administrative duty because of an investigation into the death of a suspect who'd been in police custody at his precinct. Manning first lied to protect his partner, but then he told the truth and was eventually reinstated. For whatever reason, he'd left the police force shortly afterward and joined the FBI. I wasn't sure why, maybe to get a new start. All I knew was that he'd been assigned to the FBI Behavioral Sciences Unit, which tracked serial killers.

I wasn't sure how he'd react to hearing from me again, so I decided to play it totally professional. Simply a journalist reaching out to a law enforcement official for help on a story. That's all it would be, nothing more than that.

"Hi, it's Clare," I said when I got him on the line.

There was no response.

"Clare Carlson."

Still nothing.

"Channel 10 News."

"What do you want, Clare?"

At least he was speaking to me; that was progress.

"So, you do remember me?"

"I remember you."

"What do you remember?"

"You're a journalist I worked with on a murder case last year."

"Well, that's true. It's also true we had mind-blowing sex together back then. It's true that you told me a lot of sweet things that night. And it's also true that you went back to your wife afterward."

I'd decided the professional approach wasn't working.

"What do you want?" Manning asked again.

"I need your help on a story. A murder story. People's lives could be at stake."

"Why talk to me? Talk to someone on the NYPD."

"Because you're good."

"There are a lot of good investigators at the NYPD."

"No, I mean you're *good*. You're a good man. I believe that I can trust you, no matter what happened between us. I need your help on this. Will you help me?"

There was another long silence. At first, I thought he might have hung up.

"Tell me about it," he finally said.

"Has to be in person."

"Okay, do you remember the bar where we met that first night on the Upper East Side?"

"Indelibly."

"Meet me there tonight at seven."

*   *   *

When I got there, I saw Manning sitting at a table. He didn't look much different than the last time I'd seen him a year ago. Not that he should have changed much, I suppose. Although he could have grown a beard or a mustache or shaved his head during those months. But he was still clean-shaven, with curly brown hair like I remembered. He looked good. Damn good. Like I remembered him, too.

He shook my hand when I got to the table. No hug. Not even a peck on the cheek. Just a professional greeting. I got the message. I decided to plunge right into the reason I was there.

He already had a drink in front of him. I ordered something for myself, too.

"I have reason to believe there might a connection between some—if not all—of a series of murders," I told him. "They're from different parts of the country and over a long period of time. I'm hoping you can use FBI resources to see if there is any actual evidence to support this scenario."

I handed him the printout of the murder victims I'd gotten from Marty's secret computer file. He read through it. Casually at first, then with more intensity.

"Thirty years?" he asked.

"Yes."

"Why do you think the murders might be connected?"

"I'm not sure."

"But you still think they might be."

"The person I got this list from suspected there's been a serial killer at work all this time, who's responsible for these killings."

"Why isn't that person here with you?"

"He's dead."

"By the same killer of all these women?"

"Not sure, but probably not."

"But you believed him—you think he was telling you the truth?"

"He never lied to me before."

"And you want me to run these cases through the FBI computers and files and field offices and anything else I can think of to see if I can find any evidence which indicates a single killer could be responsible?"

"That's my idea."

This was the part where I half expected him to stand up and walk away. But he didn't do that. He kept looking at the piece of paper with the list of victims that I'd put in front of him.

"From the notes you put on here, it looks like some of the murders have already been solved. People are in jail for committing them. How does that square with your idea of a single serial killer?"

"I'm not sure if all of them are connected. They might have been guesses by the person I got this list from. Which doesn't change the fact that I still need to determine if there's a possible connection between the others. Some of them could be by a serial killer, but not all of them."

"Or maybe they put the wrong people in jail for the convictions here while the real killer went free?"

"That's possible, too."

He finished his drink. I'd barely started mine. I hoped he'd have another one so we could spend more time together. But, instead, he stood up. He was still holding the piece of paper with the names on it in his hand.

"Can I keep this?" he asked.

I nodded. I tried to think of something to say so that our conversation could go on a little longer.

"How's everything with your wife?" I asked.

Hey, he could have divorced his wife by now. I figured it was at least worth asking the question.

"We're fine," he said.

"That means you're still together?"

"I'll see what I can do with this," he said, gesturing to the list of murder victims I'd given him. "Probably nothing. But I will check it out and let you know if I find out anything interesting. I'll do that for you, Clare. But only on one condition."

"What's the condition?"

"This is totally business between us—all professional, absolutely nothing else will be involved."

"I wouldn't have it any other way."

CHAPTER 22

"I REMEMBER MY father," Lucy said to me.

"Remember him how?"

"In a good way. I used to look forward to him coming home. I'd run to him and hug him as hard as I could. Those were good times. In the beginning, my mother was a part of those happy moments, too. At least in my memory she was. But then there was the bad stuff that started happening between her and me. Afterward, my mother and father would have these terrible arguments. Arguments about me. I used to hide in my bedroom and play my video games with the sound turned up as high as possible. Trying to escape into my own little fantasy world, I guess, so I didn't have to listen to them. It worked most of the time. For a while anyway. But then my mother would come into my room, and it would start all over again."

This was becoming increasingly painful for me to do. Sit here and listen to my daughter talk about the nightmare she'd endured as a child in that house. A nightmare I'd unwittingly helped create by abandoning her as a baby.

"Can you tell me what you remember about your mother?"

"I don't."

"You don't remember anything at all?"

"I remember too much."

"But . . ."

"I don't want to talk about it."

Anne Devlin, her mother, had done terrible things to her. I knew that, and I was pretty sure Lucy did, too. Eventually the physical and emotional abuse—most of it coming because of her insane jealousy of her beautiful daughter—resulted in a "kidnapping" by a vigilante group that found her a new home. Lucy Devlin disappeared forever, presumably dead—and eventually became Linda Nesbitt, the woman I was with now.

Of course, I was really Lucy's mother, not Anne Devlin. Her biological mother. But she didn't know that. And I wasn't sure at this point if she ever would. The only parents she ever knew back then were Anne and Patrick Devlin.

For maybe the zillionth time I wondered why I was doing this. Why I was putting myself—and my daughter—through such an ordeal. There was a part of me that wanted to jump up out of my seat, run out of this house, and never come back. But I didn't. I sat there and listened to her talk.

"Do you know what happened to my father?" she asked.

I hesitated before answering. I wasn't sure how much I should tell her about Patrick Devlin and his new life. Or what part he might have played—I still wasn't sure whether he did or not—in the abduction that got her out of that house and found her a new identity. But she deserved to know the truth. At least some of it.

"I saw him a while ago," I said. "He lives in Boston now. He relocated there and started all over again with his life after you . . . well, disappeared."

"Did you ask him about me?"

"Yes, that's why I went there to see him."

"Does he still miss me?"

I thought about that answer, too. About his new wife and his new children and the new company he had started there. He had moved on from the nightmares he left behind in New York. He'd managed to shut himself off from all that now. Just as he shut himself off from the child he once had named Lucy. She was dead to him now, just as she was dead to the rest of the world.

"Yes, he asked me about you," I lied.

"But he has no idea that I'm still alive?"

"No."

"No one else does, either?"

"Only me."

"And Elliott Grayson, the man who took me away from my mother."

"That's right."

"I still don't understand why you're doing all this. You say you're not going to do a story about me. That's what you promised."

"I won't, Linda. Not without your permission. You don't want people to know yet, do you? Or find out about your past life as Lucy Devlin, the most famous missing child in the country? That's what you told me. And that's what we agreed to when we began talking about all this."

"Then why are you spending so much time here with me?"

Because you're my daughter, dammit! Because I desperately want to spend this time with you. Because I want to make up for all the lost time when I never was with you. Because I want to be your mother again, even if I never really was your mother. But I want to try, Lucy. I so much want to try and be the mother that you never had.

Yep, those are the words I wanted to say to her.

It was the perfect moment—the opening I'd been looking for—to tell my daughter the truth about us.

Except . . .

There was a picture of her family on a mantel in the living room where we were sitting. Her husband, Gregory Nesbitt, was a good-looking guy—probably in his early thirties. They were at a backyard barbecue in the picture, and he was wearing a chef's hat and a cooking apron. Their little girl, an eight-year-old named Audrey—who, of course, would be my granddaughter—was looking up at him with what seemed to be total adoration for her dad. Linda Nesbitt aka Lucy Devlin stood by his side with a big smile on her face. It was a nice picture. They had the feel of the perfect All-American family. But then so had Anne and Patrick Devlin when she was a little girl Audrey's age growing up in New York. You never know about people. Not until it's too late. But, from what I could tell, Linda Nesbitt had found happiness after all the terrible things that happened to her.

Was I going to somehow mess that up by being back in her life?

"I'm just doing my job as a journalist," is what I told her.

* * *

On the way back to New York, I tried to take stock of my current situation with the young woman I now knew to be my long-lost daughter, Lucy.

There were a couple of options I could have pursued after finally tracking her down: 1) walked away and let her live her own life happily without me or 2) tell her everything—who I was, what I'd done, and try to explain why I had waited so long to reveal I was her biological mother, the woman who had set all this in motion a long time ago by giving her up for adoption as a newborn baby.

But I had done neither of these things.

Instead, I had lied to her.

There were also two logical scenarios for me to pursue professionally as a journalist here. 1) Abandon the Lucy story once and for all, because I could never tell it publicly without revealing the secrets I had hidden along the way, which would compromise my journalistic reputation and probably destroy my career; or 2) come clean and tell the whole story—the real story, the true story—of Lucy Devlin on air. It would be the biggest story of my life, even if it turned out to be my last. At least I'd go out in a blaze of glory.

But I was caught up in this deadly trap that I had created for myself with my own lies.

Sooner or later, I was going to have to make a decision on what to do about Lucy.

On both fronts.

But right now, I had a big story to do.

I tried to concentrate completely on that for the rest of the trip home.

Yep, a big story was all I needed to pull me out of this funk I was in right now.

A big story always made everything better.

CHAPTER 23

I INTRODUCED GARY Weddle to everyone at the Channel 10 morning news meeting.

I started off by repeating the same line about consultants I'd used with Faron: "Gary is a consultant who's been hired by management to help us with our newscasts. And, you know what they say about consultants. Those who can, do. Those who can't, teach. And those who can't do either become consultants." Then I followed it up with a few new jokes: "A consultant is a person you pay to borrow your watch and tell you what time it is." And finally: "Why is a consultant like a prostitute? They both screw their clients for money."

Everyone laughed, including Weddle.

Then I told them a bit about Weddle's qualifications and why he was here. I also ran through some of the ideas he had told me about improving our newscast. And that I liked a lot of his proposals. My hope was that showing I was onboard with the consultant idea might temper some of the opposition to Weddle that I knew was coming. But it did not.

"You want us to throw our material up immediately on the web for everyone to see?" someone asked. "Why would they tune in to our newscast then? That would kill our ratings."

"How would we even do it?" another editor asked. "Work twenty-four hours a day, seven days a week in here putting up news on the website all day and night. That's crazy."

And, as I expected, Brett Wolff and Dani Blaine—our two co-anchors—wanted to know how it would impact them as the stars of the newscast, the ones people wanted to see and advertisers paid big bucks to have on the screen delivering the news in their living rooms each night.

"We're the face of Channel 10 News," they both said in different ways, but pretty much with the same message. "Not some dopey website."

Gary Weddle patiently went through it all with them. He talked about how more and more people—especially young people, the target of our advertisers—were not watching traditional newscasts, but instead, got most of their news in real time on smartphones and their tablets.

He explained that his "The News Never Stops" concept would help the ratings, not hurt them, by promoting the station's newscast and its newscasters—most prominently Brett and Dani—throughout the day.

He also said that a series of procedures could be established so that any big breaking news story we would be covering anyway that day could transition easily to the station's website as part of the normal news coverage process, without involving a great deal of extra work for anyone.

"If you're at a fire that happens at 11 a.m., you're going to shoot video of that fire then, while its occurring. All we do then is put that video up on our website quickly, rather than holding onto it for the 6 p.m. newscast. Then, for the newscast itself, we do it all the better, with the star power of our two anchors and all the rest of our resources.

"Nobody's going to be working all day on it. And it's not like we'd put up every bit of news that goes on during the day. We'd only do it for a big breaking story that we're covering anyway—and giving that news to people as it happens, without being locked into the constraints of a specific newscast time like in the past.

"Look, here's the bottom line for 'The News Never Stops.' It's a promotional gimmick. The idea that we're out there doing this 24/7 is all bullshit. We don't have to actually do that, just make viewers feel like that's what they're getting from us. It will give us a brand—a promotional sizzle—that no other station in town has. And that will translate into even higher ratings for us."

Sizzle.

Brand promotion.

Bigger ratings.

Now those were concepts TV people could relate to.

Weddle was winning the room over now, getting them all to buy in for "The News Never Stops."

Even Brett and Dani.

Weddle wrapped his talk up by saying that he would be talking individually to more people in the newsroom over the coming days; I told another joke or two; and then I said how much I looked forward to working with Gary Weddle to implement all this for our Channel 10 coverage.

I gave him a big smile when I was done.

He smiled back at me.

It was a nice smile.

*　　*　　*

"What was that all about in there?" Maggie asked me when we were back in my office after Weddle left.

"Do you mean the 'The News Never Stops' stuff?"

"No, I mean what's going on between you and this Weddle guy?"

"What are you talking about?"

"You were so nice to him."

"I'm always nice."

"No, you're not."

"I'm trying to develop a good working relationship with him—the way Jack Faron asked me to do."

But Maggie wasn't buying it. I've never been able to BS Maggie.

"Are you hot for this guy, Clare?"

"What makes you think that?"

"I could pick up the vibes between you two. You're pretty obvious when you're attracted to a man. Not to mention that smile-athon thing you two had going at the end. That looked like more than just a good working relationship with Gary Weddle."

"Okay, maybe I do find him attractive. So what?"

"He's not your type, Clare."

"Everyone keeps telling me that."

"Maybe you should start listening."

CHAPTER 24

BEFORE I WENT on the air about the eight mob-related buildings and the rest, I wanted to make sure I'd exhausted every possible way to get more information for this story.

That's what I was doing with Maggie. I'd asked her to do more research on the three key people who appeared to be involved: Victor Morelli, Terri Hartwell, and Chad Enright.

Morelli was the most obvious target because I now knew he was the silent owner of the buildings. I wasn't sure exactly what roles Hartwell or Enright might have in this—but there was certainly enough to suspect Morelli could be paying off powerful politicians, under the guise of campaign contributions, to look the other way when it came to buildings owned by Morelli and others.

I also didn't know how Thomas Wincott fit into the whole payoff picture, but I put Wincott aside for now. He was not the owner of the eight buildings we were looking at. Although he did seem to be part of the bigger problem of wealthy landlords who could be getting special favors for paying off powerful political figures in the city.

For now, though, I was going to focus on the eight Morelli-owned buildings that I had visited.

Maggie started by telling me what she'd found out about Morelli.

"Victor Morelli has been the head of one of New York City's biggest crime families since the nineties. He began moving up in the ranks soon after John Gotti got convicted of murder and sent to prison for life. That's the thing about mob bosses. You get rid of one, another comes along to take his place.

"Morelli is smart and tough and brutal. He's lasted a long time because of that. He ostensibly runs a sanitation company, a construction business, and manages real estate interests as a legitimate businessman. But he makes his real money from loansharking, extortion, and other illegal activities run by his men.

"He's been compared to Gotti because of the Teflon Don thing. Like Gotti was for a long time, Morelli never seems to get convicted of any crime. The charges always go away or he beats the rap in court. One of the reasons for that might be because Morelli plays the role of the legitimate businessman so well. Goes to social events and art galleries and Broadway openings. Raises money for charities and helps people in his Brooklyn neighborhood, where's he's beloved by many people.

"But the bottom line is he's a stone-cold killer. And reputed to have a terrible temper. Especially if he believes anyone has betrayed him or double-crossed him in any possible manner.

"There's a lot of stories about this. One of his top mob capos was found dead in the East River with—well, his genitals—missing. At first, authorities thought it was a rival mob hit. But now they believe Morelli did it himself because the guy had been showing an interest in Morelli's wife. There was a neighbor in Brooklyn who complained to the police that the fireworks in Morelli's backyard were too loud one Fourth of July. That neighbor mysteriously disappeared afterward. And a few years ago, a cop was found dead in his car in the Bronx, shot in the mouth with his own gun. It was ruled a suicide, but there are people who think that the cop was taking payoffs from Morelli—and he tried to renege on the deal or squeeze more money out of him. No question about it, Morelli is a violent man if anyone crosses him."

"Nice guy," I muttered.

"Morelli's top henchman is a mobster named Michael Grasso. Or Michael—The Enforcer—Grasso, as he's known in underworld circles. He's supposed to carry out most of the heavy-duty violent work for Morelli."

She showed me a picture of Grasso on her laptop computer screen. I recognized him right away. He was the same man with the gravelly voice that I'd met the first night outside the Manhattan building where the kinky BDSM dungeon was being operated. The same man who'd given me the warning to forget about this story. And the same man who I was pretty sure gave me the follow-up warning in the gravelly voice on the phone.

Should I be worried about him and the Morelli temper if I named Morelli on the air as the owner of the buildings? Not really, I decided. I knew the mob didn't normally come after journalists. Besides, what was I going to do? Drop the story because I was afraid of Victor Morelli. That wasn't going to happen.

"Speaking of bad guys, we come now to Chad Olsen Enright," Maggie was saying. "Everyone I talked to agrees with you he's a prick. But an extremely successful one so far. He started out as a producer on Terri Hartwell's radio show, helped make her a star there, and got promoted to a top aide since she ran for and won the district attorney's job. He is supposed to be insufferable, but he's gotten away with it by staying so close to Hartwell. At least for now."

"What do you mean?"

"The word in political circles is there's going to be a shakeup in Hartwell's office soon. She's gearing up for a run at the mayor's office, as you know. Rumor is she will bring in a big political operative to run her mayor campaign—instead of giving Enright the job. He could even be out in the shakeup. So maybe she isn't quite as much of a big Chad Enright fan as everyone has always thought."

I thought about the conversation between Hartwell and myself that day in her office. The way she overruled Enright and agreed to see me after he said no. The way she made fun of him and his pomposity a bit during our conversation. I remembered, too, the pictures in Enright's office of him with the celebrities and the fancy cars and the beautiful women on his arm. Chad Enright had been living the good life because of his relationship with Terri Hartwell. Maybe that was going to end soon.

"Does Enright know about the shakeup coming in Hartwell's office for the campaign?" I asked.

"If I heard about it, Enright must have some inkling, too."

"He can't be very happy about that."

"You think?" Maggie laughed.

As for Hartwell herself, pretty much everything Maggie found out was what I already knew about her. Happily married, mother of two teenagers, former crusading lawyer, former popular radio show host, now a successful political figure running the Manhattan DA's office with her eye on the mayor's job. She'd spent her life waging war one way or another against crime, special interests, and corruption without a hint of any scandal.

"There's got to be something more going on," I said.

"With who?"

"Morelli. Enright. Hartwell. All of them."

"Well, if there is, I sure don't know what it is."

"Maybe I'll try one more thing. Some old-school journalism."

"Old-school journalism?"

"A stakeout," I said.

CHAPTER 25

I BOUGHT TWO hot dogs with sauerkraut and a Coke from a sidewalk vendor, then settled down on the steps of a church outside Terri Hartwell's office and waited.

I wasn't waiting for Hartwell though.

I was waiting for Chad Enright.

I had the feeling that he was the key to whatever was going on here.

Maybe it was just my reporter's instinct.

Or maybe it was because I didn't like Chad Enright.

But Enright was the one I wanted to learn more about before going on air with this story.

* * *

It had been a long time since I'd done a stakeout. I'd done my share as a young reporter though, enough to remember how difficult they were.

There was the food and drink thing. Which eventually led to the bathroom issue. Sooner or later, you had to heed nature's call. Which meant you had to leave your watching spot, even if just for a few minutes. But that few minutes could be enough to blow the whole story.

When I'd worked at the *New York Tribune* newspaper, we had a reporter who staked out a key witness in a murder trial for three days without the person emerging. Then, on the third day, the reporter left for less than five minutes to take a leak and the witness walked out the door. A *New York Post* reporter who had happened by at the right time got the exclusive Page One interview.

From that moment on, our guy at the *Tribune* had to live with the ignominy of being the reporter who "pissed away" the biggest story of his career.

But probably the worst part of a stakeout was the boredom.

Absolutely nothing happened for long stretches of time.

Which is what I was dealing with right now.

Lots of people went in and came out of the building. But no Chad Enright. No Terri Hartwell, either. Or anyone else I cared about—or at least knew enough about them to care.

I tried to pass the time by making lists of my favorite things. Favorite foods. Favorite movies. Favorite actors. That was a tough one, and I had to make some real decisions in my rankings. I finally gave up when I couldn't break a tie between Bradley Cooper and Ryan Gosling.

At some point, I got around to a Top 10 list of my favorite female newscasters of all time. Barbara Walters was on the list. The early Barbara Walters, who did news and interviews—not the host of *The View*. So was Connie Chung, one of the first women anchors at a major network when she did the *CBS Evening News* back in the early nineties.

Others on my list included Diane Sawyer, Katie Couric, Leslie Stahl, and Andrea Mitchell—all for obvious reasons. I did not include Julie Chen or Megyn Kelly, also for obvious reasons. And I threw in Maria Bartiromo's name on the list, too, mostly because she was the only female newscaster to ever have a song about her sung by Joey Ramone. How cool is that?

I looked over at the building. Still no sign of Enright or anyone else I cared about. I bought another hot dog from the vendor and ate it. Then a big salted pretzel with mustard. I was starting to get heartburn. I wondered if Katie Couric or Diane Sawyer or Barbara Walters ever had to deal with that problem.

I also knew that Jack Faron wasn't happy about me doing this. He'd given another speech about needing me to focus more on being news director when I told him about my stakeout plan. He said that's the job he was paying me a big salary for—not to chase around on the street after stories that my reporters were supposed to do.

Sooner or later, I was going to have to listen to him if I wanted to keep my job at Channel 10. I was getting too old to start over again at some new place. Would anyone even hire me again at my age if I lost this job? So, in addition to the heartburn and boredom, I was also having a bit of a career anxiety attack.

Gotta love these stakeouts.

Finally, a little after six p.m., Enright came out of the building, got in a cab, and rode home to a high-rise on Fifth Avenue just below 14th Street. I followed him in another cab until he went in the door, waited to make sure he didn't go out again—and then went home.

*　*　*

The next morning, I was back outside his office again, armed with a thermos of coffee and a supply of bagels. I was starting to think about what I was going to do for lunch when something happened.

Enright came out of the building, hailed a cab, and headed up-
town. I followed him again.

It took a while.

When he got to Third Avenue and 59th Street, he got out and
stood on the corner like he was waiting for someone. Five minutes
later, a steel-gray Cadillac pulled up and Enright got in. The
Caddy inched its way through midtown traffic, across 59th, up
First Avenue, and then disappeared into an underground garage
of a high-rise building at 79th and First.

I walked into the lobby and was met by a doorman.

"I'm trying to find someone I think lives here." I smiled.
Friendly, nonthreatening. Just a confused woman looking for
some help. "But I can't quite remember the name. I think it's
something like Findlay."

The doorman smiled back.

"Findlay? Let me check the board for you, ma'am." He walked
over to a lobby directory. I followed him and rapidly began scan-
ning the names, hoping to find one that might mean something
to me.

"How about Feely?" the doorman asked.

"I don't think so."

When I got down to the Ms on the directory, one of the names
jumped out at me. Morelli. Victor Morelli. Victor Morelli had an
apartment in the building. Could Chad Enright—Terri Hartwell's
top aide—be meeting here with Morelli? And, if so, why?

"Maybe I have the wrong building," I told the doorman.

Outside, I turned into the parking garage where the Caddy had
gone. There was no attendant around. I spotted the Caddy, walked
over to where it was parked. I opened the door—which was unlocked—and rummaged through the glove compartment. I found
something there indicating the car was registered to Morelli.

Just then an elevator door opened, and three men stepped out. They headed toward the Caddy. I ducked behind a car alongside before they saw me. Then, as quickly and carefully as I could, I crawled low behind more of the cars, made my way back to the garage entrance, and got the hell out of there. But not before I was able to recognize all three of the men I'd seen getting into Morelli's car.

One of them was Victor Morelli himself.

Another was Michael—The Enforcer—Grasso, his top henchman.

And the third man was Chad Enright.

CHAPTER 26

"How come you've never gotten married?" I asked Gary Weddle.

"How come you've never stayed married?"

"I guess I never found the right person."

"Me either."

We were having dinner together. And we were eating in an actual restaurant this time. I'd abandoned the cafeteria idea once I decided I liked him. The question was how much I liked him. Well, I'd already decided I liked him a lot. Sure, I know everyone kept telling me he wasn't my type. But shouldn't I be the one who decided what my type of romantic interest should be?

I still wasn't sure if this was a business dinner or a personal one. I'm not even certain who suggested it first. But it seemed like a good idea to both of us. So here we were.

I'd come up with a plan though to get a reading on exactly how he felt about this dinner. If he saw it as simply a business dinner, he'd say we should put it on our Channel 10 expense accounts. But, if he viewed it as personal—a date or whatever—he'd offer to pay the bill. I, being the liberated woman I am, would then suggest splitting it with him, and we'd be on an official date.

It was a pretty clever plan, if I do say so myself. And I was eagerly looking forward to getting the check at the end of the meal to put it into motion.

We talked as we ate about a lot of stuff at the office, including my upcoming on-air appearance about the Morelli-owned buildings. That was scheduled to lead our newscast the following evening. I told Weddle everything I'd found out about the buildings and also about my sighting of Morelli and Terri Hartwell's top deputy, Chad Enright.

"Do you think Hartwell is taking payoffs from Morelli?" he asked. "Maybe disguised as campaign contributions from a third person like say this Wincott guy you mentioned?"

"Something's going on there between them."

I'd discussed this in detail with Faron earlier after seeing Morelli, Grasso, and Enright together.

"I can't say there are payoffs. I don't know what Enright and Morelli were saying to each other or doing together in that garage. But I can point out all the illegal activities going on at the Morelli buildings, without any action being taken by authorities. I can say that Channel 10 has learned exclusively of disturbing communications between Hartwell's office and the Morelli crime family. And then I can call on Terri Hartwell to come forward and answer all these questions for us. I think that ought to be enough to set off some real fireworks and shake up Terri Hartwell's political aspirations."

Weddle said he liked it a lot, that it was the kind of enterprising story that could set us apart from other media in town and help spike our ratings. He also said he was happy so far with the way the newsroom staff at Channel 10 had worked with him to implement his "The News Never Stops" concept into our daily news operation. It was only baby steps so far, he said, but it had been a promising beginning.

"I've got you to thank for that, Clare. The way you stood up for me at that first meeting is a big reason this has worked well so far. I generally run into a lot more opposition when I go to a new place with my ideas. But they like you, they respect you. So when you supported me the way you did . . . well, it made a big difference."

At some point, I filled him in on some of the office gossip. He wanted to know more about Faron, Maggie, the on-air reporters, and—most of all—he had questions about Brett and Dani.

"What's the deal going on between those two?" he asked.

"They're sleeping together. Or at least they were the last time I checked. It's kind of a fluid situation."

"Why?"

"Well, for one thing, Brett is married."

"Ah, I see . . ."

"He also is"—I made some air quotes with my hands—"'sort of engaged' to Dani."

"Fluid." Weddle smiled.

"Very fluid."

"Isn't that a problem—a situation like that in the office—with all the controversy these days on sexual relationships or affairs in the workplace?"

"They say they're in love." I shrugged.

"What exactly is the rule about that for two people working in the same office?"

"I'm not sure what the rules are anymore."

I wondered if he knew I might be thinking about him and me as well as Brett and Dani.

Weddle had ordered a steak and baked potato. I liked that. I'm not usually into vegetarians or salad eaters. One more indication that this guy could be my type, despite all the naysayers. I'd gone for the chicken alfredo, which was good but pretty much filled up my calorie count for the rest of the week.

"You know, I almost got married once," he said at one point. "This woman and I lived together for a year. We made plans for a wedding and a life together. But, in the end, things didn't work out between us."

"Why not?"

"When I'm working on a big project, like this one at Channel 10, I became obsessed with it. Throw myself into it. I work day and night, almost forgetting everything else—including the woman I'm with. I guess I've always put my career priorities first. It's a character flaw. And it's cost me a few relationships."

"It sounds like you and I would be a good fit together," I blurted out before even realizing what I had said.

"What do you mean?"

"I have the same character flaw. If you and I got together, we could both be obsessed with our jobs and not worry about having to spend time with each other outside the job. My God, it would be the perfect relationship."

He laughed. I did, too, but it all seemed to be moving in the right direction between the two of us. Then, when the bill came, he offered to pay, as if this were a real date. We wound up splitting it, as I'd planned. As George Peppard used to say on *The A-Team*, "I love it when a plan comes together."

The real test, though, was going to be the "good night." Did we go our separate ways after leaving the restaurant or did he escort me home? It turned out he escorted me home. Walked me right to the front door of my building, where he gave me an awkward kind of hug and said, "I'd like to see you again, Clare."

"You see me every day in the office,"

"No, I mean I'd like to see you ... like this ... just you and me ..."

He was stammering, which I thought was kind of adorable. I impulsively kissed him. It was a quick kiss, but a kiss, nevertheless.

"I'd like to do that, too," I said. "But I don't think it's that easy. Because of all the stuff going on now about sex in the workplace, especially between a boss and an employee. I'm an executive with the station, and we hired you. I'm technically your boss. That could cause real problems."

"Well, my contract with the station is a temporary one, for a few months. Once that's done, we could revisit the issue, Clare. I'm willing to wait, if that's better for the both of us."

"Let's leave it like that for now and see what happens."

"What about another kiss?" he asked. "Is that allowed?"

"I think we could slip one in if we promise to keep it a secret from everyone."

"I won't tell if you don't."

Then he leaned down and kissed me.

For a long time.

It was a nice kiss.

The kind of kiss that promised even better things ahead.

*   *   *

When I got upstairs to my apartment, I called Janet. I told her I needed some advice.

"Legal or personal?" she asked.

"A combination of both."

I told her about my evening with Gary Weddle. About our decision to hold off on going any further while we worked together. And yes, about the kiss we shared at the end.

"That's a situation filled with potential downsides for you, Clare. Like you said, you're his boss. If the relationship breaks up and the station decides to fire him—or even just doesn't renew his contract—he could say that's retaliation from you because of a personal relationship. It's not as common for a woman supervisor to be accused of sexual harassment as a man, but it can happen. You could find yourself in a legal mess. That's one scenario."

"What's another one?"

"He comes up with a plan for the station that doesn't include you. Based on his consultant advice, the station fires you and gets a new news director. You claim it's because you refused his advances and wouldn't sleep with him. Under that scenario, you would have a legitimate sexual harassment lawsuit against him."

"Uh, Janet, is there any possible scenario here between Weddle and I that doesn't wind up in a lawsuit?"

"Well, you could live happily ever after."

"I'm good with that."

"Doesn't seem very likely given your track record with men."

"There's always a first time for everything."

"'Those who ignore history are doomed to repeat it.' Winston Churchill said that. But I think it applies to your love life, too."

Cute.

"So that's your legal advice for me?"

"Personal, too."

"Thank you."

"I'll send you a bill in the morning."

CHAPTER 27

"It's the News at 6 with the Channel 10 News Team. Brett Wolff and Dani Blaine at the anchor desk; Steve Stratton with sports; and Wendy Jeffers with your up-to-date weather forecast. If you want to know what's happening—you want it first and you want it accurate—Channel 10 News has you covered.

"And now, here's Brett and Dani..."

> BRETT: Good evening. There's been a bus accident on the George Washington Bridge—no one is seriously injured, but it's making a mess of the evening commuter rush; the mayor says he wants more bikes and less cars in Manhattan; the Mets found a new way to lose a ball game; and—well, if you haven't had enough rain already—there's a lot more on the way.

> DANI: But first, we open with exclusive coverage of a new housing crisis in New York City from Channel 10's own Pulitzer-Prize-winning journalist, News Director Clare Carlson.

> ME: It's always been tough to find a good place to live in New York City. The rents are too high, the apartments too

small, and the demand too much for the supply. But now the problem is even worse because more and more New Yorkers are being shut out of affordable housing by powerful and corrupt forces using these spaces instead to make themselves big profits or carry out illicit enterprises.

The screen cut to a shot of the first apartment building I'd visited:

ME: Many of the residents of this building on the Lower East Side have lived here their entire lives. Families have grown up here, and memories were made over the years. But now people are being forced out by a landlord who wants to make more money from the property. I spoke with one of the tenants still living there, a 68-year-old retiree named Joseph Moskowitz.

A video of me interviewing Moskowitz in front of the building was on the screen now.

MOSKOWITZ: They don't do repairs for me, they don't provide adequate heat in the winter, my water is sometimes shut off for days. And the only elevator in this building . . . well, it isn't just that it doesn't work. It's dangerous to all of us. Not long ago, a little boy fell down the abandoned shaft and died. The authorities ruled it an accident. But it never would have happened if the building was maintained properly. I've complained to everyone I can think of, but no one does anything.

I talked about the boy who died in the elevator shaft, a six-year-old named Danny Fields. I did an interview with his parents, too. Showed pictures of him growing up, looking happy and joyful. It was heartbreaking stuff. Especially when the mother broke down in tears on the screen.

> MRS. FIELDS (DANNY'S MOTHER): We called and we called to get them to fix that elevator. Or at least make sure the door was shut so that no one could fall into it. We told Danny to stay away from there. But he was only six years old, and he was so inquisitive about everything. And then one day . . .

That's when she broke down in tears.

> MRS. FIELDS: All they had to do was send someone over to fix that elevator and my little boy would still be alive. But they never answered any of my calls. They never got back to me no matter how many times I tried. And they didn't even bother to call or contact us with any kind of condolences after Danny died. What kind of people are they?

I showed video then from the other buildings I'd visited. Interviews with residents who talked about the traffic and other woes resulting from the mob-run pizza place, the gambling operations, the sex industry spots, and all the rest. I was careful to just recite the facts of what we did know to avoid any libel issues. But that was enough. The facts were pretty powerful.

At the pizza place, one longtime neighborhood resident complained that he no longer could find a place to park his car when he came home from work.

> RESIDENT: I get parking tickets from police all the time. The people who double park outside that pizza place never

get ticketed at all. That's not fair. I complained to police, but they ignored me. I complained one time to the manager of the pizza place. The next day, the windshield on my car was smashed. But no one listens to us.

ME: No one listens. That's a constant refrain from the people at all these locations. The owner of the buildings doesn't care about their complaints. The police don't seem to care either. Or any of the elected officials that are supposed to be protecting their rights as hardworking New Yorkers.

Then I got to the trickiest part of the report. The stuff about Victor Morelli. And about Terri Hartwell.

I said that all of the buildings in this report were owned by a faceless conglomerate called Big M Realty Corp. Which, I told the viewers, turned out to be a front for the company called More-Land Management. Finally, I revealed that More-Land Management was run by Victor Morelli, one of the city's most notorious crime bosses.

ME: Not surprisingly, Big M Realty Corp, More-Land Management, and Victor Morelli himself all refused to return calls from Channel 10 with our questions about these buildings. They don't return calls from the people in the buildings or the neighborhoods around them either.

Next, I brought up the possibility of a connection between Morelli and payoffs—disguised as political campaign contributions—to get authorities and city officials to ignore his building violations. Faron and I had gone over all this with the station's lawyers beforehand. We decided not to make a specific reference to my sighting of Morelli and Enright, since we had no idea of the context of their meeting. Instead, I said:

> ME: Channel 10 has discovered disturbing questions about the relationship between Morelli and the office of Manhattan District Attorney Terri Hartwell, who is a potential candidate for mayor. Including contacts between the Morelli and Hartwell camps. There is no evidence that Morelli has contributed money directly to the Hartwell mayor campaign. But it certainly raises the possibility of Morelli money being funneled into the Hartwell campaign through a third-party contributor. We will continue to pursue this issue. And so, we call on District Attorney Hartwell tonight to publicly disavow any connection with Morelli and to declare now that she has not received—either directly or indirectly—any campaign contributions from Victor Morelli. The people of New York have a right to get that answer from you, District Attorney Hartwell.

I mentioned Martin Barlow, too, in my report. I said he was the journalist who had first uncovered illegal activities at the buildings I'd cited. I did not say anything about a possible connection between any of this and Barlow's death. Because I wasn't sure there was one. And because I certainly didn't have any evidence to back that idea up. And I did not even consider going public with Marty's serial killer theory, which had no facts whatsoever at the moment to back it up—and seemingly had nothing to do with any of the rest of this.

I thought again about Marty and his contempt for the type of news I usually did for TV. Everything from Kardashian/Bieber to breathless weather reports to miracle diets and weight loss programs that passed for news on television. But we weren't about news on TV news shows. Not real news anyway. It was all about ratings and advertising dollars and demographics.

Except this time, I'd broken out of that format.

I'd done an actual news story.

Damn, it felt good to be a journalist again.

CHAPTER 28

TERRI HARTWELL HELD a press conference the next day that quickly turned into a tidal wave of news.

Hartwell announced that the District Attorney's Office—in conjunction with housing and other city officials—was taking immediate action against the buildings I'd featured in my broadcast.

They were all being taken over by the city, she said. The illegal operations taking place in them would be shut down. The legitimate tenants would be allowed to stay and their complaints—heat, broken elevators, and all the rest—would be dealt with in a professional and compassionate and expedited manner.

Hartwell also said that swift action would come soon at other buildings around the city with questionable ownership practices. A number of other buildings had already been targeted, several of which turned out to belong to Thomas Wincott. I didn't figure I'd get invited back to the Wincott house anytime soon.

She also denounced Victor Morelli as a "violent criminal who belongs behind bars." She said she would use the full power of her office to prosecute him for this and other crimes. She said that she never received any campaign contributions from Morelli. And—if any money had been somehow given to her campaign by him through a third party—it would be immediately returned.

"Wow!" Maggie said as we listened to Terri Hartwell's comments.

"Wow, indeed," I echoed.

"You did it, Clare! You broke this whole story wide open!"

Yep, I sure did. In my entire career, I don't think I'd ever experienced a story of mine creating so much immediate news as I'd done with this.

But there was even more from Hartwell.

"We had been working on this investigation for some time in my office," Hartwell said. "It has been one of my top priorities for months to put Victor Morelli and other unscrupulous landlords out of business.

"I originally planned to announce these actions at a later date, but we are doing it now in response to Channel 10's report highlighting these shocking abuses discovered in buildings around the city. Let me take a moment to salute Channel 10 News—and their news director, Clare Carlson, who broke the story—for an outstanding example of responsible journalism. I'm proud of what we're doing here to right these wrongs, and the people at Channel 10 should be proud, too, for their role in this."

*   *   *

By the end of the day, the elevator on the Lower East Side had been fixed. The double-parked cars outside the pizza place had been towed away. And the gambling operation and the BDSM sex business had been shut down or moved elsewhere. There was no activity that anyone could see going on at any of these locations anymore.

We covered all this big on Channel 10—first on our website as part of "The News Never Stops," which made Weddle happy—and then as our lead segment on the evening newscast.

"Thank you, Channel 10 News," a resident of one of the affected neighborhoods said at the end of the report. "Our city leaders let us down, but Channel 10 came through for us. Thank God we have journalists looking out for us when the politicians aren't."

Damn, it didn't get much better than this.

And then it got even more interesting.

Terri Hartwell called me up personally at one point to thank me for what I'd done—and to explain a bit more about why she had been less than truthful to me that first day when I asked her about the buildings in her office.

"I apologize for misleading you that day," she said. "Obviously, I knew all about those buildings even though I denied it. I had to at that point. I wasn't ready to go public yet with what we were doing. We were still trying to accumulate all the necessary evidence we needed to act. But you changed that timetable—speeded it up, I guess is the best way to put it—by breaking that story of yours. I respect that. Please respect me for doing what I had to do, Clare. I hope you understand that. I hate lying."

"Me, too."

"See, I knew we'd get along." She laughed. *Okay*, I thought to myself, let's put that to the test. I still had questions about her office and Morelli. Despite everything she'd said at the press conference, that was the one part of all this that didn't make sense to me. I told Hartwell about the scene I'd secretly witnessed in the garage of a meeting between Morelli, his top lieutenant Grasso, and her man Enright. I asked her to explain that to me.

"You really saw Chad there?" she asked.

"Yes."

"With Morelli?"

"They seemed very friendly."

There was a long pause at the other end.

"Are you sure it was Chad?" she asked finally.

"Chad Enright is a pretty unforgettable character. Hard to miss."

"And Morelli?"

"Same thing. Unforgettable."

"Maybe they were both accidentally in the garage at the same time."

"I don't think that's too likely. Why would Chad Enright be meeting secretly with Victor Morelli?"

She didn't answer me.

"What the hell's going on here, Ms. Hartwell? You make these great-sounding statements at your press conference about going after a vicious mob boss like Morelli with all the resources at your disposal. And at the same time, your top aide is meeting him in an underground garage. Whatever is going on with your office and Morelli is going to come out, sooner or later. So why not make it sooner and tell me everything you know about Morelli and Enright and all the rest?"

"There are things happening that I can't share with you yet," she said.

"I thought you said you were going to stop lying to me."

"I'm not lying about this."

"No, but you're not telling me all of the truth either."

Hartwell sighed on the line.

"Look, how about you and I get together sometime soon," she said. "We'll grab a few drinks, maybe dinner—we'll do it off the record. Just the two of us having a candid conversation. We can talk about all this stuff then."

"Including the relationship between Chad Enright and Victor Morelli?"

"Everything."

CHAPTER 29

ONE OF THE newsroom traditions I'd brought over with me to the TV news business was the Page One bar celebration. Whenever a reporter scored a big front-page scoop, the staff took him or her out to celebrate with drinks that night.

We didn't have a front page at Channel 10. But breaking a big story on air like I did was the equivalent. So, after the Terri Hartwell announcement and all the accolades started pouring in for the story we did, everyone took me to a place called Headliners that was not far from the station.

It used to be a legendary newspaper hangout, but these days—with newspapers dying out and staffs at them being drastically cut back—it was more of a journalism bar. Filled with people from TV news, magazines, websites, and all sorts of other media. So it was still a good place to celebrate a big scoop. Tradition, history, colorful surroundings. And they served liquor, so there was that, too.

Everyone was there when I got to the place. Faron, Maggie, Brett and Dani, Cassie O'Neal, Janelle Wright, Wendy Jeffers, Steve Stratton, and most of the other reporters and editors on staff. Even Brendan Kaiser, the station owner, showed up. And, even more importantly to me at the moment, Gary Weddle was there, too. I was the big star. The center of attention. That's happened to me a few times in the past during my journalistic career, but do you want to know something? I still love it!

There was a big bar surrounded by pictures of famous reporters over the years who had scored big scoops and won awards. One of the pictures on the wall was of me. Not the today me, the me from nearly twenty years ago when I won a Pulitzer Prize for my coverage of the big Lucy Devlin disappearance story. I looked at myself now in that long-ago photo. I looked so young and so pretty and so . . . well, happy. No idea that the Lucy Devlin story was a long way from being over.

Next to the bar was a buffet table with chicken, cold cuts, and a bunch of seafood appetizers—shrimp, oysters, salmon.

As I surveyed the offerings, Jack Faron was one of the first people to come over to congratulate me on our big success.

"Jeez, I can't ever remember a story coming together as fast as this one did," he told me. "Everything fell into place perfectly. And the public praise from the DA—well, that was icing on the cake."

I hadn't told him about my phone conversation afterward with Terri Hartwell. Because I wasn't sure what to make of it. I wanted to hear Hartwell out, listen to whatever she planned to tell me later about everything. I still had a lot of questions about the relationship between Enright and Morelli. Something was going on there. The biggest question was whether or not Hartwell was involved, too. I sure hoped not. I kinda liked her.

"Carlson's the name, scoops are my game," I said brightly to Faron.

I took a big swig of the drink I'd gotten from the bar.

"How much have you had to drink?" he asked.

"I'm just starting."

"I was afraid of that."

I started to sample the food. I couldn't decide between the shrimp, the boiled ham, and the chicken wings, so I filled a plate with all of them. Moderation is not one of my specialties. While I was doing this, Cassie O'Neal came over and started looking over the seafood selections, too.

"They say fish food is good for the brain," I whispered to Faron.

He looked at me questioningly.

"If I was Cassie, I'd eat a very large amount," I said.

Cassie is an enigma to me at Channel 10. She looks great, she's one of the most popular on-air reporters we have with the viewers, but she's also, well . . . dumb as a plank. I'd recently had a go-round with her when I assigned her to cover a hearing on First Amendment rights for the media. She asked me if that was the amendment that you took when you didn't want to testify in court. I said no, it was the one that repealed prohibition. She laughed, but I still don't think she quite comprehended the whole free press concept. The worst part was she made a lot of money. Even more than me. That's because rival stations had tried to hire her away from us several times; each time, Faron made me give her big money to stay at Channel 10. It was a source of constant frustration with me about the state of journalism in the world today.

"Are you going to start up again with all your jokes about Cassie being stupid?" Faron asked.

"Let's face it, her elevator doesn't go to the top floor."

"Jeez, Clare . . ."

"She's a few beers away from a six-pack."

"My God, you never stop, do you?" Faron said, shaking his head.

"All I'm saying is if she ever grew another brain, it would die of loneliness."

At some point, Faron asked me about the serial killer stuff again.

"I don't know, Jack, I don't have anything substantial. To be honest, I don't think we're gonna be able to do anything to back that up. Or come up with any answers on that Becky Bluso killing in Indiana after thirty years. The trail is long cold. There are better stories—easier stories to get—for us to go after now. That's what I'm going to do."

"Does that mean you're going back to being my news director again?"

"Bright and early tomorrow morning."

"Now you're talking sense, Clare."

There was a lot more praise and adoration for me before the evening was over. A few people like Faron and Maggie and Brett and Dani stood up to toast me and the story I'd broken wide open. The best toast came though from Brendan Kaiser, the media baron who owned Channel 10 and a jillion other media properties. He called me "the embodiment of the best of journalism, TV or newspapers. We're just so glad to have Clare Carlson with us here at Channel 10."

"Do I get a raise?" I yelled out.

I'd had a few more drinks by that point.

"You're the hotshot investigative reporter, you figure it out," someone shouted back.

*   *   *

All in all, it was a great night. Weddle and I kept a respectful distance away from each other for most of the party. But, when things were close to wrapping up, I found myself sitting next to him. Lots of people had been hugging and kissing me during the night. I wondered if maybe I should do that with Weddle now. Probably too soon. Maybe after a few more drinks.

"You're really something, Clare," he said, looking around the place at all the people who'd turned out for my big night.

"You mean as a journalist?"

"I mean in a lot of ways."

Weddle was wearing jeans, a T-shirt, and a checkered sports jacket. He almost looked cool. Well, the sports jacket didn't quite match the T-shirt, and the jeans were a bit too baggy. But I was never a stickler for detail in this kind of situation. His face was very near to me now. I took it all in. His blue eyes. A cute dimple on his cheek.

"How much time is left on this consulting contract between you and the station?" I asked.

"Two months, two weeks, and three days to go."

"I'll be counting the minutes," I told him.

Then I kissed Weddle quickly—without anyone seeing us—and moved away to mingle before either of us had a chance to succumb to temptation.

When I looked around a little later, he had left.

I went home, too, a bit after that.

Alone.

I walked into my empty apartment, took off my clothes, grabbed a box of Chocolate Mallomars out of the refrigerator—my favorite guilty indulgence after I've been drinking a lot—plopped down on the bed, and watched a forgettable movie on TV until I drifted off to sleep.

Virtue thy name is Clare Carlson.

CHAPTER 30

THERE WAS A ringing sound coming from somewhere.

I shook my head from side to side, hoping the ringing would go away. But it didn't. It kept getting worse and more insistent. I closed my eyes and tried to ignore it. That didn't work either. Damned sound just wouldn't go away.

I opened my eyes again and suddenly the events of the night before—most notably how much I'd had to drink—began to come back to me.

The ringing sound was still there. Ring, ring, go away. Come again some other day. I reached over to swat my hand at it and found my phone. I picked up the phone, dropped it on the floor, and finally got it up to my ear. The ringing stopped.

"Hmmm," I said.

"Clare, is that you?"

I recognized the voice. It was Rob Kinsey. The overnight guy who answers phones for us in the Channel 10 newsroom until everyone else gets to work. I looked over at the clock next to my bed. 6:15 a.m.

"No, Clare Carlson died several hours ago. Let her rest in peace."

"You sound bad."

"I feel worse."

"What happened?"

"I may have partied a bit too hard last night. What's up?"

"Terri Hartwell's office is looking for you."

"I talked to Terri Hartwell yesterday. She thanked me for everything we did on the story. What does she want now?"

"Maybe she wants to thank you again."

"What did she say?"

"It wasn't her who called. It was someone from her office."

"Who?"

"A guy named Chad Enright."

"Chad Enright called to talk to me?"

"Yes. He wasn't too nice about it either."

"He never is."

What the hell was Chad Enright calling me about at 6:15 a.m.? Did he know about me spotting him and Morelli and Grasso in that parking garage? Maybe Hartwell had told him after our conversation yesterday. But why call me now about it?

"You got Enright's number?" I asked.

Kinsey read it to me. It was a cell phone number.

"Okay, I'll call him when I get to the office."

I figured I might be able to go back to bed and get another hour of sleep.

"Enright wants you to call him right now."

"It can't wait until the sun comes up?"

"He said it was urgent."

I hung up with Kinsey, pulled myself up into a sitting position, and punched in the number Enright had left. He answered on the first ring.

"I have to talk to you, Ms. Carlson. There's a lot of things going on here. You think you know the story, but you only know part of it. I want everyone to hear the real story before it's too late. I'm prepared to tell you everything. About me. About Morelli. And about Terri Hartwell."

"Okay, tell me."

"Not on the phone. It has to be in person. This is too important to talk about on the phone. Meet me. Meet me right now. It will be a blockbuster story for you. And I'm going to lay it all out for you exclusively."

Jeez, who did this guy think he was? Deep Throat? On the other hand, if anyone knew what secrets Hartwell was hiding—assuming she was hiding secrets—it would be Chad Enright, her top aide. Enright wasn't my idea of the perfect source. But you don't always get to pick and choose your sources in the journalism business. And I've had even less desirable sources than Chad Enright in the past. I think.

"Where?"

"Meet me downtown at our building. In an hour. Less if you can make it."

"Okay, I'm on my way."

*　*　*

I drank some coffee—well, a lot of coffee—took a shower, and got dressed as fast as I could. I called Kinsey back and told him I was going to meet with Enright so I might be late getting into the office. I left voicemail messages for both Faron and Maggie with more specifics about my conversation with Enright and the meeting I was headed to. "Should be interesting," I told them both.

Then I took a subway downtown to the district attorney's offices. The subway stop was a few blocks' walk from the building on Foley Square. As I got nearer, I saw Enright standing on the sidewalk in front.

This guy sure was eager to see me.

"Okay, let's go upstairs to your office and talk," I said as I approached him.

"No, I don't want to go inside."

"Why not?"

"I have my reasons."

"Are we going to have this big important conversation you told me about right here on the sidewalk?"

"No, let's do it in there," he said.

He pointed to a car—a large black Lincoln Continental—sitting at the curb next to us.

"Your car?"

"Yes."

It didn't look like the kind of car Chad Enright would drive. I walked over to it. The windows of the Lincoln were dark and tinted so I couldn't see inside.

"I'm more comfortable out here," I said.

"No, this has to be private. Just the two of us. No one else can see us or know about us meeting like this. Please, get in the car."

I hesitated. This was all making me uncomfortable. But I wasn't too worried yet. I mean it was daylight now. We were standing there during the morning rush hour on a busy New York City street. Nothing bad could happen to me with all these cars and people around, right?

"Believe me, this will be well worth your time," Enright said.

I was still trying to decide what to do when the rear door of the car came flying open. A man reached out, grabbed me around the waist, and dragged me into the back seat with him. I looked over to see who had done that. Not Enright. Enright climbed inside the back seat of the Lincoln now, too. But there were three other men in the car.

One behind the wheel.

A second in the back seat who was holding on to me and also had a gun pointed at me now. He was the one who had pulled me off the street and into the car. I recognized him right away. Michael Grasso—Morelli's top henchman.

And now I saw the third person.

Sitting in the front seat next to the driver.

I recognized him, too.

Victor Morelli.

CHAPTER 31

I TRIED TO quickly take stock of my situation.

I was in a car surrounded by three mobsters and a crooked politician in Enright, who had set me up to be grabbed by them.

Enright was on one side of me in the back seat and Grasso was on the other. Grasso had his gun pointed at me and was still holding on to me. The other two—Morelli and the driver—were turned around and looking at me from the front seat.

My instincts told me that my best chance for survival was to get out of the car, even though the odds were against me being able to do that.

I jerked myself free of Grasso and made a try for the door handle.

But he grabbed me before I could get it open and pulled me back onto the back seat beside him.

"I warned you that first night you came out of the building to leave this alone," Grasso said in that gravelly voice I'd come to recognize all too well by now. "Then I called you and gave you a second warning. No more warnings. You try anything stupid like you just did there with the door, and you'll see what I mean. Understand?"

I said I understood. There didn't seem to be much else I could do at the moment.

"See, I told you I could get her for you," Enright said, speaking very rapidly. He seemed extremely nervous. "She thinks she's so smart. She's so smug. But I outsmarted her. I delivered her to you. Just like you asked me to, Mr. Morelli."

Morelli glared at me and didn't say anything for a long time. His contorted face was scary. I remembered all the things I'd heard he'd done to people who crossed him. I never thought he'd come after a journalist for doing a story. That was almost unheard of in the world of mob protocol. But there was a first time for everything. And I was afraid I might be the first here.

Finally, Morelli spoke. But not to me.

"What about the other one?" he asked Enright.

"She'll be here, too."

"Are you sure?"

"I called her, just like I called Carlson. Told her I needed to see her right away about everything that had happened. She'll show up here soon at her office. You can grab her then, same as you did with this one."

"And she won't have any security with her?"

"No. Terri's never needed protection like that."

"Well, she does today," Morelli grunted.

I couldn't believe what I was hearing. They were talking about Terri Hartwell. They were going to kidnap the district attorney. I wasn't sure what they planned after that, but it sounded like they were going to kill Terri Hartwell. And the fact that they were talking about it in front of me meant they weren't planning to let me walk out alive to tell the story.

The only thing I could think to do was keep everyone talking in the hopes that something—or someone—could save me.

"You need to reconsider what you're doing here, Mr. Morelli," I said, trying to keep my voice as calm as possible under the circumstances. "I'm aware of your reputation. I'm sure you think this is business as usual for you. But it isn't. Kidnapping a journalist is bad business. A district attorney is even worse. There's a reason no other mob leader has ever done something like this. If you murder a district attorney, law enforcement will come after you with everything they've got. And killing a journalist, any journalist, will put you in the media spotlight like you've never been before. You'll never get away with it."

"I've gotten away with everything else in the past," Morelli said arrogantly.

"This is different. They're going to track it back to you. I told my boss and another person at Channel 10 where I was going. To meet Chad Enright. I think Hartwell knows about you and Enright too, based on my last phone conversation with her. She's probably going to tell someone else, too, where she's going. Why take that kind of a chance? Why is this so important to you over a couple of buildings?"

Morelli didn't answer me, but Grasso did. "It's not just the buildings. Hartwell broke her promise to Mr. Morelli."

"What promise?"

"When Terri Hartwell started talking about running for mayor, Mr. Morelli helped her with a sizable contribution—an extremely sizable contribution. He got a lot of his friends and associates to make financial contributions to the Hartwell campaign, too. All he asked was a few little favors in return. She agreed, like the last district attorney agreed, to work with us. It was all business, everyone got something out of it."

I remembered how the previous district attorney had suddenly dropped an investigation into Morelli's building operations. Now I knew why—he'd gotten a payoff. Terri Hartwell had gotten the same kind of payoff. But then she went after him anyway. Why?

"Not long ago, Mr. Morelli tried to collect one of those favors from Terri Hartwell," Grasso continued. "But she refused. Said she didn't know what he was talking about. She threw him out of her office. She disrespected him. And now she's talking about putting him in jail."

There was something in all this that didn't make sense to me. It was the idea that Terri Hartwell took mob money—and then abruptly reneged on the deal. Why would she do that? I had a theory.

"You said Hartwell acted as if she didn't know what Morelli was talking about," I said. "Did Morelli or any of you ever talk directly with Hartwell when you were setting this deal up or giving her the campaign money? Or did you meet with someone else about all that? Someone like Chad Enright, here?"

Morelli and Grasso both turned toward Enright now. Enright looked like he was about to be sick. I knew then that I was right.

"Chad has a pretty exorbitant lifestyle," I said. "Big boat. Vacation house. Fancy cars. Expensive girlfriends. Awfully hard to maintain that on a government official's salary. So Chad figured out a way to boost his income big-time. He'd take your money on behalf of his boss, Terri Hartwell, in return for supposed favors she was going to do for you. Except he never told her anything about it. He kept the money."

"Is that right, Chad-boy?" Grasso asked. "Did you double-cross us? Were you playing both sides of the fence?"

Enright started talking, almost incoherently, in an effort to save himself.

"You don't understand," he said. "She was going to get rid of me. She was bringing in someone else to do my job once she announced she was running for mayor. She was going to take away my authority. I helped create her career, and now she was going to cast me aside. I had to do something."

"So, you worked out this deal with Morelli," I said. "It was perfect for you. You got the money, you got to keep living your lifestyle—and you figured it was payback against Hartwell because of what she was going to do about you. Then, when she went public with everything yesterday and Morelli decided to get rid of her, that was even better. Because if he killed Hartwell for reneging on your deal, then she could never figure out it was you double-dealing all along."

Enright was sobbing uncontrollably now. I turned away from him to face Morelli in the front seat.

"This changes everything, Mr. Morelli. Don't you see? Terri Hartwell didn't cheat you; she didn't break her word to you. You don't have to kill her. And Enright here will go to jail once people find out he was on the take. Isn't that enough for you?"

Everyone waited to hear what Morelli would say. But I could tell from his eyes what the answer would be. They were stone cold. A killer's eyes.

"Kill all three of them," he said to Grasso.

Enright started to plead for his life.

I knew we were almost out of time. They were still waiting for Hartwell to show up. When she did, they'd grab her in front of the building like they did with me. I didn't figure they'd kill us right there. They'd take us somewhere else—away from the DA's office and the crowds on the streets. I had to get out of the car before that happened.

I decided to try again to open the door and run. If I could make a break for it while Grasso was still focused on Enright, I might have a chance. Not much of a chance, but it was worth a try.

I was about to reach for the door handle when I heard the sirens. Suddenly, a dozen police cars, red lights flashing, squealed up and surrounded us. Armed police got out of the cars. A police loudspeaker from one of them blared: "Get out of the vehicle. Drop your weapons and keep your hands up."

Morelli and his men hesitated briefly, then calculated the odds, and surrendered meekly.

There were New York City cops, investigators from the district attorney's office, and then—most surprising of all—Terri Hartwell emerged from one of the cars.

"We've had a tail on Enright," Hartwell told me as the cops led him and Morelli and his men away. "He led us to Morelli first, then here with you. We weren't sure what was going on inside that car. We were ready to follow if you went anywhere. But then I realized they were waiting for me to show up because of Enright's ruse. That's when we decided it was time to make our move."

*   *   *

I broadcast live from the crime site soon after it was over, standing next to the car where I'd been abducted and reporting the dramatic details of everything that had just happened.

There was a lot of emotions running through me right then. Fear. Relief. Gratitude. And anger, too, that I'd been put in such a dangerous situation. People said those emotions—and especially my fear—came across in my live appearance as I reported the story.

There was a moment when I almost lost it and had to stop talking briefly to regain my composure. A video of that emotional moment wound up going viral on the web. Some people in the newsroom asked me afterward if I'd faked that for the ratings. But it was real. I was shook up pretty badly. Nearly getting killed can do that for you.

The news was filled with lots of follow-ups after that, with us at Channel 10 still in the lead and all the other media trying to play catch-up.

The stunning arrest of Hartwell's top aide, Chad Enright, was the focus of the first day's coverage. Plus, the arrest of Victor Morelli and other members of his mob family. There were more details and developments, including the arrest of Thomas Wincott, as a co-conspirator with Morelli in the housing scandal. Other details remained sketchy, and some of them might never be known for sure.

But Enright was talking—desperate to make a deal to shorten his prison time—and the picture he painted confirmed a lot of what I'd already figured out. He'd made a deal with Morelli to take campaign contributions without telling Hartwell. In return, he promised Morelli a free rein on his housing activities without any interference from the DA or other city officials. But, when Morelli finally went to Hartwell directly, she became suspicious and began looking into his properties. She'd already decided to get rid of Enright as her top aide, and she had made that clear to him. So Enright was happy for Morelli to think it was Hartwell who had double-crossed him—and even helped set her up to be killed, partly so his role in this could never be revealed by her.

There was no indication that Thomas Wincott was involved with—or even knew anything—about any plan to murder Hartwell. But he had been making campaign contributions to Enright, too, some on behalf of Morelli, to cover up their illegal housing activities. So he faced corruption charges growing out of the entire investigation.

I still didn't know how Marty had found out about all this.

But Enright did remember being at Wincott's townhouse one day to discuss campaign contributions for Hartwell. At some point, when Wincott left the room to talk to his wife, Enright made a call on his cell phone from the Wincott townhouse to Victor Morelli to discuss Terri Hartwell and the protection

Morelli thought he was buying from her. All in generalities, he said, and he didn't think anyone else had heard him.

But Marty lived in that townhouse, too. Maybe he got suspicious about what his son-in-law was doing. Maybe he had a hunch something funny was going on. Maybe he had already been looking into his son-in-law's housing activities. We would never know for sure now that Marty was dead.

And none of this answered the question I'd started out with—who killed Martin Barlow and why?

Enright insisted he had nothing to do with that, and the authorities believed him. There was no evidence either linking Morelli or any of his people to Marty's death.

In the end, the murder of Martin Barlow seemed to be just what it appeared at the beginning.

A senseless, random murder in New York City.

PART II

THE NEWS NEVER STOPS

CHAPTER 32

ANY STORY—NO MATTER how sensational—has a short life span in today's media world. Within a few days, or even hours, another big story has come along to take its place and grab the public's attention.

The media has always operated like this, even back in the heyday of newspapers. Yesterday's screaming front-page headline was today's back-page follow-up story. It got even worse in TV news where there was constant pressure to deliver big ratings—the demand for something new to keep people from switching channels.

And now, in the age of the internet and social media, everything is about instant gratification. We are all looking for that sensational story, that ratings bonanza, that traffic click bait for the web—then we're quickly on to the next story.

Which is what happened with the Terri Hartwell story.

Eventually all of us—Channel 10 and the rest of the media—moved on.

The big buzz at the moment was bike riding on the streets of New York City. Environmental groups had succeeded in getting the bike lanes dramatically expanded, so there were more people—a lot more—riding bicycles here now. At the same time, taxi and limousine and automobile groups complained about the increased number of bike riders hurting their businesses and making city streets more difficult—and more dangerous—to navigate.

It was true that more and more accidents were happening involving bicycle riders. The worst came when a teenaged girl on a bike and a family of six riding in an SUV collided at a Manhattan intersection—killing the girl as well as all six people in the SUV when it swerved into an oncoming truck in a futile attempt to avoid the biker.

Then, in the middle of all this, transit officials announced they were raising fares 25 percent, making the third option of buses or subways even more difficult for people. It was a perfect commuter chaos storm, and we at Channel 10—along with other news outlets in town—milked the story for all it was worth.

There was a big controversy going on about bathrooms in city schools. Activist groups were demanding the city build new "third gender" bathrooms to serve students who didn't identify with being either male or female. Me, I remember when it was "boys" and "girls" on the doors of school bathrooms. But the world was changing very rapidly. And all of us in the news business had to keep pace with it.

We covered a lot of crime stories, too. There are always crime stories. Murder. Rape. Robberies. Crime was the staple of local TV news everywhere, and we were no exception at Channel 10.

All of this kept me very busy, the way the news always does.

Jack Faron asked me one day about the serial killer story. I told him that I'd made a few inquiries, but I didn't see anything to move forward on in terms of coming up with a story we could put on the air. He agreed.

"There's too much other news to cover right here in New York," I said. "I can't chase around the country after some wild speculation that might or might not be true. I hate to admit this, but maybe

Marty Barlow had gotten a bit crazy in his old age. He got lucky on the Hartwell corruption story. He was right there, even if he didn't know the details. But this is too much to believe. I think he was desperate to come up with a big scoop—the scoop of a lifetime—because he knew he didn't have much time left and he felt the news business had passed him by."

* * *

Terri Hartwell met up with me for drinks, as she'd promised. There had been a question after the Hartwell story broke about how it might affect her politically. I mean, her top aide had been taking payoffs from the mob. On the other hand, she had cracked the case, and now it looked like she was finally going to be able to put Victor Morelli behind bars after years of him eluding justice. The latest polls showed her popularity with the voters to be even higher than before. She was still the favorite to become the city's next mayor.

I planned to ask her about this and the case against Morelli and other stuff when we met, but she surprised me with a preemptive strike in the conversation that threw me off balance.

"How would you like to come work for me?" she asked as soon as we sat down

"Doing what?"

"I need a new Chad Enright. Well, not actually like Chad. A nicer version. Not to mention one who won't plot to kill me. But I need a strong number two like that. Someone tough, smart, and used to dealing with crises exploding all the time. You fit the criteria better than anyone I know. What do you think?"

"I already have a job. Running the news operation at Channel 10 isn't too shabby."

"This could be a better job for you."

"You mean more money?"

"I'm not sure about that. Government salaries might not compare to what you're getting now. But better in terms of a career and a future for you. If I get elected mayor, you'll be my top person. Maybe the second most powerful person in the city. And who knows what might happen after that. There could be even more high-profile jobs for me, and for you, too, if things work out the way I hope."

Holy cow, I thought to myself. She was already looking ahead to a political future beyond the mayor's office. Senator? Governor? Maybe even the White House down the line. And she was offering to let me become a political superstar along with her.

I knew that I would never do it. It wasn't just about the money. I was a journalist at heart, not a political operative. But I figured it couldn't hurt to play along like I was interested. Maybe it would help me get some more stories out of her office.

"Does that idea interest you, Clare?"

"It certainly is an intriguing prospect."

"Then you'll consider it?"

"Definitely."

*　　*　　*

"The News Never Stops" seemed to be succeeding, at least so far.

We used Weddle's concept to report on a number of stories with live video and streaming and a lot of other stuff that we passed off as actual news coverage. Most important of all, we promoted the "live" concept intensely on air and in other media as well. The ratings had jumped since we started doing all this, so I guess Weddle knew what he was talking about.

Our personal relationship was in the same holding pattern it had been before.

We snuck off together for a few private conversations, even a quick kiss or two. But no, we had not slept together. Not yet. We both realized the career dangers involved here, so we cooled it on the relationship front until his consulting job with Channel 10 was over. Of course, the station might decide to extend his contract, which would be good for the station but bad for my sex life.

Anyway, it wasn't like I was busy doing anything with anyone else in this area. I'd never heard back from Scott Manning after our meeting, my ex-husband Sam Markham wouldn't even take my phone calls anymore, and there was no one else breaking down my bedroom door to get in at the moment.

So I'd wait for Weddle.

As long as I had to.

I just hoped it didn't take too much longer.

* * *

Brett and Dani had broken up again. Then they were back together. If that sounds confusing to you, imagine how it is for me.

It turned out that Dani discovered a receipt that showed Brett had bought something expensive for his wife on her birthday. Dani blew up and announced their "engagement" was off. But, before I could bring them into my office to sort it all out in terms of office policy, they were back together again.

Brett explained that the gift was a farewell thank-you to his wife for being such a great mother to their kids, and nothing more. Dani accepted that. Whew! Talk about fast-breaking news. I was having trouble keeping up with the latest on Brett and Dani. I wondered if I could somehow spin the two of them off as a TV reality show. Now that would get us a lot of ratings!

There was another sexual issue with one of the cameramen, a guy named Ted Fleckman who had worked there for a long time.

Cassie O'Neal had come to the office one day wearing a low-cut blouse, and Fleckman made a breast joke in front of her. She filed a formal complaint about his "inappropriate" comment. I suspended Fleckman for two weeks without pay and ordered him to attend sensitivity training classes. I could have fired him, but I took into account his long service to the station.

"Why did you do it?" I asked him.

"It was a joke, Clare."

"You can't say things like that in the workplace."

"It's an old joke. I've said it here in the past. Hell, I think I've even said it to you. No one ever got upset before."

"Times have changed," I told him. "You need to change, too."

"So I get suspended for telling a joke I've told a lot of times in the past? It was a damn joke. All I was trying to do was get a laugh."

"It wasn't that funny a joke anyway," I told him.

All of this made me even more certain it was the right move for me and Weddle to keep our relationship under wraps as long as we were working together in the newsroom. I was the supervisor responsible for making sure no inappropriate sexual stuff was going on here. It was important for me to make sure everyone understood the rules of sexual behavior—what was acceptable and what was not—in the workplace today.

Even the news director.

*　*　*

"I've been thinking that I need to settle down," I told Janet. "Get married, buy a house in the suburbs, maybe even have a family."

"Do you have someone in your life to settle down with?"

"Not at the moment."

"Any prospects?"

"That guy Weddle I told you about."

"But you said you haven't even had sex with him yet."

"Well, there is that . . ."

"Where would you live in the suburbs?"

"No idea."

"And the family?"

"What about it?"

"I asked you about this not long ago—are you considering having a baby at your age?"

"No."

"Then where would the family come from? Adoption?"

"Can't tell you that either."

"This idea doesn't seem like a well-thought-out plan, Clare."

"I'm still working out some of the details . . ."

The thing was, the family part was as much on hold as my relationship with Gary Weddle.

I hadn't gone back to see Lucy in Virginia for a few weeks now, ever since she'd asked me disturbing questions about my interest in her life that I couldn't answer. Sooner or later, I was going to have to make a decision on Lucy. Either tell her the truth about who I am, her biological mother—or else simply walk away from her forever.

*   *   *

It all might have worked out. The marriage stuff to Weddle. The home in the suburbs. The family with me and Lucy and my granddaughter. But life is a lot like the news cycle—sometimes it hits you with a big breaking surprise development when you least expect it to happen.

Maggie told me that Scott Manning was on the phone for me. Damn.

Scott Manning—and all the pain and heartbreak and regrets I had about him and our doomed relationship—was the one thing I didn't need right now.

I decided to make that clear to Manning, once and for all, right at the start of the conversation on the phone.

"Look, I'm sorry about a lot of the things I said and did after you went back to your wife, Scott. But I was jealous and I was angry at you then. Not now. I'm not interested in having a relationship with you anymore. I've got someone else. I'm happy with him. So, you're with your wife, I'm with him—and I don't plan on ever having any kind of a sexual relationship with you again. I just want to make that clear."

"That's all very interesting to know, but it's not why I called."

"Huh?"

"I've got news for you. About that list of murders you gave me. We just got a DNA match on some of them. Not all yet, but enough to indicate a real pattern. It looks like it was the same person who killed these women, Clare."

"A serial killer," I said.

"A serial killer," he repeated.

PART III

THE WANDERER

CHAPTER 33

LESS THAN AN hour later, I was sitting in Manning's office at FBI headquarters in Lower Manhattan.

"There are definite DNA matches with five of the names you gave me," Manning said. "Likely matches in a half dozen more. The others—all except one—came back with varying degrees of DNA confirmation data, making it possible, but not absolutely certain, they were done by the same person."

"That includes the murders people have already been sent to jail for?"

"Yes."

"Which means they must be innocent."

"It looks like that."

"Jeez!"

"Yeah, it's gonna be a major legal nightmare. But that's not my concern. I just want to catch the son of a bitch who's been doing this for so long. Now that we know he does exist."

No serial killer—at least none that I could think of—had ever gone undetected for such a sustained period of time without anyone realizing the deadly predator even existed.

Sure, there had been serial killers who worked in anonymity for shorter periods in the past.

A lot of people don't know this, but David Berkowitz, aka Son of Sam, was shooting and killing people in New York City for months before anyone knew about it. Berkowitz's spree began with the stabbing of two teenaged girls in 1975. After that, Berkowitz began using a gun—the infamous .44 Bulldog revolver—in a series of attacks against women—and sometimes the men with them—throughout 1976 and into early 1977. But they all seemed like separate, random crimes until police matched up the ballistics in all the slayings to find out they came from the same gun. That's when the terrifying serial killer who would become Son of Sam exploded into the public consciousness. After that, Son of Sam/David Berkowitz went public with his killings, sending taunting notes to the authorities and media about his victims.

Ted Bundy was able to abduct and murder women in secret at the beginning, too, but authorities eventually connected the pattern and linked the various murders to Bundy after a few years of disappearing women—and bodies found later throughout the Northwest.

No question about it though, "The Wanderer"—that's what I was calling him, too, now—was a different kind of serial killer. A serial killer who had carried out his deadly spree in secret for three decades while no one even knew he was out there. Until now.

"Which one of the murders was the only one that didn't have any kind of DNA match?" I asked.

"The first one."

"Becky Bluso in Indiana."

"That's right."

I was surprised.

"I don't understand," I said. "How could Becky Bluso's murder not be connected to all the rest? The person I got the information about the serial killings from started it all out by looking into the Bluso murder. And it was at the top of the list of victims he put together. It doesn't make any sense that there'd be no DNA match on her."

Manning shrugged. "I'm only telling you what the DNA results showed."

He explained that DNA testing was difficult in such old cases. DNA deteriorated at different rates—depending on a variety of variables—including how it had been stored. In cold cases like this, many of them ignored for years without any arrest, DNA preservation was not a big priority.

"That's why these cases are less than a perfect DNA match," he said. "But there's enough DNA evidence for them to make us believe they are connected. The other five are slam-dunk matches. No question about it. Same person did them. Probably did all of them. Except for Becky Bluso. We got nothing from DNA there."

"Maybe the DNA match wasn't there because evidence samples had eroded or whatever after thirty years."

"Or maybe someone else murdered Bluso, a different killer from whoever did the rest."

"Then why would her name be at the top of the list of victims?"

"You tell me. You're the one who came to us with the list."

He asked me then for more information about how I'd obtained the names. I'd told him some of it in the meeting we'd had in the bar that first night, but he wasn't that interested in the details then. Now he wanted to know everything.

"Any idea how Barlow came up with the names?" Manning asked when I was finished.

"Only that he was interested in going back to the Bluso girl's murder—which he had remembered from his days as city editor at the Indiana paper—and that led him to these other dead women."

"Except the Bluso killing doesn't seem to have anything to do with the rest of them."

"As far as we know," I said.

My mind was racing at a million miles an hour right now. Not only with questions about Bluso and the other dead women. But mostly, how I was going to break this big, blockbuster story. I figured I'd race back to the office, get Maggie and the others to pull together whatever background and old video footage we could find from the other murders, and then I'd report the whole thing myself on the 6 p.m. newscast. Maybe I could even get Manning to go on air with me to talk about these revelations.

But, as it turned out, Manning had other ideas.

"I need you to sit on this story for now and not tell anyone about it," he told me.

"Are you kidding me? This is a huge story, and I'm the one who discovered it. I came to you, remember? Why wouldn't I put it on the air tonight?"

"Because right now we know about this serial killer being out there, but he doesn't know about us. That is, he doesn't know we know about him. That gives us a big advantage in looking for him. If you air the story, it will jeopardize our investigation. That's why I'm asking you not to do it."

"Look, I understand what you're saying. And I want to be a good citizen and help the FBI and police just like anyone else. But the investigation is your job, not mine. My job is to report the story. And that's why it's going on the air on our 6 p.m. newscast tonight."

"You can't do that, Clare."

"How are you going to stop me? I have the same information you have, and you've told me now about the DNA matchup results that confirm there's a serial killer at work. We weren't off the record or anything when you did that. I'm going with the story."

"I think there's a way we can both get what we want out of this."

"Huh?'

"I have an offer for you."

"There's nothing you can offer me that will stop me from airing the story on our newscast tonight."

"Listen to my offer to you first."

"There's no point—"

"Please, Clare."

"Okay, what's your offer?"

"I'll let you inside our investigation."

CHAPTER 34

I TOLD JACK Faron everything when I got back to the office. Well, almost everything.

"This could be one of the biggest serial killer stories of all time, Jack," I said after running through the details of my encounter with Scott Manning. "Bigger than Son of Sam, bigger than the Zodiac Killer, bigger maybe even than Ted Bundy. We're talking about close to twenty potential victims—and there might well be more we don't know about yet. But we can do even better than report this story; we can *own* this story. 'The Wanderer' will belong to Channel 10—all the way until they finally catch him—if I'm a part of the FBI investigation."

"Or we could go with the story we have on air tonight," Faron said. "Break it wide open. We'll get all the attention; we'll get big ratings, too. That's what we're here for, Clare, to report stories to our viewers. Whatever it is we know at the moment. Our job is not to sit on a big story to meet the demands of law enforcement as to when we can run it. I say we put you on the air tonight with whatever you've already got."

"That's not an option."

"Why not? You told me the FBI guy confirmed there was a solid DNA match on some of the cases, and likely matches on many of the others. You also said you never went off the record with him on anything he revealed. What's the problem?"

"I gave him my word we'd hold it."

"Tell him you changed your mind."

"I can't."

"Why not?"

"Because you can't tell someone you're giving them your word, then say you changed your mind about it afterward. That kind of defeats the whole purpose of the 'I'm giving you my word' pledge."

"You shouldn't have done that without consulting with me first."

"Let's give it a try, huh? I'm supposed to go back there tomorrow and meet Manning's boss to get a fuller briefing on the status of the investigation. We can always revisit the decision after that. All we'd be doing is holding off on the story for a day. But, if I am part of the FBI team going after this guy, we would have the complete story from the inside."

"Unless someone else breaks it first."

"No one else knows about this."

"What if someone from the FBI office leaks it to another media outlet?"

"That won't happen."

"How can you be sure?"

"Scott Manning gave me his word," I said.

"Are you even certain that this guy Manning can pull off something like this? He's new to the FBI, right? He only left the NYPD last year. He might have said anything he could think of to get you not to air this story, but that doesn't mean he can back up his promises with the bureau."

"Manning was the first one at the FBI who found out about The Wanderer. He's bringing it to the FBI's attention. That makes him a big player in all this, no matter how new he is. And I'm the one who brought the information to him. That's how we can sell this all to his boss. In any case, we'll know more about how all this will play out—or if we should just go ahead on our own and not work with them—once I meet Manning's supervisor tomorrow."

"Just to be clear, isn't Scott Manning the same guy who was involved with you on the Grace Mancuso/Dora Gayle story last year? The same guy you had working for us then? And the same guy you were sleeping with at the time, which I didn't find out about until later?"

"We only slept together once."

"Not the point."

"I thought you'd want to know."

"But you don't have that kind of relationship with him now?"

"That's right."

"You're not still having sex with him?"

"No sex whatsoever except for that one time last year."

"You have no personal feelings of any kind toward Scott Manning right now?"

"Absolutely none," I said.

That was the part where I said before that I wasn't being completely, 100 percent truthful to Faron about everything.

I went through with him next what my people would be doing on this for the rest of the day. I was going to ask Maggie and others to gather more information for me on the victims—and the crimes themselves—from the list. I knew Manning and the FBI were surely doing the same thing right now. But I wanted to have as much information as possible with me when I met with Manning's boss.

Before I left Faron's office, he asked me about Gary Weddle.

"How's everything going between you and the consultant?" he asked. "I've been meaning to ask you about that. It seems to be working—based on what I've seen so far in the newsroom and in our ratings numbers."

"Yes," I told him. "We've accomplished a lot in terms of meshing the 'The News Never Stops' concept of Weddle's together with our normal newsroom schedule. Feeding stories in instantly via texts, tweets, video streams, and the rest. But we've still maintained the integrity of the actual news broadcasts. Gary Weddle and I are working extremely well together."

"I'm surprised."

"Why?"

"You don't generally get along with people like that. And you were resistant in the beginning to me bringing him in here at all. Why the change in your attitude?"

I shrugged. "I like him, Jack."

"Like him how?"

That question startled me.

"What do you mean?"

"People here tell me you two seem to get along maybe too well. Nothing obvious, but there seems to be some sort of bond there, I'm hearing. Are you having a personal relationship with this guy, too, Clare?"

I thought about the conversations Gary Weddle and I had had about our future. About the times we'd managed to sneak away to spend a bit of private time together. About the stolen kisses between us.

"Of course not."

"Good. Because you know how complicated that kind of a relationship can be in an office these days. I'm already getting enough stress about what's going on between Brett and Dani. I mean, I'm not sure whether they're going to have sex on the air some night or file lawsuits against each other. I don't need another Brett and Dani situation in this office. Which is why I asked about you and Weddle."

"My interest in Gary Weddle is simply putting out the best—and most profitable—newscast we can do here at Channel 10."

"Glad to hear that," Faron said.

Okay, that was the second untruth of the conversation.

But who's counting?

*   *   *

I called Maggie into my office afterward and gave her the list of crime victims to check for more information. I said I wanted newspaper articles, TV broadcasts, videos, social media coverage—anything she could find out about any and all of them. I did not tell her why I wanted this. Which was the first question she asked me.

"I can't tell you that, Maggie," I said.

"You can, but you won't."

"Okay, I won't."

"Then I'm not doing this assignment for you unless you tell me what this story is all about."

"You're my deputy, Maggie. You're supposed to do whatever I tell you to do. No questions asked."

"I'm also a journalist. I ask questions for a living. My question now is what's going on here? Wouldn't you ask the same kind of question if you were in my place?"

Maggie was right.

I'd promised Manning that I wouldn't tell anyone else at the station so that it couldn't leak out. But I'd already told Faron because I knew I had to cover myself that way in case this all blew up in my face. Now I decided to tell Maggie, too, making it clear about the need for secrecy from anyone else in the newsroom.

"Wow!" she said when I was finished. "That is a helluva story!"

"It will be once we're able to put it on the air. Hopefully soon."

"And you're working with that ex-cop Scott Manning again?"

"That's right."

"The same guy you slept with last year?"

"Not the point."

"Are you sleeping with him now?"

"Everyone keeps asking me about that."

"It's an obvious question, Clare."

"No, I have no personal relationship of any kind anymore with Scott Manning. Please try and put together as much of this stuff as you can before the end of the day so I can have it when I go back to the FBI tomorrow. That's all I'm concerned with right now."

It was a nice little speech, and it sure sounded good.

And there was no question that I was focused on the story—which could be the story of a lifetime—at the moment.

That was the only reason I was looking forward to returning to the FBI office again tomorrow, I told myself.

Except why was I still so excited thinking about seeing Scott Manning again?

CHAPTER 35

SCOTT MANNING'S BOSS was a man named Gregory Wharton. Wharton was about fifty with short-cropped hair, dressed in a blue suit that looked so bland it could have been FBI-issued, and gave off every vibe of being a lifer with the bureau. He might have been nice-looking except for the perpetual scowl on his face—at least when he looked at me. He was not happy I was there or happy with the reason for it.

"This is a very unusual situation," Wharton was saying to me now as we sat in his office. Manning was there, too, looking slightly uncomfortable. "An unprecedented situation, at least in my time here, Ms. Carlson. We have great respect for the media and the job you do, but we don't allow journalists to be part of investigations we're running. This is an especially sensitive investigation—both in terms of avoiding a public panic or compromising the investigation itself—so it is crucial that all of us are extremely discreet about it."

"Discreet," I repeated.

"Yes. I'd like to think of us both working for the public good. You came to us with some important information about a series of murders, and we are grateful for that. In return, we are prepared to work with you on this story as it develops. I think that's a fair arrangement. A good quid-pro-quo, as they say."

"Quid-pro-quo," I said.

I was starting to sound like an echo.

"The first thing we have to establish is the secrecy of this investigation. Between you and I and Agent Manning here. Everything we say and do here is completely confidential. This is all totally off-the-record, as I guess you journalists say. I need you to promise me that right now, Ms. Carlson. Do I have your word on that?"

"Cross my heart and hope to die," I said, making an imaginary X on my chest.

"Excuse me?"

"I'm giving you my word."

"I'm serious about this. I need to be sure you're telling me the truth about this."

"Hey, my pants aren't on fire or anything."

Wharton looked confused.

"You know, liar, liar, pants on fire. Mine aren't."

He smiled now, but it looked forced. I had a feeling where all this was headed. I found out that I was right.

"Now, Agent Manning here overstepped his authority when he promised you would be a part of our investigation. I do understand his reasoning for doing that. You obtained the valuable information that alerted us to this series of crimes, and he felt it was important to convince you not to make this information public yet. Unfortunately, allowing you to participate in the investigation itself is not going to be possible. It's simply not a feasible option here. I'm sure you understand the reason for that."

I sat there and waited. Here it comes, I thought.

"So, I'm going to propose a different scenario. One that I think will benefit both of us. We will keep you informed as best we can on all the developments in our investigation, right up to—and including—the time we capture the killer. Until then, you will not be able to use any of this. But, as soon as the killer is in custody, you will have the complete story ahead of anyone else."

"How long do you expect that to take?" I asked.

"Hard to say. It could be a matter of days or weeks or more."

"And you expect me to sit around and twiddle my thumbs waiting for you during all this? Not good enough."

"That's my offer, Ms. Carlson,"

"It's not much of an offer."

"Take it or leave it."

I heard a sigh and a sharp outtake of breath from Manning. He knew what was coming. I stood up and started walking toward the door.

"Where are you going?" Wharton said.

"Back to my station to put this story on the air."

"Now wait a minute . . ."

"No, you wait a minute. I have an executive producer at Channel 10 who wanted to put this story on the air last night. I talked him out of it, but now I think he was right. You don't want to honor the deal I made with Agent Manning? Fine. You can hear all about it on the Channel 10 newscast tonight. We're going to lead with it, then go big again at 11 and blow it up to go viral all over our website. Everyone will pick this story up from us. Serial killer running wild, FBI clueless about it. That's a win-win situation for us, Wharton. I can't lose doing that. But you can. You can lose big-time. Good luck with your investigation."

I was halfway to the door when he called me back.

"Okay," Wharton said. "You win. We'll go back to the original deal. The one you made with Manning."

"I'll be a part of your investigation?"

"Yes."

"Thank you."

"You're welcome."

He gave me that smile again.

The phony one.

Yep, no question about it, Gregory Wharton didn't like me.

On my way out, Manning whispered to me: "Well, that didn't go so badly as I feared it might."

"Are you kidding me?" I asked. "How could it have gone worse?"

"I thought the two of you might kill each other." He smiled.

*   *   *

An hour later, I was sitting in at an organizational meeting by the FBI team conducting the investigation. There were about ten agents in the room, plus Manning and me and Wharton. Wharton was clearly in charge and ran the meeting.

He started out by listing the basic facts I'd provided to Manning about the various murders, then told about the DNA results, which indicated they were the work of the same person.

He said they were calling that person "The Wanderer"—the same name Marty had given him in his notes—because they needed a code name for the task force's investigation. The Wanderer seemed perfect, Wharton said. I thought about how Marty had come up with that name based on an old Dion song he listened to as a kid. Now it was the name of a major law enforcement operation. Marty was back in the big time of crime reporting, even if it was too late for him to enjoy it.

At one point, Wharton introduced me as the journalist who had given them the original information and told everyone how I would be taking part in their investigation moving forward. He assured everyone I had agreed to keep whatever I learned confidential until the killer was apprehended.

I saw a lot of scowls on the faces around the room, not unlike the scowl from Wharton back in his office. None of these people wanted me there any more than he did. But that was okay. I was getting used to rejection.

Because of the massive number of potential murders by the serial killer, Wharton said it was important to focus the bureau's investigation on the places most likely to produce results. In this case, he said, that meant the five murders with the definite DNA link. After that, they could move on to the other cases.

Agents were assigned to travel to all five areas where those definite DNA murders had occurred. Others were told to prepare a psychological profile of the suspected killer based on techniques in identifying serial killers that had proved successful in the past. And the remaining agents would comb through data and other material in the FBI files looking for some link to the person who was doing this.

When the meeting was over, Manning asked me if I planned to go to one of the areas where the murders had taken place.

"That's what I'm going to do, all right."

"Which one of the five targeted areas are you going to?"

"None of them."

"What do you mean?"

"I'm going back to Eckersville, Indiana. The Becky Bluso murder. I can't do anything more at these other places than your agents can do. But maybe I can find out something more in Eckersville."

"But that murder is the only one that's not been linked to any of the rest of them."

"I know. And that doesn't make sense to me. I still think it is connected. I have to find out how."

CHAPTER 36

"ARE YOU SURE this is a good idea?" Janet asked me

"No."

"I don't like it, Clare."

"You mean the story?"

"No, the person you're working on it with."

We were talking on the phone. I'd called Janet to tell her about Manning and the rest. I didn't tell her a lot about the details of the story. Only that it involved a series of murders that might be related. Not that I didn't trust Janet. But I'd promised Manning and the FBI I would keep all this information to myself. I'd already broken that promise twice—with Faron and then with Maggie, albeit for necessary reasons—and I didn't want to make it worse by telling Janet everything, too.

Besides, Janet and I had this policy where we tried not to reveal to each other sensitive stuff about the things we were working on: my exclusive stories and her sensitive legal cases. We had agreed that we both had big mouths—okay, that was mostly me that had a big mouth—and could inadvertently leak privileged information without even knowing we were doing it. Anyway, it seemed to work out better for our friendship this way.

"It's just a story," I said now. "He's an FBI agent working on it and I'm a journalist. That's all this is."

"Except for the fact that you have a torrid sexual relationship with this guy."

"Had a torrid sexual relationship with him—past tense," I pointed out.

"And you have no interest in having that kind of a relationship with him now?"

"He's married."

"That's a non-answer."

"I'm only interested in the story, Janet."

"And he's okay with that, too?"

"He insisted on it. Said it had to be strictly business right from the start when I approached him again about this. We're both on the same page. He's back with his wife and I'm interested in somebody else besides him."

"That guy Weddle at your station?"

"Right."

"Who you haven't actually consummated anything with yet, because you both decided to hold off until he stops working for the station. Meanwhile, you'll be with Scott Manning on this other story."

"Uh-huh."

"I think this whole situation is fraught with peril."

"Fraught with peril? Talk to me in English, Janet—not legal-speak."

"It could all blow up in your face."

*   *   *

I went back to the office and ran the afternoon news meeting. The big story was a tornado warning for New Jersey, Staten Island, and parts of Long Island. That made the lead story choice for the newscast easy. Tornadoes rarely caused major damage in the New York City area, but tornado warnings still scared the hell out of people and guaranteed big ratings.

At the end of the meeting, I informed everyone that Maggie would be running the news meetings for the next few days while I was on special assignment. Everyone wanted to know what the special assignment was, of course—the room was full of nosy journalists. But I just made a joke of it by saying: "I could tell you, but then I'd have to kill you all."

I told Faron and Maggie privately all about my meeting with Manning and the FBI and why I was going back to Indiana. Faron seemed dubious about the FBI keeping its word on cooperation, and I think he still regretted not going on air with the story right away. Maggie seemed dubious about me working with Manning again, which she'd never approved of. There was a lot of dubious reaction in the room. But both agreed it was good in the end that the FBI had allowed me into the investigation.

I found Weddle then and told him I was leaving for Indiana the next day. I said it was a big story that I was working on, along with an FBI agent named Scott Manning who had helped me last year break all the Dora Gayle/Grace Mancuso murder news. I didn't tell him much more—about the story now or about Manning.

He didn't ask either. I was hoping he might suggest we get together that night for a farewell of sorts. Maybe some dinner. Maybe some snuggling. Maybe a secret kiss or two. But he wished me a good trip and then said—rather abruptly, I thought—he needed to go back into the office he was using to crunch some new ratings numbers.

Maybe he knew about my past with Manning and was jealous.

Maybe he was upset because he was going to miss me so much while I was out of town.

Or maybe he did need to get back to work on the ratings numbers.

Sometimes I overthink this kind of stuff.

I went home, packed for my trip, ordered pizza, and finally fell asleep still wearing the same clothes I wore to work in front of the TV watching as Jimmy Fallon did his "thank-you letters" reading bit. I'd put on an expensive new dress yesterday morning in hopes of impressing either Manning or Weddle with how great it looked. But neither one mentioned it.

Now here I was all alone in my apartment.

Clare Carlson, media superstar.

All dressed up and eating pizza to go.

CHAPTER 37

UNLIKE ALL THE unfriendly FBI people I'd just left, Jeff Parkman—the police chief in Eckersville—seemed happy to see me again. Maybe that's what happened when you were the top cop in a small town where serious crime hardly ever happened, except for one big high-profile murder case thirty years ago. You liked talking about that moment when this peaceful little town had a real, honest-to-goodness big crime.

I brought him up to speed on why I was there, but he already knew most of it because the FBI had contacted him before I got there.

"Any idea why the Becky Bluso murder doesn't seem to be linked to any of the other murders they're investigating?" I asked him.

"Any idea why it should be connected?"

"No."

"So maybe it isn't."

"Let's just theorize for a minute that there is a serial killer out there. Maybe Becky Bluso was his first kill. Then he goes on from there to carry out a series of other murders on young women like Bluso, without anyone ever connecting any of the crimes until now. Isn't that possible?"

Parkman shrugged.

"I suppose. That would mean if we solve the Becky Bluso murder now, it would reveal the answer to who killed those other women."

"Exactly. That's why I'm here."

"Only thing is, we've never been able to figure out who killed Becky Bluso for the past thirty years. What makes you think we can solve it now?"

"Better late than never." I smiled.

Parkman went through the details of the crime again. Becky going on a shopping trip with her younger sister that day. Coming home to meet a girlfriend while the sister went off to the pool. The friend knocking on the door, finding it open, and then discovering Becky's bloodied body in the upstairs bedroom. The friend running out of the house screaming. Police arriving to find the horrifying crime scene. Parkman even offered to take me back to the neighborhood if I wanted to see the inside of the house today. I did.

As we pulled up in front of the address, I thought again about what a peaceful neighborhood it seemed to be. All the houses looked alike, all the lawns were neatly trimmed, and all the people seemed to live quiet, uneventful lives. It was like a scene from a long-ago Norman Rockwell painting of middle America.

The woman who answered the door at what used to be the Bluso house didn't seem surprised when Parkman said he wanted us to see the inside. She said they'd had other curiosity seekers in the past who stared—and sometimes even knocked on the door—at the most infamous crime site in Eckersville history. She said she hadn't known about that when she bought the house, but she'd gotten used to the attention. She led us through inside where three children played and watched TV in the living room.

Then we went up the stairs to the bedroom where Becky's friend had found her brutally murdered. There were bunk beds in the room now, and it turned out to be one of the bedrooms where two of the boys slept. There were toys and games and clothes scattered all around.

I wondered about what it was like living in a house where someone had died so horribly. Did the people here now worry about demons or ghosts or evil spirits haunting the place? On the other hand, a lot of people didn't know what happened in their homes before they lived there. I sure had no idea who lived in my apartment before I got there. In any case, none of this helped me answer any of my questions about the Becky Bluso murder. Nothing more to see here.

When we got outside again, Parkman pointed to the house next door to the Blusos. "That's where Ed Weiland, the neighbor who was at the barbecue with the Blusos the night before, lived back then. He was a widower with a son, Seth. Like I told you last time you were here, they had a lot of guns and knives and seemed a bit weird, people said. Both of them were questioned at the time as potential suspects, but nothing ever came of it. A lot of people were questioned as potential suspects, but nothing ever came of that either."

Then he looked at another house on the block. "That's where Teresa Lofton lived. She's the friend that discovered Becky's body. Imagine what that must have been like for a seventeen-year-old girl."

I nodded.

"What happened to her?"

I figured she might be a good interview.

"Oh, she was so messed up by it all she had to drop out of school. I understand she underwent a lot of grief counseling and other therapy. The family moved away not long afterward. Too many memories here, I guess."

I sighed.

"It was a long time ago," Parkman said. "People die. Move away. Start different lives. Victims, suspects, potential leads, and witnesses. That's why this cold case is so damned cold. Thirty years is a long time."

On the way back to his office, he told me again about the sad history of the Bluso family after the murder. The younger sister dying from leukemia. The father gone with a heart attack. The death of the mother after that. "They seemed to be a cursed family," he said, shaking his head sadly.

"What about the older sister?" I asked.

"Betty. She was two years older than Becky. Betty was away at college in Maine when the murder happened."

"She still alive?"

"As far as I know. She wound up being a professor at a college in Maine. A place called Eaton College, as I remember. She was back here a few times—after the murder, of course, and then for all the funerals. But she's never lived in Eckersville again since then. Too many bad memories here, I guess. Same as with the Loftons."

I made a note to try to track down Betty Bluso—or whatever she called herself these days.

I figured maybe she could tell me something about Becky or her family or the rest of it that I'd missed so far. And she was the only person I knew how to find—so there was that, too.

We pulled up in front of the police station and got out. It was a nice new building with the new courthouse and new library and new government offices all attached. Parkman was proud of it and walked me around the grounds to show it off. I asked some questions and pretended like I cared. I figured it couldn't hurt to keep this guy on my side. Besides, what the hell else did I have to do in Eckersville? It seemed to be a dead end.

But that's the thing about being a good reporter. You keep asking questions, even if there doesn't seem to be any reason for it. Because every once in a while, you get an answer that you weren't expecting.

"Bet you haven't had such interest in the Becky Bluso case for a long time, huh?" I asked Parkman. "First the woman newspaper reporter who did the article for the Fort Wayne paper. Then Marty Barlow, my friend from New York you told me was here. Followed by me. And now the FBI is all over it, too. All four of us wanting to know everything you knew about the Becky Bluso case. Weird, huh?"

"Well, there was the other guy before that, too."

"What do you mean?"

"Oh, this was a few years ago. A guy asked me a lot of questions about the old Bluso case. He never told me why. But the mayor and other political leaders made a big thing out of me working with him in any way possible, so I did whatever I could. I even took him over for a tour of the Bluso house, like I did with you. Of course, I understand why everyone wanted me to be so nice to him. After what he did for this town."

I was confused. "What did he do for the town?"

"He made a huge financial contribution to build this library and help us put up this whole municipal complex you see here."

Parkman pointed to a plaque in front of the library. It said:

"This library is dedicated to the town of Eckersville. A good place to read. A good place to learn. A good place to live."

Underneath that was the name of the generous benefactor to the town.

The name of the man who had donated the money.

The name of the man who had made the library and this beautiful building in the center of Eckersville possible.

The name of the man who had been so interested in the Becky Bluso case.

The name was Russell Danziger.

CHAPTER 38

"Russell Danziger?" Manning asked. "The big-shot New York political operative? Is that who we're talking about here?"

"Same one. I checked."

I'd called Manning from the Indianapolis airport, while I was waiting to board a flight.

"Why would Russell Danziger donate such a big amount of money to the town of Eckersville?" Manning wanted to know.

"That's my question, too."

"Is Danziger from Eckersville?"

"No. And, as far as anyone is aware, he's only been there one time. When he came to donate the money to build the library and—oh, by the way—ask a lot of questions about the old Becky Bluso murder case."

"It just doesn't make any sense for Danziger to do that."

"There's only one scenario where it does make sense." I'd been thinking about this since leaving Eckersville. "Guilt. Danziger is guilty about something, so he tries to use money to assuage that guilt in the only way a man like him knows how to do—with money. But what is he guilty about? Becky Bluso's murder. At least he's very interested in it. Maybe because he was the one who murdered her a long time ago."

"C'mon, Clare, you're reaching here."

"Do you have a better theory?"

"I don't have any theory. I do know that Russell Danziger is one of the most powerful men in New York City—hell, one of the most powerful in the country—and there's absolutely no evidence to indicate he had anything to do with killing the Bluso girl."

"Then why did he donate all that money to the town? Why was he so interested in her murder?"

"There could be a lot of reasons."

"Sure. And one of them is he killed the Bluso girl thirty years ago. Plus, maybe a lot more women. And years later, he gave the money to assuage his guilt over Bluso's death. I know that doesn't make a lot of sense, but it makes about as much sense as anything else in this case. Let's check the towns where the other women died. Find out if Russell Danziger gave any money to them any time after the murders, too. If he did, then we'll know we're on the right track."

"Okay, I'll make some discreet checks on Danziger. But we have to tread carefully here. The guy's got a lot of clout. Enough clout to deal with a curious journalist or even a curious FBI agent."

"Understood."

"Where are you now, anyway?"

"Getting ready to fly from Indianapolis to Portland, Maine."

"What's in Maine?"

"Becky Bluso's older sister, Betty. She's the only member of the Bluso family still alive. I think it's worth it to interview her to find out if she remembers anything about her sister that might help."

"Ask her if she ever knew Russell Danziger." Manning laughed.

"Wow, I never thought of that. Thanks for the FBI crime-solving tip, J. Edgar Hoover."

*   *   *

I'd tracked down Betty Bluso by googling her and Eaton College. That was the easy part. Getting her to agree to talk with me was tougher. She said she'd put that part of her life behind her a long time ago. But, when I said I was going to show up at her door one way or another, she agreed to see me.

I met her in her office later that day in the faculty building of Eaton College, a small school just outside Portland on the Maine coast. She was an attractive woman of about fifty—she'd been a few years older than Becky—and you could see a lot of the same beauty I'd seen in the pictures of her dead sister.

Her name was Fulger now, and she said her husband was a history professor at the college. She taught English literature and had written several nonfiction books on the topic. They had no children—their choice, she said—but did have two dogs, a cat, and even a horse at the house they owned not far from the college.

It sounded like a nice life, and I was sorry I had to interrupt it with something so disturbing as her sister's murder.

"I was gone when it happened," she told me. "I came home afterward for the funeral and all the rest of the grieving. But it wasn't for long. I'd enjoyed my time away at college, and all I wanted to do was get back. Eckersville was never a particularly interesting place for me when I was growing up and then—after what happened to Becky—I wanted to stay away from it as much as possible.

"My parents never got over it. My younger sister, Bonnie, was the most affected. She blamed herself for leaving Becky alone at the house after their shopping trip. Which was crazy, but she kept talking about it until the day she died. I'm the only one left in the family now. I try to put it all out of my mind. But I suppose I'll never be able to accomplish that. I'll live with the memory of what happened to Becky until the day I die.

"The worst part—for my parents, for Bonnie, and for me—was not understanding why. Why would someone take the life of a beautiful young girl like Becky in such a brutal fashion? If they'd caught someone for the murder, maybe all of us could have experienced some kind of closure. But that never happened. And I don't expect it ever to happen now, no matter how much you dig into it, Ms. Carlson. Not after all this time."

We talked about the possible suspects Parkman had mentioned to me. Guys at school who were interested in Becky. The girl who might have had a lesbian crush on her. The next-door neighbor at the barbecue the night before and his son.

"Ed Weiland and his son, Seth," she said when I mentioned the last two. "They always gave me the creeps. Especially the kid. He was good-looking, but I don't know . . . creepy. They were friends of my parents because they were our neighbors, and we spent a lot of time together with them. But Seth—I guess if I had to pick someone from back then who might have done it—would have to be on that list. But then he died, so I guess any secrets he had about Becky died with him a long time ago."

"Anyone else you ever suspected?"

She started to say something, but then stopped. I could tell she was hesitant about answering. Which made me even more interested in what she had to say.

"I think Becky might have been seeing someone," she said finally.

"She had a boyfriend she'd been dating. The police questioned him, according to the accounts I read. But he had an alibi for that day. He was away at a summer camp. They cleared him."

"No, I mean someone else."

"Who?"

"I'm not sure. But she was interested in someone. She wouldn't talk about it much the last time I saw her, right before I went back to college at the end of the summer. But she did say he was older than her. And that even though he wasn't available to her now, she was going to change that soon."

"Older? Could she have been talking about Ed Weiland, the next-door neighbor?"

"No, she'd never have been with anyone like him. I think she meant someone a year or two ahead of her in school. She mentioned something about him graduating recently."

"Could that have been Seth Weiland, the son?"

"No, he was in the same class as Becky."

"Then who?"

"I have no idea." She shrugged. "Not that it matters, I suppose. The police questioned pretty much every guy in town after she was killed. They never found evidence linking any of them to Becky's death."

I waited until the end to ask her the most important question in my mind right now.

"Did you ever know anyone named Russell Danziger?"

"Who's that?"

"He donated a lot of money to the town of Eckersville."

"What does that have to do with Becky?"

"I was hoping you might know."

"Know what?"

"If your sister ever mentioned the name of Russell Danziger to you before she was killed?"

"I never heard of him."

I was disappointed by her answer, but not surprised. I knew going in that the whole Danziger thing was a long shot. Maybe

Manning was right. I still had no idea why Danziger had donated all that money to the town of Eckersville. But that didn't mean he'd killed Becky Bluso or anyone else.

Before I left, Betty showed me a picture of the whole Bluso family at a barbecue in their backyard. It was old, tattered, and frayed. She said it was taken July 4th that summer, a few weeks before Becky was murdered. They were all smiling and happy and looked as if all was right in their world. None of them had any inkling of the tragedy that lay ahead. Happy memories before everything went bad for the Bluso family.

Betty Bluso had spent her life since then trying to forget about all those memories from back in Eckersville.

And now I had opened up the painful wound for her all over again.

I left her like that sitting in her office and staring at that picture.

Sometimes being a journalist is not a fun job.

CHAPTER 39

THE PROBLEM WAS I was still flying blind on this story. I didn't exactly know where I was on it, where I was going, or what any of it meant. All I had was a list of possibly related murders from Marty that had seemed unbelievable, but turned out to be true. And now this mysterious revelation about Russell Danziger and one of the murder locations. Except that murder was the one that didn't seem to link up in any way with all the others. None of it fit together.

God, I wished I could talk to Marty again. Ask him more questions, get his guidance, hear him say: "Clarissa, don't you see what it is you're missing? Didn't I teach you anything as a reporter?"

Yep, that would be swell.

But—unless I acquired a supernatural way to communicate with the afterlife—it wasn't going to happen.

All I had was what he'd left behind. But had I missed anything? I'd been through his computer and the paper files in his room at the 68th Street townhouse, and he'd talked about a bit of it that day in my office. But not enough to help me now. So who else might he have confided in? Well, I don't think he would have told his daughter, Connie, anything, and I was even more certain he wouldn't have talked about it with Thomas Wincott.

But there was one person in his family that he might have confided in.

His granddaughter.

He was close to his granddaughter, Michelle. He encouraged her in her acting career, he supported her in her battles with her father, and he talked about his newspaper career with her. Hell, he even told her about me. And she was the only one in that house who showed any emotion after he died.

*　　*　　*

Michelle Wincott lived in a cramped studio apartment in a not-so-great building on the Lower East Side of Manhattan, just off the Bowery. The Bowery used to be synonymous with poverty and down-and-out inhabitants. But, in more recent years, it had been transformed into an area of luxury apartment buildings, Starbucks-like coffee shops, trendy restaurants, and all the other elements of a hip neighborhood.

The hip people hadn't gotten around to Michelle's building yet, which stood out like a sore thumb in the middle of all this affluence. Michelle Wincott told me her father had offered to foot the bill for a better apartment, but she refused. She didn't say it in so many words, but the meaning was clear: She'd rather live like this than take money from her father.

She didn't seem very concerned about her father's legal situation now. In addition to criminal charges from the Morelli/Enright fallout, Thomas Wincott had been targeted with several civil lawsuits, his realtor's license was suspended, and he was under intense scrutiny from various local, state, and federal agencies. When I asked Michelle how he was dealing with all this, she just shrugged. Like I was talking about someone she hardly knew, not her father.

They didn't seem to have an ideal father-daughter relationship.

"I came to see you because I'm hoping to find out some more information about your grandfather in those last days and weeks before he died," I told her. "I got the impression when we talked earlier that you were close to him. Maybe even closer to him than your mother was—and certainly more than your father."

"What exactly are you looking for?"

"I'm not sure."

"Then how do I know what you want to hear?"

"Tell me everything."

"Why?"

"Maybe we can figure out together what it was we don't know." I smiled in encouragement.

She smiled back. She seemed like a good kid, Michelle Wincott. And why not? She was Marty's granddaughter, his own flesh and blood. But what had happened to Marty's daughter, Connie? Was she like Michelle when she was younger and growing up with Marty and his wife? Did she change when she met and married Thomas Wincott? Or had she always been like that, and that's why she and Wincott were attracted to each other? Maybe the good genes in a family skipped a generation.

Michelle talked again about how much Marty had encouraged her acting career. Cheering for her successes, helping her feel better during the disappointments, and always telling her to keep reaching for her dream. There's no limit to what you can do if you believe in yourself, he told her. Never give up that dream. I realized as I talked to her that Marty had told me the same thing a long time ago when I was close to her age.

There were some pictures on the wall of her apartment. Most of them were acting shots of her taken for promotion or her in various acting roles. But one of the pictures—placed prominently on the wall behind where she was sitting now—was of her and Marty. It showed the two of them outside Radio City Music Hall, and it must have been taken a number of years ago. Michelle was a young teenager at that point.

"He took me to see the Rockettes show there," Michelle said now, pointing to the picture. "It's one of my favorite memories. He took me to see other shows, too, on Broadway and elsewhere around the city when I was growing up. Even back then, I had aspirations to be an actress. So he told me he wanted to make sure I saw the best in the business. That way one day I could be just as good, or maybe even better."

I noticed there were no pictures of her mother or her father in the apartment.

"Did you see much of Marty before he died?"

"A lot. More than ever before. I mean, he was always talking to me about the news stories he was working on around town. Battling against politicians and that sort of thing. He used to get himself so worked up when he talked about it. I mostly listened and tried to calm him down. Most of the time it worked. But at the end, well . . . it was different. He asked me for my help before he died. He'd never done that before. So I knew it was important to him. That's why I did what I could."

"What kind of help did he want from you?"

"He used that laptop computer of his to put his notes into— he'd been able to be part of the 21st-century technology that way—but he still didn't understand how to do a lot of things online. Me, I grew up with all that and know all about cell phones and laptops. So I showed him how to do things he didn't know how to do on the computer."

"Give me an example."

"Well, we built a website for him. The one where he posted all those news stories of his. I think it was important to him, almost like he was writing for a newspaper again. I helped him organize a lot of other stuff, too. I even helped him set up a special password-coded area that he wanted for posting material in case anyone ever gained access to his computer."

Damn. The site with the password Clarissa.

"I also did a lot of research for him. Most of it on my computer here. It seemed easier that way, to do it myself and give him the results, rather than try to teach him how to do all that on his own."

"What kind of research did you do for him?"

"Oh, looking up material on a big story he said he was working on. Of course, they were all big stories to him. But this one seemed especially important."

"Was it about the series of buildings in New York City that wound up involving your father?"

"No, it was a bunch of other stuff. He had asked me to look up things about the buildings at first. I didn't know at the time it had anything to do with my father. But he stopped asking me about that and became obsessed, instead, about something else. A bunch of old murders that he was interested in. Most of them were a long time ago, and not even from around here. I asked him why he cared. He told me he was working on a book about unsolved murders. Anyway, he gave me this list of names—people who'd been murdered over the years in all sorts of places around the country—and I looked up a lot of facts and information online for him."

"Do you still have that information on your computer?" I asked, trying to make the request sound as casual as I could—even though I was desperate to see what was on her computer.

"I believe so."

"Would it be all right if I looked through it?"

"Don't see why not."

She showed me the materials on her computer she'd assembled for Marty.

On the murders, there were more details about the crimes and their aftermath and the police investigations, but no idea of why Marty had thought there was a link between any or all of these long-ago killings. I started to go through it all painstakingly, making whatever notes I could as I went along. I realized at some point that I would need to ask Michelle Wincott to print it out for me to take back to the office. But I continued to look through the computer files as we talked.

"You're sure he never told you what this was all about?" I asked her.

"Not exactly."

"What do you mean?"

"Well, he mentioned one name. A name he was especially interested in. My grandfather asked for all sorts of biographical background—and anything else I could find out—about this guy. It wasn't easy either. This person is someone who is very secretive and avoids any kind of public exposure. An extremely private person. But I learned everything I could about him. I never got a chance to ask my grandfather what it was all about though. Grandfather died before I could do that."

"Who's the person Marty was so interested in?" I asked.

"A man named Russell Danziger," Michelle Wincott told me.

*   *   *

The material she'd compiled on Russell Danziger for Marty painted an incredibly sinister picture of a powerful, corrupt political mover and shaker who would do anything he needed to achieve his goals. Break rules. Skirt the law. Use bribes, extortion, and work with anyone—even the mob—to get what he wanted. And to put the people in office that he wanted. All consistent with what I'd already heard about him.

There were more details, too, about how secretive and mysterious a person he was. He had no wife. No children. No real friends that anyone knew about. No one even knew exactly where he lived or even if he had an office. He had various contact points around the city, but nothing that was officially listed anywhere.

Danziger was sixty years old. He'd been born in Eugene, Oregon—and grown up as the son of a decorated Army general who'd served on the Joint Chiefs of Staff. The father had been in Vietnam and other war zones and had been attached to the CIA for a number of intelligence assignments.

Russell Danziger's mother had died when he was five, so he was raised by his father at military bases around the country. Later, he followed in his father's footsteps and began a military career. He was accepted into West Point in the late seventies and graduated as a second lieutenant in 1981. He moved steadily up the ranks in the Army until he reached the rank of colonel. While in the Army, he also took advantage of college courses in business and eventually earned a master's degree in business administration.

He then resigned his commission in 2003 and went into private business—where he quickly became extremely successful. That led to his political consulting business and his fame as a kingmaker—or at least a maker of senators and governors—and, if things worked out with Terri Hartwell's campaign, a big-city mayor.

People who worked with him told of how he ran his business like a commanding officer—with tight schedules, rigid rules and regulations, him barking orders to everyone. A total no-nonsense guy. I thought again about the way he barged into Hartwell's office that day I was there. Even Hartwell—a powerful person in her own right—seemed to jump to attention as soon as she found out it was Danziger who wanted to see her.

He was now an extremely rich man. He had a massive apartment somewhere in New York City, people said; a house on an island off the coast of New England; he owned a boat; and he even had his own private plane. But there was no specific information about any of this, any more than there was about the location of his office or his personal life or anything else. The man had managed to shroud himself in secrecy and live his life out of the public spotlight. He was the ultimate loner, but an incredibly wealthy and successful loner.

All this was interesting enough, but then I found something even better.

A map. Marty had gotten together a map. At first, I didn't know what it was. Just a bunch of locations around the country. But, when I studied it closer, I realized it was the various locations Russell Danziger had been stationed while he was in the military. A few of them were overseas, but mostly throughout the U.S. Like most military people, he'd moved around every year or so.

Then I saw a second map.

Another series of locations around the country.

The crime sites for the twenty murders on his list.

I must have gasped at that, because Michelle asked me quickly if I was all right.

I nodded.

"Did you find what you were looking for?" she asked.

I sure did.

And more.

Marty must have found out about Russell Danziger's connection with Becky Bluso and Eckersville, as I had when I went there.

And now he was tracking Danziger's movements around the country at the time of the other murders.

There were a few possible reasons for this, I suppose.

But only one that made any sense.

Marty thought Russell Danziger could be The Wanderer.

CHAPTER 40

THE NEXT FBI meeting I attended with Manning, his boss Gregory Wharton, and the rest of the bureau's "Wanderer" team was different from the first one. Not better, just different. The mood toward me being there had changed from shocked disapproval to a mere grudging acceptance of my unwanted presence. I tried to stay as quiet and unobtrusive as possible at the beginning while Wharton updated everyone on the status of the investigation.

They had focused mostly on the five female victims where a definite link now had been determined from the crime scene evidence. There had also been some investigation done on the cases on the list where there had been a possible or likely DNA link, but their main concentration right now would be on the five definite matches that gave them the best chance of pursuing more evidence that might provide a clue to the killer.

The five definite links from the victims' list were:

LEIGH STOCKER, 1992—Ohio University coed; 21 years old; killed while hitchhiking home for spring break from the OU campus in Athens, Ohio, to her home outside Youngstown; body found stabbed to death and mutilated in a wooded area alongside Interstate 71. She was last seen at a rest stop fast-food place along the highway. A manager there remembered her talking to a man at a table before her murder, according to police accounts at the time. The manager couldn't remember much about the man, but he positively identified Leigh when shown a picture of her.

MONICA CARSTAIRS, 1994—A 24-year-old gymnastic teacher in Denver. She was found stabbed to death inside her car in the gym parking lot one night. Authorities at the time believed it was a random robbery or attempted sexual attack—and never linked it to any other crimes.

TONI GENARO. 1997—Schoolteacher in Allentown, PA. Stabbed to death in a wooded area near the school by an unknown assailant. Police had suspected either a troubled student or a disgruntled parent, but no arrests had ever been made.

SANDI NESS, 1999—19-year-old waitress at a beachside restaurant near St. Petersburg, FL. She was found strangled on the beach not far from where she worked. There were minor stab wounds, but the cause of death was determined to be strangulation—with the killer using his hands, not a rope or other device. Friends said Sandi liked to take long walks on the beach, and the assumption was that was where she had been confronted by her killer.

WENDY HILLER, 2001—Divorce attorney in Seattle, WA. She was the oldest victim at 36 years old. Found stabbed and strangled in her bedroom by her boyfriend when he returned home. The boyfriend was a suspect for a while. So were some of the clients and their spouses involved in messy divorce cases. But Wendy Hiller's murder remained unsolved nearly two decades later.

"In all of these cases, the murder was initially determined to be an isolated, random case by local law enforcement officials. There was never any indication they might be part of a larger spree of killing," Wharton told everyone.

"As you can see from the material I passed out, the circumstances were different in each case. The majority of victims had brown or black hair, but some were blond and one—Wendy Hiller—was a redhead. Their ages vary from nineteen to thirty-six. Different parts of the country—with no apparent link between any of the locations. And the method of murder varied between stabbing—in most of the cases—to strangulation and even physical beating. A gun was never used. In many cases—but not all— rope was used to restrain the victim prior to the murder.

"There never was—and I believe this is highly significant—any evidence of a sexual attack on any of the victims. No semen, no bruising around the sexual organs, and all of them were still fully clothed when they were found."

"If the motive wasn't sex, what was it?" one of the agents asked.

"Oh, it still could have been sex," Wharton replied. "Just not the kind of sex we can identify with. But we presume the killer got some sort of sexual thrill out of what he was doing. Otherwise, he wouldn't have targeted attractive young women the way he did. Except he never made an effort to claim credit for any of the murders. They were all done under the radar with no publicity. Other serial killers have wanted public attention. Not this guy. That's what makes him so scary. He breaks all our rules."

Wharton pointed to a map on the wall that displayed the Wanderer's murders and the locations of each. All of them—both the confirmed DNA ones as well as the others on the list.

"Several of the early murders were in the eastern part of the U.S.," he said. "That made us suspect that was the killer's original location where he targeted women, but that theory didn't hold up. The second killing was in Denver, and many of the later ones jumped all over the place—Florida, Nebraska, Alabama, Texas, California, then back to Massachusetts and the East Coast.

"We've been in touch with local law enforcement authorities at each of these locations to get them to reopen their investigative files. Maybe we'll get lucky and stumble onto something significant by combing over it all again like this."

I found that last part disturbing. That meant a lot of people were now aware of the existence of this serial killer. I understood the FBI's need to do this. But it increased the chances of a leak to other media. If that happened, I would be scooped on my own story.

I'd have to talk to Faron about this when I got back to the office. At some point, we might have to reconsider our decision to work with the FBI—and go with the story we had. But I'd worry about that later.

"Does anyone have anything else to add?" Wharton asked, looking around at everyone else in the room while at the same time managing to avoid eye contact with me.

"What about the Russell Danziger angle?" I asked.

"Russell Danziger?" an agent said. "The political powerhouse? What's he got to do with this?"

I looked over at Manning. He hesitated for a moment, or so I thought, but then nodded and joined in. "Clare uncovered a possible link between Russell Danziger and one of the murders on the list. Nothing specific yet. But she—well, we both—feel it deserves further examination."

"Which murder?" someone asked.

"Becky Bluso."

The other agent chuckled. "The only murder that doesn't have any connection to any of the others. Beautiful. Just what you'd expect from a dumb-ass reporter, looking for something at the one murder we don't really care about."

I ignored the "dumb-ass reporter" remark and simply recounted everything I'd found out about Danziger and the library money, plus his curiosity about the Bluso case when he was in Eckersville. I also told them about his military background and how he'd moved around the country over the years, as we believed The Wanderer did.

"Are you saying that these military assignments matched up with locations of all these murders?" someone asked.

"Not exactly, but . . ."

"What does any of this even mean then? Lots of people move around the country. Lots of people donate money to worthwhile causes like building a library. So what?"

"I don't know what it means," I said. "But I want to find out."

Wharton had not made any comment yet. But he was glaring at me again so I could tell he was unhappy. I knew Manning had briefed him about all this before the meeting. The fact that he hadn't mentioned it meant he didn't take it seriously. Or maybe he didn't want to ruffle any feathers with someone as powerful and politically connected as Danziger. In any case, I knew I wasn't going to get any support from him.

"I don't want to waste any of our valuable time or resources on a wild goose chase like this," Wharton said. "So, the man donates money to build a library in a town where one of the murders took place—and asked some questions about it while he was there. Why should I even care about that?"

I decided I'd been polite for long enough.

"You should care," I said. "Because your whole vaunted FBI investigative team here has turned up jack squat so far. There's nothing you told me here today that I didn't already know about this story. A story, by the way, you wouldn't even know about except for me. So far, there's only been one person we know about with any possible link to any of the murders. That's Russell Danziger. If the FBI chooses not to pursue this information about Danziger I've provided, I will do that for my TV station. You can either work with me on this or watch it on the Channel 10 News."

That was a bluff. I didn't have any information about Danziger I could put on the air at this point. Only suspicions and unanswered questions. But I figured the threat of my doing it would get their attention. I was right.

I looked over at Manning, who looked as if he wished he could hide under the conference table. Everyone in the room, especially Wharton, seemed shocked at my outburst. This was the ultimate fear for them. A goddamned reporter in the midst of their mass murder case going rogue—taking it public—in the middle of their investigation.

"Okay, we'll look at Russell Danziger," Wharton finally said. "Make some checks, find out a bit more about him."

"That isn't going to be easy," one of the agents said. "No one knows much about this guy."

"Then we need to talk to someone who does know something about Danziger," Wharton said.

He looked around the room.

"Does anyone here have a contact who actually knows Russell Danziger very well?"

"I think I do," I said.

CHAPTER 41

I MET TERRI Hartwell for dinner at the Union Square Cafe on the East Side of Manhattan. I'd told her that I wanted to talk more about her job offer. I figured that was the best way to get access to her in a hurry. It worked. She called right back with a dinner confirmation for that evening.

The Union Square Cafe used to be right off Union Square. Now, like most things in Manhattan, it had moved to a new location. But it was still one of the highest-rated and highest-priced restaurants in New York City. Hartwell said she was paying. So I guessed I still rated pretty high with her.

I figured I should make some small talk before bringing up the name of Russell Danziger.

We discussed a lot of things. Her campaign plans for mayor. I asked her more questions about the job offer and did my best to pretend I was seriously considering it. The status of the criminal case against Enright and Morelli and the others. It was a good conversation. We both drank wine while we talked, making the conversation even better. I realized—just as I had that first day in her office—that I liked Terri Hartwell. She seemed to like me, too.

At one point—after a fair amount of wine—we began to talk about personal stuff. She talked about her husband, his job in the pharmaceutical industry, and their two children. She asked me if I was married. I said I had been, several times. But not at the moment.

"Any children?" she asked.

"No," I lied, thinking about Lucy.

"Do you think you might ever get married again?"

"I'd certainly consider it if the right man came along."

"Any likely candidates?"

I'd drunk enough wine by now that I was probably a bit more candid than I might have been otherwise. And I'd been thinking a lot anyway about my relationship with Gary Weddle. It was good. But I also still found myself fantasizing about Scott Manning and the time we'd spent together. I told her about this and said I was a bit confused about my feelings.

"I mean I like the new guy. He's a great guy. Everything about him and me being together makes sense. But I still can't forget about the other one who doesn't make sense for me at all. Crazy, huh? I guess you can't relate to something like that because you've been happily married for so long."

"You'd be surprised," Hartwell said.

"What do you mean?"

"We all have an unrequited love in our life, Clare. A guy that makes no sense for us. On any level. But somehow, we can't forget about him. I love my husband, but I knew someone like that, too."

I suddenly wondered if she might be talking about Russell Danziger.

I asked her if Danziger had been the other man in her life.

"Oh, my God, no!" She laughed. "Russell is certainly not the love of my life. I don't think he's the love of anyone's life. He's a very unusual man when it comes to his personal—or sexual, in this case—stuff. He's never been married, never even been with anyone as far as I know."

"Is he gay?"

"No. I don't think he's anything. I've never heard him even talk about sex or personal relationships. He's an intense man. Focused completely on his work, which he excels at. In terms of his personal life, I always figured he was a bit like Ed Koch used to be when he was mayor. Lots of people said he was kind of asexual. I guess that's the best way I'd describe Russell Danziger."

I wondered how the idea of him being asexual—or at least not showing any interest in sex—squared with the idea of him being The Wanderer. The Wanderer never had sex with any of his victims, which seemed unusual. And I knew that there had been serial killers who got a sexual thrill simply from the killing of women. Son of Sam didn't have sex with his victims. Zodiac didn't either. Ted Bundy preferred to have his sex with his women victims' corpses after they were dead. Maybe Danziger had repressed sexual urges like this that came out only through murder. This was all speculation at the moment. But Russell Danziger sure did seem like a man who had a lot of secrets.

"Russell had a very difficult childhood," Hartwell said when I pressed her more about him. "I think he had to repress his emotions to survive that. Which is probably why he still does that today. You don't get any emotion or real human feeling from Russell. At least, I've rarely seen it. And I know him as well as anyone."

I remembered reading how his mother had died when he was young. I asked her if that's what she meant by a difficult childhood.

"It wasn't just that she died," Hartwell said. "She shot herself in the bedroom. Used one of her husband's service revolvers. He was on duty at the base at the time. Russell was there alone with his mother. He heard the shot, ran into the bedroom, and found her lying dead in a pool of blood on the bed. He was a little five-year-old boy. He didn't know what to do. So he hugged her. He stayed in that room with her like that until someone found them hours later. Can you imagine what that must have been like for a five-year-old?"

That explained a lot about why Russell Danziger grew up as emotionally screwed up as he was. But was he emotionally screwed up enough to become a serial killer?

"Any idea why the mother killed herself?" I asked.

"Russell's father."

"What do you mean?"

"Russell's father, Joseph Danziger, was a control freak, a perfectionist who ran his family with an iron fist like they were part of the military. He punished the mother, beat her badly, if he found a speck of dust in the house after she cleaned; monitored her every move; and made her life a living hell if she disobeyed him in any way. Maybe now a woman like that would have more options to escape an abusive, controlling husband. But she only knew one way out, and she took it.

"Russell hardly ever talks about any of this, as you might expect. You won't find it in any articles or biographical material about him. But he did talk to me about it one time. It was the only time I ever saw him let his guard down and show any emotion. He said that his own life with his father became even more difficult after his mother died. He was terrified of his father. That's why he went into the military, he said, because that's what his father wanted him to do. His father retired from the Army in 2002, died a year later in 2003. That was the same year Russell resigned his commission as a colonel and went into private business. I always felt that was more than a coincidence."

All of this—the mother's suicide, the emotional trauma he'd gone through as a little boy, the abusiveness of the father—painted a picture of a man who was looking better and better to me as a potential serial killer. Like many children who had been the target of abuse, I wondered if he took that rage and resentment out on others in the same way now. I knew Danziger was abusive and controlling to people he worked with. But how far did the demons buried deep inside him go? Did those demons extend to killing women as some sort of emotional release for him? That might sound crazy, but it was demons just as crazy that drove Ted Bundy and Son of Sam and other serial killers.

"It sounds like you're as close to Danziger as anyone," I said.

"I wouldn't be surprised, but that's not saying much. There's not a lot of people in Danziger's life you could call friends. He's all business."

"Why you?"

"I have no idea."

"Did you ever ask him?"

"No, I never did. Hey, I'm glad to have him on my side. He's a helluva political operator."

But was he secretly a serial killer, too?

"Can I meet Danziger?" I asked her.

"Why?"

"I'm curious about him."

"Russell doesn't meet with members of the media."

"You asked me to come work for you. You said you wanted me to be a key part of your campaign team. I said I would consider it. Part of that is finding out more about the other people on your team. There's no one more important to you than Russell Danziger. Everyone knows that. That's why I want to meet him. Can you arrange it?"

"That's a pretty big ask."

"I know."

"If I got him to agree, it would have to be an off-the-record conversation. You wouldn't be able to use any quotes."

"Understood."

"I'll see what I can do," Terri Hartwell said.

CHAPTER 42

IT HAD BEEN a while since I'd been to the house in Winchester, Virginia, where Lucy Devlin lived as Linda Nesbitt with her husband and young daughter. The regular trips had become too much for me—both in terms of time away from work and the emotional toll it took.

At first, I thought she might be upset with me when I showed up at her door again after an absence of several weeks. But she greeted me warmly and led me into the living room, where she served coffee and pastries. It was almost as if she'd missed me. Although I realized that it could just be me fantasizing about a mother-daughter relationship that I'd never had.

"I've been thinking a lot about it," she said to me as we sat there. "Thinking about whether I should go public with my story. Let you put it on the air and tell the world everything. Maybe it could help some other people—especially children like I was—to avoid going through everything I had to go through."

I nodded as if I thought that was a good idea. Even though I knew it wasn't. For me, anyway. Because if she did that—if the full story of Lucy Devlin ever came out—it could destroy my career because of the lies I had told and the journalistic transgressions I had committed.

But I needed to maintain the illusion that I was this TV reporter still covering a story—the biggest story of my life so far—instead of revealing the truth that I was there as her mother, desperately searching for a way to maintain contact with the daughter I walked away from a long time ago.

Why was I doing this charade? Part of it, I told myself, was so I could be around my daughter. But I also believed I needed to confront the guilt I felt over everything young Lucy Delvin had been forced to endure as a child.

"You've been asking me a lot of questions about what I remember back then when I was a little girl living in New York City before my disappearance," she said at one point. "Now I have a question for you."

"Fire away."

"I've never understood much about what happened when you covered my original story. How did you get all those scoops back then? How did you get such access to my mother and father during the search for me? How did you find out all that stuff when no other reporter could? Both when I first disappeared, and then again last year, when you did my story on TV. I mean, you won a Pulitzer Prize for it at the newspaper. Then you became a media star all over again with it on TV. That's pretty impressive."

"Carlson's the name, Pulitzers are my game."

She laughed. "You're funny."

That made me feel good. I'd made my daughter laugh. That was a big step for me.

"Seriously, how did you do it?"

"A lot of it was just luck. Being in the right place at the right time. That's what happened to me when you disappeared. I got lucky, I guess."

"No, I mean how *exactly* did you get so close to my family? The stories you did came from inside the house, while all other media were outside. You were close to my mother; you must have known her well. It sounded as if you knew my father, too, before everything with me even happened. But how? That's the part I haven't been able to figure out. It doesn't make a lot of sense."

She was right—it didn't make a lot of sense. Unless you knew the real facts. That I didn't just happen to know her father, Patrick Devlin. I'd been sleeping with him. I'd tracked Lucy down before she disappeared. Started an affair with Patrick Devlin after I discovered he was Lucy's adoptive father as a bizarre effort to get close to Lucy. And afterward, when Lucy was suddenly gone and presumed dead or kidnapped, I had continued to report the story like I was just another journalist—a story that made me a media star, won me a Pulitzer, and catapulted my career to where it was today. No, I couldn't tell her the truth. The lie was better.

"I'd interviewed your father a few weeks earlier for a story I was doing on the construction industry in New York City," I said. "That's how I knew him and got to know your mother, too. That's all. Like I said, sometimes it's all about being lucky enough to be in the right place at the right time."

At some point, her daughter, Audrey, came into the living room.

My God, I thought to myself, this is my granddaughter!

I'm sitting here right now with my daughter—and my granddaughter.

It made me happy. But sad, too. Waves of guilt surged through me as I remembered all my actions that had brought me to this place and time.

I'd met Audrey before on my visits. Not for long then. But this time was different. She seemed very interested in me. Almost as if she knew . . . well, that I was her grandmother. Of course, that was more fantasy stuff on my part. No way this little girl could be aware of who I really was.

Unless there was some unspoken connection—some basic genetic instinct—that drew my granddaughter to me in the same way as I was drawn to her at that moment.

I found myself hoping desperately that was somehow the case.

Audrey was playing a video game on an iPad. Just like people said Lucy used to do when she was her age. She showed me the screen now and proudly pointed to her score.

I am one of those adults who still like video games. I've played them for a long time—all the way back to Mario and Pac-Man and the classic games on Nintendo. This one was a modern update on one of those long-ago concepts. Building blocks of different colors you needed to complete a puzzle. Much more complicated and detailed and colorful than the games I remember, but the same concept when you stripped it down to the basics. I played along with Audrey for a while and showed her a few tricks on how to run up her score even higher than she already had.

I'm not sure how long we played together on the game. It seemed like only a few minutes. But I realized afterward when I looked at my watch that it had been much longer.

"Do you have children, Clare?" Lucy/Linda asked.

"Uh, no, I never have."

"Why not?"

"Too busy with my career, I guess."

"Lots of women have successful careers and families these days. Maybe you should think about that."

"I'm too old to be a mother," I said.

"You'd make a good mother," she said, pointing over to Audrey looking expectantly at me for my next move in the game. "I think you'd make a very good mother."

"I need to get going," I told her, not knowing what else to say. "I've got a long trip back to New York."

I said a quick goodbye to her and to Audrey, then got into my rental car and drove away as fast as I could.

Before I pulled away, I looked back and saw them both standing at the open door, waving goodbye to me.

I waved goodbye back to them, too.

I wasn't sure if I would ever come back.

CHAPTER 43

"WE'VE PUT TOGETHER a profile of the killer," Scott Manning told me.

"Does it include his name?" I asked.

Manning looked confused.

"No. A psychological profile based on theories and FBI studies . . ."

"I know what an FBI profile is," I said. "I was being sarcastic."

He smiled now.

"Right, I forget about that little trait of yours."

"I don't believe in this profile stuff about unidentified serial killers. I think it's bogus. You guys put out a profile packed with every little detail about a serial killer. He's left handed; he walks with a slight limp; he's married and a loving father at home, but he goes out and kills women because his mother didn't love him enough or the female babysitter hit him for wetting the bed when he was growing up—or maybe because he saw *Silence of the Lambs* and thought it would be a swell idea to be like Buffalo Bill or Hannibal Lecter. Then, when you finally catch him, none of these things actually describe him. But you focus on one or two details that fall in the ballpark and play them up. Then you do another profile when the next serial killer case comes along. Me, I think profiles are a waste of time."

"Do you want to hear what's in this one?"

"Yes."

I was sitting in front of Manning's desk at FBI headquarters. He was wearing a light blue tweed sports jacket, open-collared blue shirt, and navy-colored slacks. His body looked fit even though he mostly sat behind a desk here at the FBI. He looked good. Not that it mattered to me, of course. There was a picture of his wife and their three children on his desk. His wife was attractive. His three children, too. I was fine with all that. Totally fine.

"The first thing we looked at was what this guy might do for a living," Manning told me. "The murders happened in so many different locations around the country that our guy might well have a job where he travels around a lot. Like a traveling salesman or a truck driver or . . ."

"Or a military man who moves around from base to base," I pointed out.

"Or a military man," he said.

"Like Russell Danziger."

"Lots of times the killer turns out to be an upstanding citizen, very successful—the last guy you'd suspect to be a murderer. People tend to think serial killers are all weirdos like David Berkowitz was as Son of Sam. But sometimes, they turn out to be seemingly normal people living normal lives. In this case, though, we believe the killer has repressed sexual feelings. That's because of the personal way he kills his victims—stabbing with a knife or strangulation or with his own hands, rather than a gun."

I told him how I'd found out Danziger was both emotionally and sexually repressed.

"Also, the guy is highly intelligent," Manning continued, "methodical and intense. He's managed to cover up these murders for a long time. He clearly thinks them out—before and after—even though the killings themselves are carried out with angry passion."

"Highly intelligent," I repeated. "Successful. Methodical and intense. Sexually repressed. Moved around the country a lot like a military man might have. Sounds to me a lot like Russell Danziger."

"Many people could fit that description besides Danziger, Clare."

"Russell Danziger is the only one on our radar right now."

"All right, the profile does seem to fit Danziger."

"Then why doesn't the FBI question him?"

"We can't question anyone—certainly not a man as important as Russell Danziger—based on a profile. Or because he once donated money to a town where a young woman was murdered. Or because some crazy old guy like Martin Barlow decided he was The Wanderer."

"That crazy old guy is the reason you found out about all of these murders being connected," I pointed out.

"Still, we need evidence before we can approach Danziger."

"What about his DNA? Can't you check that, too, see if it matches the DNA at the murder scenes?"

"We can't demand a sample of Danziger's DNA without confronting him with solid evidence linking him to the murders—solid evidence that we don't have."

"Maybe the Army has his DNA on file. I remembered doing a story a while back about how the military now collected DNA from all service members."

"They do. But that's for identification of body remains, especially in a war zone. Those DNA files are only available to law enforcement if we obtain a court order. To do that, we'd need the same kind of evidence required to get it from Danziger directly. Evidence, which again, we don't have."

I had another idea.

I talked about the case of the Golden State Killer in California that was in the news recently in which DNA had been used to identify the suspect decades after the murders. "They got a possible DNA match from a family member that had submitted it for a genealogy website. It was close enough that they started checking out this person's relatives—and found him that way. Even if you can't get Danziger's DNA now, maybe you can see if the DNA from any of the crime sites matches someone related to him. That would be a start."

"Danziger's parents are dead. He's an only child. No other living relatives show up anywhere."

"You already checked?"

"I checked. I checked out all the possibilities. None of them will work."

"What happens next then?"

"We've got another FBI team meeting scheduled for this afternoon to go over all of these findings."

"Called by Gregory Wharton?"

"Of course."

"Am I invited?"

"Does it matter?"

"No."

"I'll see you there."

I picked up the printout of the profile and put it in my handbag. It was time to go. I looked over again at the picture of Manning's wife and family. I wanted to say something about them, but I knew that wasn't smart. I needed to go back to my office and do my job; let him do his job, too. This was going to be all business between us; we had agreed. For me to ask him about his marriage would be wrong and inappropriate. But, from long practice of saying wrong and inappropriate things, I asked him anyway.

"Good. We've been making progress. Slower between me and my kids. But we're working at it. One day at a time, as they say. Thanks for asking."

I nodded and pretended like that was the answer I was looking for.

"How about you?" he asked. "Are you seeing someone?"

"I am. A very nice guy. You'd like him."

"Think you might get married again?"

"We're taking it kind of slow at the moment. I want to make sure that this time it works out."

"That makes sense."

There was a long silence.

"Well, this is a bit awkward," I finally said, standing up. "I better go now."

"I'll see you at the meeting this afternoon."

"See you then," I said.

CHAPTER 44

I HAD COME up with an idea. Not about The Wanderer or how to find him or even how to break the story. I was still confused by all that. No, my idea was about me and Gary Weddle. I shared it now with Weddle.

"We give ourselves a onetime mulligan," I said.

"A mulligan?"

"Yes, like in golf when you get a free shot."

"Actually, a mulligan isn't a free shot. The shot before then is the free one. A mulligan means you don't count that, only the second—or the mulligan—shot in your score. So technically . . ."

"Okay, so maybe mulligan isn't the right word. Let's say we give ourselves a free pass—one time only, at least for now—to do something without it counting. No consequences about it for either of us. Are you in?"

"Exactly what are we talking about here?"

"Sex."

"I'm in."

We were sitting in my office after the morning news meeting. Ostensibly talking about the big news stories we'd focus on for the day. But the subject of our conversation turned to him and me. And what we did with our "relationship" going forward.

I knew the safest approach was for Weddle and me to bide our time and wait until we weren't working together anymore. That was the mature, logical, responsible approach. Except sex doesn't always lead to mature, logical, and responsible outcomes.

The plan we eventually worked out went like this: We would spend one night together. We agreed not to tell anyone about it while Weddle was still working at Channel 10—even if things didn't work out between us. The upshot—this could be the beginning of a beautiful relationship. And, if it didn't work, nothing would be lost, and there'd be no office scandal. That was my plan—a pretty good plan. Okay, it wasn't a plan without flaws, I understood that. But I needed to do something here. Move forward. Weddle was eager, too.

"What happens if we have wild, wonderful, torrid sex and then can't keep our hands off each other?" he said.

"That's good, right?"

"How do we handle this if we don't want to stop?"

"We'll make up the rules as we go along."

"I'm saying that could be a problem."

"Sounds like a good problem to have."

* * *

The day before we scheduled our nighttime tryst for was a long one for me. I sat in meetings with Weddle—talking about ratings and demographics and ad rates—as if everything were normal. Except I was fantasizing about how he would look naked. Maybe he was having the same thoughts about me. At least I hoped so.

I don't think that anybody noticed anything. Except maybe for Maggie. She gave me a strange look a couple of times while Weddle and I were interacting. Not surprising. Maggie always picked up sexual signals. I thought she might ask me again about me and Weddle afterward, but she didn't. Maybe she already knew.

At the end of the day, Weddle and I made a big point of leaving the office separately. Different times, different goodbyes to everyone. We even left by different doors. I went out through the front lobby of the building, and he went out the back door onto an adjoining street. We would meet for dinner after that and then . . . well, I was pretty sure what was going to happen.

An hour later, we were sitting at a secluded, romantic Italian restaurant in Greenwich Village. We ate pasta, drank wine, and made small talk the way people do when they're eager to have sex, but not sure how to make the first move.

We talked about the big news events of the day. We talked about "The News Never Stops" and how that was going. We talked about the off-again, on-again relationship of Brett and Dani in the office. We talked about how intellectually challenged I thought Cassie O'Neal was. I told him stories about my early days as an on-air reporter, until Jack Faron decided I'd be better off behind the camera than in front of it. He told me stories about crazy TV people he'd worked with over the years.

Eventually, we ran out of small talk.

"Isn't the uncertainty killing you?" I finally asked him.

"Uncertainty?"

"Sure. There's always uncertainty the first time you have sex with someone. Wondering how it's going to go. Good, great—or not so great. Sexual chemistry is such a tricky business. You never know what the results are going to be."

"So, I guess it's time to find out." He smiled.

At that point, I wiped some marinara sauce off my lips with a napkin, took a big gulp of wine, and leaned over across the table to kiss him.

He kissed me back.

Everything was going according to plan. A few minutes later, we were getting ready to pay the bill. We'd decided to go to his place. I'd never been to his apartment. I wondered what it was like. My guess was it would be a lot like him. Messy, disorganized—with papers and clothes scattered around it. Weddle was definitely a kind of a klutz, but that was a lot of why he was so adorable. I wondered if he might be a bit of a klutz in bed. Either way, I was looking forward to finding out.

That's when my cell phone rang.

I looked down and saw the call was from Scott Manning.

Jeez, talk about perfect timing.

"Where are you, Clare?" Manning asked when I picked up.

"I'm on a date."

"You need to get down here to FBI headquarters right away."

"What part of 'I'm on a date' didn't you understand?"

"We caught a break on The Wanderer," Manning said. "You're gonna want to be here for this."

CHAPTER 45

THERE IS ALWAYS a moment in a big story when something un-expected happens. You ask all the right questions, make all the logical moves—do everything a good journalist is supposed to do to break the story. And then, totally out of left field, an event blindsides you—for better or worse.

In this case it was better.

"There's a potential new victim of The Wanderer," Manning said. "A real estate broker named Dianna Colson in Boca Raton, Florida. She was attacked inside one of the houses she was showing nine years ago. No one was ever caught."

"Is there a DNA match?" I asked.

"No relevant DNA in this case."

"Then why do you think it's the same guy?"

"We've got something better than the DNA. We've got an eye-witness. Dianna Colson herself."

"She's alive?"

"That's right. She managed to get away. She's alive and talking. Talking right now to our people from the Miami bureau in Florida."

*   *   *

The FBI agents in Miami made a video of the interview with Dianna Colson. She was twenty-eight years old at the time of the attack, had long blond hair—very attractive—like the rest of the The Wanderer's women victims. He clearly picked his targets on the basis of looks.

On June 16, 2011, Colson had received a phone call from a man asking to see a house she had listed for sale. The house was vacant, had been on the market for a while, and she was eager to show it to a prospective buyer.

But Colson said when she got to the house, no one was there. Or so she thought. Then, as she walked through the empty house to check on a few things, a man grabbed her from behind. She screamed, but he put his hand over her mouth. She tried to get away from him, but he was too strong for her. As she struggled to get free, he put a choke hold around her neck and dragged her up the stairs to one of the bedrooms. She gasped desperately for air from the choke hold, but he squeezed even tighter. So tightly that she eventually passed out.

She woke up, bound and gagged, on the bedroom floor. At first, she wondered if the intruder raped her. But she was still clothed—tied up, making it difficult to move.

Then she saw a figure in the room. He approached her with his right hand held high in the air. That's when she saw the knife. It was a huge knife. Like a butcher knife, she remembered thinking in terror. He leaned over her, the knife in midair as she screamed helplessly into the gag—and then plunged the knife downward toward her. But he didn't stab her. He simply brought the knife down close to her, the blade stabbing the floor next to where she lay. Then he did it again. And again. She lost track of how many times he did this with that knife, convinced each thrust would be the one that would kill her. But then, each time, overwhelmed with relief—albeit temporary relief—when the knife didn't stab her.

Was this some sort of kinky sex game, she remembered thinking to herself.

Then he left her alone in the room, saying he would be back soon to finish playing with her.

During this time, she managed to loosen one of the ropes binding her hands. He must have been in such a hurry that he hadn't tied it tightly enough. From that, she managed to wriggle out of the rest of the ropes and remove the gag. She found an open window and jumped to the yard below. She ran away, screaming for help. A neighbor heard her and called the police.

When the police went into the house, the intruder was gone.

"Recorded as an unsolved attack," Manning said. "No one ever linked it to any other cases. Nothing similar had occurred around Boca Raton around that time, and, of course, no one had any idea about the other women victims throughout the country. But, when we began digging into possible other cases involving The Wanderer, this popped up. Everything about it sounded like The Wanderer. Except this victim got away. She's the only one who did. At least, the only one we know about."

On the video, the agents showed Dianna Colson a series of photos.

Most of them mug shots of known sex offenders from the Miami area as well as a few others in the mix to make for an objective video lineup—one that would hold up in court if she identified her attacker. And, there was also one other photo—which Manning had insisted on—a photo of Russell Danziger.

Colson looked at the photos in front of her for a long time, then finally pointed at the picture of Danziger.

"It could be him," she said.

"How sure are you?"

She shook her head.

"He came up behind me. I didn't see him at first. Then, up in that bedroom, it was dark; the shades were down. Plus, I was scared. and it all happened so quickly. I still have nightmares about it, but I never see his face in the nightmares. I guess I've blocked that out."

"Look at the picture again that you pointed at, Ms. Colson," one of the agents said to her. "Could that be the man who attacked you nine years ago?"

She nodded.

"It could be."

"Can you say for sure it was him?"

"It could be," she repeated.

*   *   *

It wasn't perfect, but it was a big step forward in the investigation. We had an eyewitness. We had a victim who was still alive. For the first time, we had a case in which The Wanderer had been stopped before he could kill.

So far, everything The Wanderer had done seemed methodical, brilliantly planned, and carried out without a mistake of any kind. But this time, he had messed up. He'd left the victim alive.

The evidence was piling up against Russell Danziger.

Now, we needed to come up with the one bit of key evidence to break this whole case—and my story—wide open.

And I had come up with a plan on how to do that.

But I needed Russell Danziger to make the plan work.

CHAPTER 46

As it turned out, I didn't have to look far for Danziger. He found me. Thanks to Terri Hartwell. He strode into my office at Channel 10, sat down without being invited to, and glared at me. He said Hartwell had asked him to meet with me as a special favor to her, and that was the only reason he was here. He clearly was not pleased about it.

"Everything we say is off the record," Danziger said. "I won't go on the air, and you can't quote me about anything on the air. Even as an unnamed source. Whatever we say does not leave this room. Is that understood?"

"That's fine, Mr. Danziger."

"And I won't talk at all—even off the record—to you about Terri Hartwell's political plans. Not about a run for mayor. Not about any other office. Not even about running for reelection as DA. All political talk about Terri Hartwell is off limits, Ms. Carlson."

"I'm good with that, too," I said.

"Then what the hell am I here for? Why did you ask me to come to your office?"

"Because I couldn't find yours." I smiled.

Danziger did not smile back. He did not seem like a man who appreciated humor. I had a reason for inviting him, of course. But I couldn't tell him what it was. I used my cover story instead.

"I've heard so much about you that I wanted to meet you, Mr. Danziger. That's what I told Terri Hartwell when we had dinner. She offered me a job with her. If she does become mayor—and I know we're not going to talk about that—you'll presumably be a big player in the city's government. We'd be working there together. So I wanted to get to know you and find out a bit about you. That's all."

Maggie came into the office at this point carrying two cups of coffee. Normally, Maggie would never bring me coffee; she'd tell me to get it myself if I asked her. But she was in on my plan. She handed one coffee cup to me and put the other one down in front of Danziger. I took a big sip of my coffee, hoping it would encourage him to do the same. But he left it untouched in front of him.

"I understand you were in the military," I said to him. "I respect that. Can we talk about your transition from the Army into the business world?"

He relaxed a bit. Once he started talking, he was quite forthcoming about the Army years. Told me about his rise in the ranks to colonel, about places he'd been on those military assignments. He was less forthcoming, though, about his business career. Or how he went from that to political power broker. I didn't press him. I was more interested in something else.

I picked up my coffee cup again and took another sip, glancing at him as I did so.

He continued to ignore the coffee in front of him.

"What about family?" I asked. "Children? Where do you live? And, if you don't mind me asking, why don't you have a designated office? It makes you awfully hard to find."

"I do mind you asking," he said. "None of that is any of your business."

I nodded and smiled. I told him I understood. I was afraid I was losing him. That he'd jump up and storm out at any minute. I needed to do something before that happened.

"This coffee is really good," I said, taking another drink from my cup. "Comes from a coffee shop downstairs. Best coffee in town, some people say."

"Huh?" he said distractedly, still upset by my last questions. "Oh, sure . . ."

He picked up the cup in front of him and took a drink.

I asked him a few more questions that he didn't object to. He must have liked the coffee. He took several more sips and emptied the cup as he talked.

I decided it was time to ask him what I really wanted to know.

"Did you ever live in Boca Raton, Mr. Danziger?"

"Boca Raton?"

"Yes. It's in Florida. North of Miami."

"I know where it is, but why are you asking me about it?"

"Someone told me you might have lived there some years ago."

"I've never lived in Boca Raton," he said, looking more confused than angry by the question.

"Okay, let's move on to another city then. How about Eckersville, Indiana?"

"What?"

"I know you've been there. In fact, you donated a huge amount of money to Eckersville for them to build a new library. Tell me about you and Eckersville."

The confused expression on his face was gone now. Replaced by one of fury. Then came the explosion. He stood up, pounded his fist on my desk, and began yelling at me.

"Is that why you wanted me here? To ask me about Eckersville? I have no idea what you're trying to do, but I'm not talking to you about Eckersville or anything else. This conversation is over."

It was a scary scene, and Danziger looked as if he wanted to hit me. The thought crossed my mind that it might not be a great idea to be in a room like this with a man who could be a mass murderer—and make him angry at me. But he didn't attack. He stormed out of my office, slamming the door so hard behind him that it felt like the walls shook.

That was okay with me.

Because I'd accomplished what I wanted with Russell Danziger.

I'd discussed it all beforehand with Manning. The FBI couldn't formally question Danziger. They couldn't demand a sample of his DNA to compare with the DNA from the killer found at the crime scenes. They didn't have enough evidence. But I could do that without him knowing. By getting him to leave his DNA on something. Then, if his DNA matched the killer's, the FBI could go after him through their normal channels.

I looked down at the coffee cup Danziger had left behind on my desk.

The one I'd gotten him to drink out of.

I had Russell Danziger's DNA on the coffee cup.

CHAPTER 47

EVERYTHING I WAS doing on this story was now falling into place perfectly. Every move I made was getting me closer and closer to breaking one of the biggest exclusive serial killer stories of all time.

And then it all exploded in my face.

I knew something was wrong when the phone in my apartment rang at 7:20 a.m. as I was getting ready for work. The caller ID said it was Jack Faron. Faron didn't normally call me at home this early to tell me what a great job I was doing. He called when there was something wrong.

"Turn on the *Today* show," he barked.

I already had the TV on, but I'd muted it while I was getting dressed. I grabbed the remote now, switched the channel to NBC, and turned up the sound.

The *Today* show usually featured soft news—cooking segments, celebrity interviews, health workouts. But there were no cooking or workouts or celebrities on the screen. Instead, it was a woman reporter, whom I recognized from *NBC Nightly News*, standing in front of FBI headquarters in Lower Manhattan.

"Once again on this breaking story," she was saying, "NBC News has learned exclusively that the FBI believes a serial killer is responsible for numerous murders of young women across the country over a long period of time. Possibly as many as twenty murders over thirty years. The FBI Behavioral Sciences Unit inside this building has set up a special task force in an effort to identify and apprehend the killer, whom they refer to as 'The Wanderer.' We'll have more on this breaking, exclusive story throughout the day and tonight on the *NBC Nightly News*. This is Leslie Gabbert reporting from FBI headquarters in New York City."

"Damn. Damn. Damn," I muttered into the phone as I watched.

"My sentiments, too," Faron said. "You said this was our story, Clare. You said we should hold it, work with the FBI, and then break the whole thing from inside the investigation. I listened to you. I wanted to go with the story right away, but you convinced me to wait. And now we're screwed. Chasing after our own exclusive. What the hell went wrong?"

I had a pretty good idea about what had happened. Gregory Wharton—or one of the other agents on the FBI task force—had leaked it to a friendly reporter at NBC News. This Leslie Gabbert woman. They never wanted me as part of their investigation, and this was their payback. They knew the story would come out sooner or later from me, but this way they could control it. Control the timing and the details of what was made public. And, I was certain, their story would give virtually all the credit for uncovering the link between The Wanderer murders to the FBI—not to me or to Marty or to Channel 10.

"I'm on my way into the office," I said.

"You better be. I won't be there when you get in. I'm on my way to Brendan Kaiser's office to try to explain to our station's owner how we got scooped on our own story. I'd been keeping him appraised of the details from you, which he's now watching on another channel. I hope I still have a job when I'm finished with Kaiser. I hope we both do."

"I'm sorry, Jack," I said. I couldn't think of anything else to say.
"I'm sorry about this. It's my fault, no one else's. I'll take the blame.
Tell Kaiser that for me."

Faron didn't answer.

Then I heard a dial tone.

He'd hung up on me.

I tried calling Manning. Then Wharton. Then other members
of the FBI task force if I had their number. No one answered.
Maybe they were busy. Or, more likely, they were avoiding me.

*   *   *

The Channel 10 newsroom was in full crisis mode by the time I
got there.

At the morning news meeting, everyone now knew the details
about what had happened. They were all furious. Mad at Leslie
Gabbert. Mad at NBC. But mostly, mad at me for working on the
story for so long without telling anyone—except Maggie and
Faron—what I was doing.

"Don't you trust us, Clare?" Brett Wolff wanted to know.
"We're supposed to be a team. A news team. But you went off and
worked on this story on your own, without any input from the
rest of us. That's inexcusable. And, what's even worse, you screwed
it up!"

Lots of other people chimed in then with the same message for
me. There were no jokes, no wisecracks at this news conference.
Me, I sat there and took it all without making any effort to defend
myself. There was no defense. Everyone was right. I had screwed
up this story, and I had no one to blame but myself for it.

But, like journalists do when they get beat on a story, the talk
eventually turned to what we could do next. How we could catch

up on this story. How we were going to play it on the Channel 10 News later.

I explained that I would go on air myself to deliver a report about everything we knew. I'd play up the angle about being inside the investigation the whole time. I'd say that we withheld the story in cooperation with the FBI. I'd include a lot of background and details that I knew about The Wanderer and his murders.

"Still sounds lame," Brett said.

"Yeah, like we're playing catch-up," Dani said.

"We are playing catch-up," someone muttered.

"Anyone else have any other suggestions?" I asked, looking around the room.

"We need something new," Maggie said. "Something exclusive about the story to make it our story again. Do you have anything else at all, Clare?"

I did. The Russell Danziger angle. There had been no mention of Danziger on the NBC report. Not surprising. There wasn't enough evidence yet to link him to the murders. But I had evidence. Or at least I hoped to have evidence. All I had to do was get confirmation from Scott Manning that Danziger's DNA—which I'd secretly obtained from him that day in my office from the coffee cup—matched the DNA left behind by the killer at the crime scenes. Then we could break it exclusively on Channel 10. A big exclusive. Big enough to blow The Wanderer story wide open. Big enough for everyone to stop being so pissed off at me and maybe save my career, too.

"I'm working on an angle," I said.

*   *   *

When I finally reached Manning, he was almost as upset as I was about the leak to NBC. He insisted he knew nothing about it. I believed him. I was certain it had been Wharton or one of the others on the task force who had stabbed me in the back by going to NBC News. But that wasn't my priority right now. My priority was nailing Russell Danziger.

"Scott, I need those DNA results. I need them now, like by this afternoon so I can break something on our 6 p.m. newscast that doesn't sound like we're chasing NBC on the story. I need to be able to talk about Danziger, too."

"I've got the DNA samples," Manning said.

"Thank God!" I exhaled deeply into the phone.

"You're not going to like the results."

I knew what he was going to tell me next, even before he said it. Everything had been going right for me on this story until today, and now it was all going horribly wrong.

"The DNA doesn't match, Clare."

"But . . ."

"Russell Danziger is not The Wanderer."

CHAPTER 48

So what did I go on the air with now?

I still needed to come up with something different about The Wanderer in the wake of the shocking news that I'd been chasing the wrong man in Russell Danziger. I needed something else that would set apart our coverage at Channel 10 from the NBC exclusive and all the other media playing catch-up right now.

Oh, I could play up the fact that I was inside the investigation. That I had the story first, that I was working with the FBI right from the beginning. But that then brought up the question: Why didn't I break the story myself, instead of waiting for NBC News to do it? It was a reasonable question. One that I had no good answer for.

I finally decided that the best exclusive angle I had—the only one—was the Becky Bluso murder. I'd gone to Eckersville. I'd talked to the police chief there about the murder investigation. I'd toured the house where the murder took place. And I'd gone to Maine to interview Betty Bluso, the only surviving member of the Bluso family, about her sister's long-ago murder.

Sure, the Bluso murder was the only one where no definitive DNA or any other kind of evidence existed to it being connected with the other murders. But Marty had obviously believed it was. In all likelihood, it was his investigation of the Becky Bluso case that led him to all the other murders on his list. He'd put her picture at the top of all the victims of the murders. And he'd made her picture bigger than any of the others. I was pretty sure I could pull off the idea that Becky Bluso was possibly—even likely to have been—The Wanderer's first murder. Which I continued to believe, too, despite the lack of hard evidence.

The one thing I couldn't use on the air was the revelation that Russell Danziger had donated big money to the Eckersville library. No way I could link Danziger to the story now. I still didn't understand what Danziger was doing in Eckersville or why he cared so much about the damn library or the Bluso murder case. But since he wasn't the killer—and the DNA results confirmed this—it didn't matter much anymore.

I spent the hours before the 6 p.m. broadcast going over all the stuff I'd found out in Eckersville about Becky Bluso's murder. I reached out to the police chief, Jeff Parkman, and got him to agree to do video footage in front of the old Bluso house—and also give sound bites to a local crew I sent there to shoot for us. I did the same thing with Becky's sister, Betty, who agreed to a video interview with us from her office at the college in Maine about Becky's long-ago murder.

I also pored over my notes from the time I was in Eckersville, looking for someone else—anyone else—I could interview. But I realized that most everyone else was dead. Everyone in Becky's family except for the older sister. So was the neighbor who had been at the barbecue with the Blusos the night before the murder. And his troubled son who police thought might be a suspect—but never could get enough evidence to arrest—had died in a car crash years ago.

Going over it all again, I was struck by the story of Teresa Lofton, the neighborhood friend who had discovered Becky's body. Parkman said she'd been so traumatized that she and her family moved away from the area soon afterward. I could only imagine how that could affect a teenager.

I'd never tried to track down Teresa Lofton. Everybody said she'd just disappeared after stumbling onto the horrific murder scene of her friend Becky, and no ever knew what happened to her. "Teresa Lofton?" Betty Bluso said when I asked her about it on the phone before we did our interview for the show. "No, I have no idea about Teresa. I tried to reach out to her after Becky's murder. But she never returned my phone calls or showed up at Becky's funeral. Everyone says she was so devastated by what she saw that she had some kind of an emotional breakdown. Her parents took her away from Eckersville right afterward, and that was the last I ever heard of her."

I decided to use that as an angle, too. I'd talk about how this young girl's life had changed irrevocably on that terrible day she discovered her friend Becky Bluso brutally murdered. How she and her family left town immediately afterward. How no one ever knew what happened to Teresa Lofton after that. It certainly added a bit more drama and emotion to my story.

While I was working on all this, Gary Weddle came into my office. He said all the right things about the story screwup not being my fault to try to make me feel better. I told him about what I was planning to do on the air tonight, and he seemed to like it. But things had been a bit awkward between us since the night I left him so abruptly—interrupting our plans for sex. I wondered again if he had found out about the background between me and Manning, the FBI agent I said I had to rush off to meet. Or if Weddle was just disappointed that our plan for a night of romance hadn't worked out. But, for whatever reason, he'd kept his distance from me since then, and I'd done the same with him. I suppose we were both trying to figure out where this relationship was going.

The truth is, I didn't know. I didn't know where the relationship with Weddle was going. I didn't know where my relationship with my daughter in Winchester, Virginia, was going, either. And I didn't know where this damn story I was working on was going.

I didn't know a lot of things right now.

*   *   *

At 6 p.m., I was on the air telling it all to the Channel 10 audience.

> ME: Now that the news of The Wanderer murders has become public, Channel 10 News can reveal that we have exclusively been a part of the FBI investigation into the killings. We first alerted the FBI to the potential links between the murders—as many as twenty over a thirty-year period, occurring in every part of the country. And we have been with the FBI Behavioral Sciences Unit team every step of the way as they try to apprehend this fiend.

I went through the details of the murders and the links that had been discovered between them, then focused on the one I wanted to play up the most for our broadcast: the Becky Bluso murder.

> ME: Seventeen-year-old Becky Bluso was stabbed to death in broad daylight inside her house on this bucolic street in the Midwestern town of Eckersville, Indiana, on August 23,

1990. It is believed—even though there is no direct evidence yet to confirm this—that Becky Bluso may have been the first victim of The Wanderer. The first woman out of at least 20 to die at the hands of this monster.

A picture of the old Bluso house—and the rest of the street—went up on the screen.

> ME: Becky Bluso was one of the most popular girls at Eckersville High School. She was an honor student. She was a cheerleader. She was on the Student Council. But, on this afternoon, someone came into her home and brutally butchered her to death.

Parkman came on the screen then to talk about the investigation into the case, all the leads the police had chased over the years without success. "We will never give up," Parkman said, as he'd told me when I was in his office. "No matter how long it takes, we are determined to bring the person who committed this unspeakable crime to justice."

This was followed by the interview with Becky's sister. Betty Bluso talked about the things she remembered about her younger sister. About the shock of learning what had happened to her. And about the destruction of the Bluso family in the wake of that tragedy.

> ME: Robert and Elizabeth Bluso died of natural causes after their daughter's murder. But there are many in Eckersville who believe they died of broken hearts. This is a tragedy that touched—and forever changed the lives—of many people in this peaceful Indiana community.

I then segued into the story of Teresa Lofton, the teenaged neighborhood girl who found Becky's body. I went through the account of how she showed up at the house to meet Becky, went inside when she saw the door was open, and then discovered the bloody scene upstairs.

> ME: Teresa Lofton was so traumatized by what she saw that day that she and her family left town soon afterward. She never returned to Eckersville. One can only imagine the horror of what this young girl had to live through, and remember, from that horrendous scene. That was 30 years ago, but the nightmare continues. And it won't end until the murderer of Becky Bluso, who is now believed to be the murderer of all these other women, too, is finally caught. Channel 10 will continue to keep you up to date on this breaking story both in our newscasts and in our "The News Never Stops" website coverage.

*   *   *

My phone was ringing when I got back to my office after the broadcast.

I thought it might be Manning. Or someone else from the FBI task force like Wharton who wanted to talk about what I'd just reported on air. But it wasn't. It was Terri Hartwell.

"What the hell is going on?" Hartwell asked.

She sounded upset.

"I don't understand what you mean," I said.

"That Becky Bluso story you did on the air. This whole Wanderer thing you were talking about. Where did that all come from? Why didn't you ever tell me anything about all this?"

I still didn't get it. None of the murders had taken place in New York City. They wouldn't have anything to do with Hartwell or her office. I pointed that out to her. I asked her exactly what it was she was asking about.

"Teresa Lofton," she said.

"Right. The girl from next door who found Becky Bluso's body after the murder, then moved away from Eckersville right after that. So what?"

"That's me," Hartwell said.

"What are you talking about?"

And then, even before she said anything else, it all came together for me.

Teresa Lofton.

Terri was a shortened name for Teresa.

And Hartwell was her married name.

"I'm Teresa Lofton," Terri Hartwell said.

PART IV

THE LAST SCOOP

CHAPTER 49

TERRI HARTWELL HAD been a part of this story from the very beginning. She was the first name Marty talked about with me that day back in my office. But I'd never made the connection.

I assumed all along that Marty started out investigating the building corruption scandal because of his son-in-law's questionable business activities in the real estate business, but then happened to get curious about the first big murder case he ever covered and went back to Indiana where he uncovered the link to the serial killings.

They were always two separate stories—first Terri Hartwell and the building scandal, then Becky Bluso and the other murders.

Or so I thought.

But I was wrong.

Marty had been working on one story.

"The biggest story of my life," he'd said.

And it was all centered around Terri Hartwell.

* * *

"I always hated the name Teresa," Terri Hartwell said to me now. "Made me sound like a nun. But my parents gave me the name, and I was stuck with it growing up and all through high school. Later, after I left Eckersville, I started using Terri. Then I got married and became Terri Hartwell, not Teresa Lofton. I changed my hair color from brunette to red, I changed the way I dressed, I changed the way I acted. I never told anyone about being Teresa Lofton or growing up in Eckersville or any of the rest about what happened there. I became Terri Hartwell. I liked Terri Hartwell better than I liked Teresa Lofton. Too many bad memories associated with Teresa Lofton."

We were sitting in her office again at Foley Square. She was still stunned by the revelation that the long-ago murder of Becky Bluso might be linked to a series of other murders being actively investigated by the FBI.

"Becky and I grew up together," she said. "We lived nearly next door to each other. We played together, we went to school together, we were inseparable for a long time. Becky and I were almost like sisters. I had dark hair then—just like her—and people sometimes said I looked more like Becky's sister than her real sisters did.

"We were very close, Becky and I. But we were also competitive. We both wanted the same things. Cheerleader squad. Honor roll. Student government office. And boys, of course. At the end, we had a pretty bad falling-out over . . . well, a boy.

"Becky and I hadn't even spoken to each other in weeks. But we were trying to patch it up. She'd reached out and asked me to come over to her house that afternoon. That's why I was meeting her. We'd decided to get together and try to be friends again. Like the old days. Except . . ."

Her voice trailed off.

All this bad feeling between the two girls brought up an obvious question. Could she have killed Becky herself? I didn't know a good way to ask Terri Hartwell that question. But I went ahead and did it anyway. I asked her if the police had ever questioned her as a possible suspect.

"Sure, they did. They questioned me. They questioned every-body. Everyone was a suspect, at first. But they were just flailing around. They never had any real clue about what happened. Still don't, from what you say. To be honest, the Eckersville police de-partment simply wasn't equipped to handle a major murder inves-tigation. I realize that now after my years in law enforcement. Maybe things would have been different if they'd done a better job. Maybe some of these other women might not be dead."

"We still don't know Becky Bluso's murder is connected to the others," I pointed out. "It's the only one where there's no forensic or DNA evidence that matches any of the other murders."

"I kind of hope it does turn out to have been a serial killer who murdered Becky. I like the idea of The Wanderer or whoever he is randomly picking the victims. Because the alternative is Becky's killer was . . ."

"Someone she knew," I said.

"Someone she knew," Hartwell repeated.

I asked her about why she and her family moved away from Eckersville so quickly after the murder.

"I was terribly traumatized by what I'd seen in Becky's house—her blood-covered body and all the rest of that horrible scene. My parents decided that was the best thing to do. They were right. I never went back to Eckersville after that. I tried to forget about Becky Bluso and Teresa Lofton and Eckersville."

There was still something I didn't understand. Well, there were a lot of things I didn't understand. But this one was a simple question.

"Did my friend Marty Barlow ever come to you to talk about you being Teresa Lofton or about the Becky Bluso murder?"

"No, I never met Barlow."

"He did talk to Chad Enright."

"I didn't know that either until later."

"Except he only asked Enright about the housing scandal questions, not about you and Becky Bluso."

"That's what Chad says. And he doesn't have any reason to lie now. He's telling authorities everything he can in hopes of getting some kind of break in a plea bargain deal."

Why hadn't Marty asked about the Bluso murder? I could only theorize an answer for that now. But it was a logical one. Marty hadn't made the Terri Hartwell/Teresa Lofton connection yet when he talked to Enright. He was still looking for information on the housing scandal. Then, at some point, when he was digging into that and the possibility of the DA's office being involved in a payoff scheme, he recognized who Terri Hartwell was. Teresa Lofton, the next-door neighbor in the first big murder story he covered as a young journalist in Indiana. That must have sparked his curiosity in the old case. He changed direction and began looking into the Becky Bluso murder again. And that, for reasons still unknown, led him to the string of other murders he believed were connected to the Bluso case.

If all this was true, he would have gone to Hartwell eventually. But I knew how Marty worked. He liked to get all his facts in order before interviewing a key participant in a story. That's what he'd been doing with Terri Hartwell. Making sure he'd accumulated all the facts he could before talking to Hartwell about Becky Bluso. Only Marty ran out of time before he could do that.

"The first time I found out about any of this was when I saw your broadcast," Hartwell said. "It completely blew me away. That's when I called you to tell you about me. You have a reputation as a dogged reporter. I knew you'd figure out about me, sooner or later. I decided it was better to deal with it sooner. What are you going to do now?"

"This is a big story. And your involvement—even if you were only a teenager back then—is a part of the story."

"Does it have to be?"

"What do you mean?"

"I've spent my entire life trying to put Eckersville and Teresa Lofton behind me. I understand you've got a job to do. But I'm not really relevant to the story you're working on. I'm only a sidelight."

"A helluva interesting sidelight."

"I offered you a job. Are you still considering that?"

"I haven't made a decision," I said.

"Sure, you have."

"Okay, I'm not going to come work for you. I wasn't when you first offered it—and I'm certainly not going to do it now."

"I can't use that for leverage then, I guess."

There was something very wrong here. Terri Hartwell, like any politician, was always looking for media publicity. And there was nothing in this to make her look bad. In fact, it might make her even more sympathetic to the voters. The crime-fighter who had to deal with her traumatic crime experience as a young girl. But here she was doing everything she could—even practically trying to bribe me with a job offer—to keep me quiet.

I also had the feeling that she was not telling me everything. That she was holding something back.

"Who was the boy?" I asked.

"What boy?"

"The boy you and Becky were fighting over."

"That's not important now."

"Who was the boy?" I repeated.

"Why does it matter after all this time?"

"He could be a suspect."

"Everyone was a suspect back then. I told you that."

"It won't take me much time to find out who it was," I said. "I'll go back and talk to people in Eckersville who went to high school then. Sooner or later, probably sooner, I'll get his name. And then I'll talk to him. Wouldn't it be easier for you to tell me who he is right now?"

"You can't talk to him. He's dead."

"What happened?"

"He joined the Army and was killed about a year later. I heard about it after I left Eckersville. I never knew much more about it. I wanted to put everything there behind me. I hadn't even thought about any of this in a long time until you brought the subject up again."

"So why won't you talk to me about what was going on back then between him and you and Becky?"

"It's a long story."

"I've got plenty of time."

And then she told me about Dale Blanchard . . .

CHAPTER 50

"DALE BLANCHARD WAS my first love," Terri Hartwell said. "You never forget your first love. Oh, I'd had crushes on boys in high school before him. A few dates, too. But he was the one. The boy I wanted to marry. Or so I thought back then. I fell head over heels in love with Dale."

She described Blanchard in glowing terms even after all these years. Good-looking, sexy guy. Drove a cool car. Was a big athlete—played football, basketball, and track. All the girls in school had a thing for Blanchard, she said. But he was smitten with her, the way she was with him. They went to school dances together. They went to movies together. And they did even more than that together.

"He was the first man I ever had sex with. Christ, I was only seventeen, barely legal. I'd hardly even been kissed before Dale. But he was older—a year ahead of me in high school, he was a senior that year when I was a junior—and he'd clearly had experience with other women before me.

"We did it in his car sometimes. We did it in the park a few times during that summer. And we'd even go back to my house on Oak Park Drive and do it in my bedroom when my parents weren't home. If they were gone for the afternoon, I'd call up Dale and we'd make love in my bed and laugh about what my parents would say if they had any idea what we were doing.

"Every girl in school was envious of me. Including Becky. That's what led to the falling-out between us. She was jealous of me and Dale. She tried to come on to him a few times, but he rebuffed her—and she blamed me. We'd grown up together as best friends, but now we weren't even talking."

Hartwell had told me about a guy in her life—someone she'd never really gotten over—the last time we talked over dinner. It happened when I was telling her about how I still had this thing for Scott Manning even though I knew he made no sense for me in any kind of a real relationship. "We all have an unrequited love in our life, Clare," she'd said. "A guy that makes no sense for us. On any level. But somehow, we can't forget about him. I love my husband, but I knew someone like that, too."

That guy had been Dale Blanchard for her, she told me now.

"My family wasn't happy about it at all. My mother and father didn't like Dale and wanted me to stop seeing him. He'd already graduated high school that June and had no real plan about what to do next. They said he was all wrong for me. But the more they said that, the more exciting it was for me to be with him.

"He was the bad boy. I'd always been the good girl, but now I could be the bad girl when I was with him. I know that probably doesn't make a lot of sense, but it did for a confused teenaged girl in Eckersville, Indiana, still trying to figure out what she wanted out of life. What I wanted was Dale. At first. And then . . . well, everything changed."

I asked Hartwell what she meant by that. She hesitated at first, clearly troubled by the memory of something from back then. I got the feeling it was something else she had tried to forget over the years—to sublimate deep in her mind—even if she hadn't been entirely successful at it.

"Dale had some problems," she said.

"What kind of problems?"

"Mental. Emotional. I realized that at some point. I tried to ignore them, but over time that became harder and harder to do. He had this terrible temper. It would explode suddenly, often for no reason. He'd be acting nice and sweet, and then he'd get angry with me. Later, he would apologize. He told me he didn't even remember some of the things he said and did when he was in that state. It was almost like he blacked out or something. Turned him into a different person. And then, later, he'd be fine again."

I knew there was more. I waited for her to tell me. And finally, she did.

"A lot of it was about sex. You see, Dale didn't like to have just normal sex. He liked to role play. Like he'd captured me and tied me up and forced me to have sex with him. Rough sex, they call it now. Sure, it seemed weird. But it turned him on, and I wanted to do whatever turned Dale Blanchard on. I thought it was fun to play those games, too.

"But then it started to get out of hand. One time he nearly strangled me. We were having sex, and he pretended to put his hands on my throat and squeeze. He began squeezing too hard with his hands until I could barely breathe. He apologized to me afterward and said he didn't even remember doing it.

"Another time he picked up a pair of scissors and cut me. The same thing happened then afterward—him apologizing, saying he didn't even know he was doing it. But when he hit me the last time, we were having sex. I decided I had enough. I told Dale I didn't want to see him again. He was crushed. I think he really loved me. It wasn't like he had any shortage of girls. Lots of girls wanted him, most of all Becky. He told me Becky had propositioned him again, but he wanted me. I told him to forget about me, I was done with him."

I wanted to ask her the obvious question. But I didn't have to. Hartwell asked it herself.

"You want to know if I think Dale Blanchard killed Becky?"

She shook her head no.

"I can't believe he did it. I know Dale was crazy, he could be violent—but he was basically a good guy. I wouldn't have stayed with him for as long as I did if I didn't feel that way. The good always outweighed the bad with Dale as far as I was concerned. I loved him. And he always stopped the rough stuff before he really hurt me when we were together.

"But yes, I thought about the possibility. When I came across Becky's bloody body that day—and remembered how she was coming on to Dale—I wondered if he could have done it. That he had gotten violent with her, like he did with me. Only this time he didn't stop until she was dead.

"But I didn't tell anyone. I couldn't. I couldn't tell my parents—or anyone else—that I'd had these violent sex incidents with Dale. Christ, I was seventeen. I'd just discovered my childhood friend and neighbor murdered. I was scared and I was confused.

"Looking back on it now, I guess I had a kind of emotional breakdown. My parents thought it was because of finding Becky dead like that. It was, in part. But all the rest of it, too. So they moved me away from Eckersville and all those memories as quickly as they could, and I never looked back."

There was a sort of bizarre irony to all this. I'm sure Hartwell realized it, too. This woman had become famous as a radio commentator fighting crime and as a law-and-order political candidate. But she walked away from one of the most sensational murders ever and never told everything she knew about the case.

"Do you think Dale Blanchard was the one who killed Becky Bluso?" I asked her, repeating the question she'd asked herself a few minutes earlier. Only this time her answer was a bit different.

"I don't know."

"What's your gut instinct?"

She sighed.

"I've thought about this a lot. Played those events over and over again in my mind. Becky had the hots for Dale, and she knew we'd broken up. She might have invited him to come to her bedroom that day. I'd told her once about the kinky sex games Dale liked to play, and she seemed excited—not horrified—by them. Maybe she wanted to play those games with him, too. And she knew that I was going to meet her there later. Maybe that's why she invited me. That might have given her a kind of perverse satisfaction for me to find my ex-boyfriend in her arms.

"I've thought about other possible scenarios, too. What if the whole thing was a mistake? What if Dale got confused? He used to come to my house and sneak into bed with me. All those houses on Oak Park Drive look alike, you saw that. Becky and I looked a lot alike as well. What if Dale was in one of those confused blackouts he suffered from, went into the wrong house, and somehow thought Becky was me? And, when he found out she wasn't, he lashed out at her in anger because he thought she was me. I'm not sure. But I still think about stuff like that."

"And after Becky's murder you left town?"

"Yes."

"You never told anyone else your suspicions about Blanchard?"

"Not a soul."

"Didn't you think that—if Blanchard did murder Becky in a rage that day—he might kill again?"

"I wasn't thinking about anything when it happened except running away from it all. And then later . . . well, you asked me what my gut instinct was? My gut instinct was—and still is, I suppose—that I can't believe Dale did something like that. I was so messed up that first year or so after we left Eckersville that I never could think clearly about it, I guess. Then I heard that Dale had died. If he was dead, then there was no point in digging up the past. I wanted it all to go away. I never went back to Eckersville or talked with anyone about Becky Bluso again. I wanted to forget Eckersville was ever a part of my life. It had no place in the life I wanted to lead."

Maybe she was right.

Maybe there was no reason then to go back and find out for sure about Dale Blanchard's guilt or innocence in Becky Bluso's murder once he was dead.

But now there was.

Blanchard could be—and I still wasn't sure how—the key to finding the serial killer we'd dubbed The Wanderer.

I told that to Hartwell.

"I've spent my entire life trying to get away from Eckersville— and from being Teresa Lofton," she said. "Ever since that day I ran away from Becky's house."

"It's time to stop running," I said.

CHAPTER 51

I STILL HAD a job to do. I was the news director of Channel 10.

I went back there after leaving Hartwell and ran the afternoon news meeting like normal. I picked a hit-and-run fatality in Times Square as our lead story; refereed an argument between Brett and Dani over who got to do the lead-in for it—I guess things weren't going well for them in the bedroom—and gave some helpful show notes to reporters, including Cassie O'Neal: "This is live TV," I told her. "That means you have to check your hair before you go on camera."

I did not tell Jack Faron or anyone else about my conversation with Terri Hartwell. I knew I probably should. I was on shaky ground after screwing up by not telling everyone what I was doing with the FBI on The Wanderer story. But I wasn't sure exactly what the Terri Hartwell revelations meant or how they fit into the entire Wanderer story, if they even did. I needed more information.

So I went to the place I usually went for information.

"I need you to find out about someone named Dale Blanchard," I told Maggie in my office after the meeting was over. "He grew up in Eckersville, Indiana. Joined the U.S. Army in 1990. Died in the Army a year later. That's about all I know."

"Why do we care about Dale Blanchard?"

"He could be a suspect in the Becky Bluso murder, which—whether it's connected or not—is still at the top of the list for The Wanderer murders."

"Who told you he's a suspect?"

"A source."

Maggie glared at me. But she didn't push it this time.

"Okay, I've got someone who can check military records for me," Maggie said. "When do you need this by?"

"Now," I said.

She nodded and got up to leave. But before she got to the door, she turned around and hit me with a question I wasn't ready for.

"What's going on with you and Weddle anyway?" she asked.

"Nothing's going on. We're both doing our jobs. He's acting like a professional, I'm acting like a professional. There's been no interaction whatsoever in the office to suggest anything else."

"I know. It's weird. Because I thought you two did have some kind of personal relationship. I don't understand, Clare."

I didn't either. I'd thought sleeping with Weddle that night might solve a lot of the questions about our relationship, but—when that didn't happen—it wound up making things more confused. We'd both kept our distance from each other since that abortive romantic encounter, like two boxers feeling each other out to see what the other one was going to do next. I wasn't sure exactly what to do, and I think Weddle felt the same way. We'd both responded by reverting to our "professional" approach with each other.

"He seems like a nice guy," Maggie said.

"He's a great guy."

"Then why don't you two get together?"

"It's complicated, Maggie."

"Do you want to talk about it with me?"

"I want to talk about Dale Blanchard," I told her.

*   *   *

Dale Blanchard had enlisted in the late summer of 1990, a few weeks after Becky Bluso's murder. Which was interesting. If you wanted to get away to hide out from the scrutiny of the law, the military was a pretty good place to do it.

Blanchard spent eight weeks undergoing basic training at Fort Knox, Kentucky, then another eight weeks of Advanced Infantry Training there. He was assigned to the First Cavalry Division at Fort Hood, Texas. In January of 1991, he was among those sent to Iraq for Desert Storm—the first Iraqi war against Saddam Hussein.

There'd been some problems along the way for Blanchard in the Army. At Fort Knox, he was disciplined for shoving a drill sergeant who had ordered him to do push-ups. He had another physical confrontation with a superior officer at Fort Hood that got him busted from PFC back to Private. And later, he spent two weeks in the stockade for pushing a second lieutenant who didn't like the way he saluted. Terri Hartwell had sure been right about Blanchard having a temper and flying off the handle easily. Is that what happened with Becky Bluso?

Any chance of us getting an answer from Blanchard to that ended in February 1991, in Iraq.

"Blanchard was in a unit that was clearing out areas of small houses outside Baghdad," Maggie told me, reading from the notes she'd compiled on her laptop. "Even though the war was very short, there was still fierce resistance from some Republican Guard units and local resistance groups in the area. Blanchard's unit was going into each house and making sure that it was clear of enemy activity.

"Inside one of the houses, Blanchard and an officer from his unit encountered an enemy soldier who was hiding out there. The enemy soldier saw them before they saw him. He threw a hand grenade into the small room where they were standing.

"The grenade should have killed both Blanchard and the American officer standing next to him. But Blanchard fell on top of the grenade before it exploded and took the full brunt of the blast. The other man was unhurt. Blanchard suffered serious wounds and was medevacked to a hospital, where he lingered for several days in terrible pain before dying.

"There's no question Blanchard saved the other man's life by what he did. He received the Army Silver Star medal posthumously. So this guy who might be a murderer wound up being a hero."

I nodded. I hadn't been sure what the Blanchard information was going to tell me, and I was even less sure after I heard this. I still didn't know whether or not he was the person who killed Becky Bluso. And he certainly couldn't have been The Wanderer who went on to murder all those other women in subsequent years. Unless . . .

"Are we absolutely certain Dale Blanchard is dead?" I asked Maggie.

"Of course he's dead. He got the Silver Star medal posthumously."

"Is there any way he could have faked his death in Iraq?"

"You don't fake your death in the Army, Clare. He died. He dived on a live grenade, saved another man's life, and lost his life doing it. The other man said afterward in the reports that Blanchard must have known they both could have been killed if he hadn't done what he did. He did an incredibly heroic thing.

Whatever else you think Blanchard might be responsible for after this—The Wanderer murders or anything else—he didn't do them."

She was right. I was grasping at straws. But I'm a journalist. Journalists ask questions like that. I had one more question to ask.

"Who was the other man?" I asked.

"Do you mean the one from his unit whose life was saved?"

"Right."

"I'm not sure. It's not in the stuff I have here," she said, looking down at her notes.

"Let's find out. Maybe we can interview him. It would be a good story if Blanchard does turn out to be responsible for Becky Bluso's murder. The absurdity of him being both hero and villain. Dale Blanchard saved one life and took another."

Maggie nodded, took out her cell phone, and made a few calls. Whatever she found out clearly stunned her by the look on her face. She hung up and then smiled at me.

"You still have your reporter's instinct to ask the right question, Clare."

"What did you find out?"

"I'm not sure what's going on here—but I've got the name of the officer from Blanchard's unit whose life he saved that day in Iraq."

"Who is he?"

"Russell Danziger," she said.

CHAPTER 52

IF RUSSELL DANZIGER had been a difficult man for me to reach the first time I tried, it was going to be near-impossible for me to do this time.

He'd stormed out of my office in anger after I lured him there to surreptitiously get his DNA because I thought—wrongly, as it turned out—that he could be the The Wanderer serial killer.

Now he unexpectedly turned up in connection with the man who I suspected murdered the first victim, Becky Bluso. Except, that man could not be The Wanderer either because he died before the other murders took place.

I had absolutely no idea what any of this meant, but I knew that I needed to find out.

I told it all to Terri Hartwell who seemed as stunned as I was by Danziger's links with Dale Blanchard and Eckersville.

"Danziger never said anything to you about Blanchard or Eckersville?" I asked.

"Not a word."

"That doesn't make any sense. He just happened to serve in the Army with the guy you had a romance with in high school? He just happened to donate a large amount of money to build a library in the town of Eckersville where you grew up? And now he works with you on your political campaign? That can't all be a coincidence."

I asked her how and when she'd first met Danziger.

"It was several years ago," she said. "I was starting to do some media stuff, and he approached me one day about helping to manage my career. He was already successful at that point. He'd made a lot of money for himself and other people. I had no idea why he was interested in me, but I jumped at the chance.

"He was the one who helped me get the radio talk show gig. Then he got me big media exposure, big ratings, big money for it. After that, he convinced me to run for the district attorney job. He pulled all the strings and got me elected. Now I'm counting on him for the mayoral race. I owe a lot to Russell Danziger. A whole helluva lot."

"Did he ever tell you why he decided to . . . well, pluck you from obscurity and make you a media and political star?" I asked.

"He said it was because I was so talented."

"And you believed him?"

"What other reason could it have been?"

"Are you sure he wasn't romantically interested in you?"

"Like I told you before, I don't think Russell is romantically interested in anyone."

"And he never mentioned anything about Eckersville or any of the people there, like Dale Blanchard?"

"I didn't think he even knew I was from Eckersville. I always just said I grew up in a small Midwestern or Indiana town in my bio material. I never talked about Eckersville. Once I left there, I became Terri Hartwell. That's the truth."

I believed her. She hadn't always told me the whole truth about everything, but then none of us really do. I was pretty sure this was all true though.

"We have to talk to Danziger," I said.

"We?"

"You and me."

"He'd never go for that. Not after what happened at your office last time."

"You gotta try, we have no other choice."

"Yeah, I know . . ." she sighed.

Terri Hartwell.

Dale Blanchard.

Eckersville, Indiana.

And now Russell Danziger.

None of this added up for me, no matter how many different ways I tried to approach it.

* * *

Terri Hartwell called me back later that day.

"We can meet with Russell Danziger at his apartment in an hour," Hartwell said.

She gave me an address on Sutton Place and said she'd meet me out front.

"Damn, how did you pull this off so quickly?"

"I can be very persuasive."

"What did you tell Danziger?"

"You'll find out when we get there."

"What do you mean?"

"I didn't tell him you were going to be with me."

"Jeez . . ."

"It was the only way to do it, Clare."

"Well, this should be interesting. Thanks, I guess."

"I want to know the answers as much as you do," Hartwell said.

CHAPTER 53

RUSSELL DANZIGER HAD that angry look on his face again when he opened the door of an apartment on Sutton Place and saw me standing there with Terri Hartwell. The same angry look I'd seen that first day he burst into Hartwell's office and again when he stormed out of mine at Channel 10. Maybe that was the only look he ever had. Did this guy ever smile?

"What's she doing here?" he said to Hartwell, talking about me as if I weren't there. "I don't want to see her. She has to go."

"We need to talk to you, Russell, about something very important."

"I'll talk to you, not her," he said, this time at least acknowledging my presence with a nod in my direction.

"We both need to talk to you."

"About what?"

"Dale Blanchard."

I thought he might slam the door on both of us. But he didn't. He seemed to have a strange connection with Terri Hartwell that I still didn't quite understand. I wondered if he really was in love with her, even though he'd never acted on it. Or at least as much in love as someone as repressed and narcissistic as Danziger could be. In any case, he let us inside. Both of us.

The apartment was breathtakingly large. Hell, the foyer we were standing in at the moment was as big as my entire apartment. I had no idea how many rooms were in the place, but it must have been a lot. He led us into the living room, which had panoramic views of the East River and the 59th Street Bridge. Expensive-looking furniture, carpets, and paintings filled the room. There was a huge TV screen on the wall tuned to CNN. This was quite a life Russell Danziger had built for himself. And now I was here to maybe take it all apart.

"What do you want to know about Dale Blanchard?" he asked after we sat down.

"What was your relationship with him?" Hartwell asked.

"We were in the Army together."

"Yes."

"And that's all?" I asked.

"No, there's more. Blanchard saved my life in Iraq. He fell on top of a live grenade that was about to rip us both apart. It cost him his life, and—because of that—I got to live mine. But you already knew all that, didn't you?"

"Did you donate a large amount of money to build a library in Blanchard's hometown of Eckersville, Indiana?"

"Yes, I did. You know that, too."

"You really spent all that money in honor of Dale Blanchard?" Hartwell said.

"Well, the man did save my life."

"So why didn't you put his name on the library plaque, instead of yours?" I asked him.

Danziger shrugged. "I guess I just have this lust to be in the spotlight of public attention and adoration." He sort of grinned when he said that. It was a strange-looking grin. I wasn't sure if it was better or worse than his usual angry expression, but at least it was different.

"Let's cut through all the BS to get to the real truth here, Mr. Danziger," I said. "Dale Blanchard was from Eckersville. Terri Hartwell grew up in Eckersville as Teresa Lofton. Teresa Lofton had a romance with Dale Blanchard in high school. Blanchard saved your life in Iraq, then he died. You later show up out of the blue to introduce yourself to Hartwell and catapult her media and political career. Those are the facts. Now you need to connect the dots for us and tell the goddamned truth!"

Danziger got off the couch where he was sitting and began walking toward us. I wondered if he actually was going to throw us out this time. He was a big man; he might even hit me. But instead he walked past Hartwell and me toward a desk in the corner, opened a drawer, and took out a picture.

He came back and showed the picture to us. It was him and several soldiers at a base camp in Iraq. Hartwell let out an involuntary gasp when she saw the face of one of the soldiers. So I knew it was Blanchard. He was very handsome with a rakish look on his face as he held a can of beer up to the camera. I could see why a young Terri Hartwell had been so enamored with him in high school.

"That picture was taken a few weeks before the grenade attack happened," Danziger said. "I didn't know him well then. I was a major and he was an enlisted man. He was just another soldier in my unit to me. I had no idea he would become the most important person I ever met in my life."

Danziger put the picture down, but he kept looking at it as he talked.

"Everything in a war is magnified. Sometimes things which at first seem to be insignificant turn out to be totally life changing. Or life ending, as it happened for Blanchard. I mean me and my men had gone into hundreds of buildings like that one without anything ever going wrong. But then, in an instant, everything went wrong.

"I don't know if Blanchard even had time to think about what he did. Or if he would have done the same thing if he had had time to think. Or if I would have done the same thing for him, if I'd been the one closest to the live grenade. I still think about that. I have ever since that day in 1991, and I do to this day.

"When George Bush died—the one who was president during the first Gulf War I fought in—the obits talked a lot about his heroic service in World War II. About how his plane was shot down—he survived, but the other two men in his plane were killed. Bush had told people that he still thought about those two men every day of his life, too, like I do with Blanchard. Most people can't understand something like that because they've never been to war. But I have, and I do understand. There isn't a day that goes by in my life where I don't still think about what Dale Blanchard did for me. I got to live my life, but he never did."

Then he told us about going to see Blanchard in the Army hospital before he died of his wounds.

"He was in terrible pain and pumped up on drugs. He knew he was dying. There were no words I could say to thank him for what he had done, but I thanked him anyway. He asked me if I could do something important for him. I, of course, said yes.

"He said if I ever had the opportunity to do something to help the town of Eckersville, I should do it for him. He said he'd done something bad back in Eckersville and wanted to make amends, as best he could. But he said it had to be anonymous. He didn't deserve to get credit for anything because . . . well, he said because what he'd done back then was too horrible for that. He just wanted to do the right thing.

"Then he also asked me to look after a girl named Teresa Lofton, who he called the 'love of his life.' But I couldn't tell her that either. He said he loved her more than anything, but he had hurt her. Now he wanted to make up for that, too. He made me promise to look after Teresa Lofton, whenever I could. But not to tell her anything about why I was doing it, either. He said he didn't deserve a girl like Teresa Lofton. I said I'd do my best. Dale Blanchard died not long afterward."

I looked over at Terri Hartwell. There was a look of shock on her face. And, unless I was mistaken, tears welling up in her eyes. She clearly was emotionally affected by all this, even thirty years later. You never forget your first love, she'd told me. Hartwell's first love had been Dale Blanchard. No matter what he might have done, some of that feeling for him still endured. And she was finding out for the first time that his last thoughts, his last words, had been about her. I think at that moment she was seventeen-year-old Teresa Lofton again, not Terri Hartwell.

"Everything I've accomplished, every moment of my life that I've enjoyed since then . . . it's all because of what Dale Blanchard did that day in Iraq," Danziger said. "I wouldn't be sitting here today if it weren't for Dale Blanchard. I owe him—and his memory—a debt I can never repay. But I've tried.

"At first, I wasn't able to do much in those ensuing years because I was in the Army, moving around to different assignments and locations. And I wasn't a wealthy man then. But I never forgot about Blanchard and my promise to him. That's why—when I left the Army and started making big money in my business enterprises—I made that donation to the Eckersville library.

"And I'd followed Teresa Lofton over the years," he said, looking over at Hartwell, "as she got married, had children, and moved ahead in her career. That's when I decided to help her even more, to look after her the way I had promised Blanchard I would. It's been a relationship that's been beneficial to both of us. But I never told her how and why it all started. Because that's what Dale Blanchard asked me to do. I've kept my word on that. Until today."

"You said Dale told you he'd done something bad back in Eckersville," I said to Danziger. "Something he wanted to try and make up for. Did he tell you what he did that was so bad?"

"No, I have no idea what it was."

"Did he confess to you on his deathbed that he had murdered a young woman named Becky Bluso? Is that why you asked questions about the Bluso murder when you went to Eckersville, and even visited the crime site?"

"I don't know anything about that."

Russell Danziger sure was a bizarre guy. A man who had repressed all emotions or kindness or human feelings over the years. Probably because his own father had done the same thing to him. But yet he had this emotional attachment to Dale Blanchard, who had been dead for thirty years. And, by extension, with Terri Hartwell, the woman Blanchard had loved and asked him to take care of. It sounded crazy to me. But maybe if someone saved your life in a war, you looked at things differently. Now I had to hope he still had one bit of decent human emotion left in him. I needed Russell Danziger to do the right thing here.

I took out a printout with the pictures of all the women we believed were victims of The Wanderer.

"These women have been murdered since Becky Bluso," I said. "We thought at first it was done by the same person that murdered Becky Bluso. That's apparently not the case now. But I still think all these murders are connected somehow. And the killer is still out there. Tell us everything Dale Blanchard told you about Becky Bluso before he died. Maybe there's something there that could help us find the answers. I know you promised to keep Dale

Blanchard's secrets for him. And I know how important that is to you. But other women are being killed besides Becky Bluso. Maybe if you tell us what you know—all of it you found out from Blanchard in that hospital—we can bring some kind of justice for these crimes. And hopefully prevent any more women from dying."

Danziger stared at the pictures—the faces of the dead women— for a long time. I asked him the same question again.

"Did Blanchard confess to you on his deathbed that he was the one who murdered Becky Bluso?" I asked.

He nodded. Almost imperceptibly at first. But it was a nod.

"He didn't mean to do it, Dale told me. He didn't even know why he did it. It just happened. Something in him snapped, he said. He'd been angry and depressed about losing you, Terri. When Becky Bluso invited him into her bedroom, she looked so much like you that, at first, he began fantasizing he was with you again, he said. He didn't remember any of the details. Just that he'd tied up Bluso on the bed and began playing games with a knife—like he used to do with you. He said he blacked out. When he became conscious again of what was around him, he saw what he had done. He'd carried all that guilt with him ever since then. And now, when he knew he was dying, I guess it was important to him to tell someone. I never told anyone after he died. Becky Bluso was dead, and now so was he. I wanted him to die remembered as a hero, not as a murderer."

"Are you the only person he ever told about killing Becky Bluso?" I asked.

Danziger was silent now.

"Mr. Danziger?"

"He said there was someone else who knew about it."

"Who?"

"Someone in Eckersville. Another student at the high school. He got drunk one night and told the kid about it. He freaked out the next morning when he sobered up and realized what he had done. He figured the guy would report him to the police. But that never happened. Dale never understood why the guy didn't go to the authorities."

"Did he tell you the name of this other student?"

"No, I don't know the name."

"Didn't you ask him?"

"Dale died before I could do that."

CHAPTER 54

THE NEXT DAY Scott Manning and I were on a plane to Indiana.

"Okay, this guy Blanchard kills Becky Bluso in a crazy moment and tells another kid at school about it," Manning said, repeating the facts I'd given to him after leaving Danziger. "Only the other kid never tells anyone. Or reports it to the police. Why? What does he do next?"

"Maybe he starts killing women, too."

"You think Blanchard kills the first one, then the other guy keeps doing it with the rest after Blanchard goes into the Army and dies?"

"That is a plausible theory. It explains why the DNA results were similar in all the crimes except the first one, Becky Bluso."

"Seems like a reach to me, Clare. Just because this other student knew about Blanchard doing the Bluso murder—and didn't say anything—doesn't mean he'd begin murdering women on his own. Hell, Danziger knew about Blanchard and Becky Bluso, too, and he's not The Wanderer."

"We know that now because of the DNA results."

"What you're saying is all we have to do is find this other guy, somehow get him to admit to us that Blanchard told him about murdering Bluso, obtain his DNA, and maybe even get him to confess to all the other murders and being one of the worst serial killers in history?"

I nodded. "It should be easy."

"Do you have any idea how many students must have gone to Eckersville High School back in 1990 when Becky Bluso was murdered?"

"One thousand four hundred and fifty-one. I checked before we left."

"Assuming half of them are male, that's seven hundred possible suspects we need to track down and question."

"At least."

"Most of them have probably left Eckersville and are living in other parts of the country or the world."

"Likely."

"Some of them will be dead."

"Also, likely."

"And a whole lot of others won't want to talk to us or won't re-member much of anything about a guy they went to high school with thirty years ago."

"Like I said, this should be easy." I smiled.

My relationship with the FBI was still a tenuous one. I hadn't talked to Wharton or any of the other agents from the task force since the FBI leak that scooped me on my own story. I dealt di-rectly with Manning now. But, once they found out I was going to Eckersville on this new lead, they assigned Manning to ac-company me. Even though he was still dubious about my theory on this.

I'd talked to Janet on the phone about what I was doing with Manning before I left. She told me for like the zillionth time I was making a bad decision by mixing my personal and profes-sional lives.

"This has disaster written all over it," she said. "It's like taking a loaded gun along with you. Sooner or later, that gun is going to go off."

"This is all professional, Janet. He's the FBI agent. I'm the journalist. That's all there is to it. We respect each other's boundaries."

Janet snorted loudly into the phone. "You've got this new guy, Gary Weddle. The media consultant at your station. It sounds like you have a chance for a healthy relationship with him. You like Weddle, right?"

"Yes, I do."

"And Scott Manning is married. He's not going to leave his wife for you. Even you must realize that. He had a chance to leave her a year ago, and he chose his marriage over you. Married guys who go back to their wives once do it again and again. You're taking a chance on screwing up a healthy relationship by not walking away from an unhealthy one, Clare."

"I know what I'm doing."

"Well, that would be a first."

"Cute."

"At least make sure you stay in different hotels while you're there."

"We're booked at the same hotel."

"Jeez..."

"Two different rooms, Janet. There are walls between the rooms, too. That way we can't roll out of bed into each other's arms or anything, if that's what you're worried about. The walls are pretty thick, too, I imagine. I mean, I'd have to use a sledgehammer to knock them down and get at Manning in the middle of the night."

"The Walls of Jericho," Janet muttered.

"What?"

"The Walls of Jericho. From the old movie with Clark Gable and Claudette Colbert. *It Happened One Night*. He's a reporter and she's a runaway heiress. They have to hide out in a hotel together, so they put a blanket up between them at night. The Walls of Jericho, Colbert called it. By the end of the movie, the Walls of Jericho have come down and they are together."

"There aren't any walls coming down in my hotel," I told her.

I thought about that now as I looked over at Manning in the seat next to me on the plane. It had been a long night for him, getting everything organized with the FBI and planning the trip to Indiana with me. Even though it was only a two-hour flight, he was fast asleep. Watching him with his eyes closed like that made me remember the last time I'd seen him sleeping. It was a year ago when we'd had sex in my apartment. This time was different though. Just like I'd tried to convince Janet. Now I had to also convince myself of that for sure, too.

I tried to keep my mind on the story, not on Scott Manning. I'd brought along a printout of names and possible locations/contact information for members of Eckersville High School in 1990 that we'd culled from yearbooks and other sources before leaving New York. I pored through them now.

I was still doing that when Manning woke up and we landed at the Indianapolis International Airport.

*   *   *

Chief Parkman had already organized his force at the Eckersville Police Station to work with the FBI on this when we got there. He said that he had nine full-time officers, plus a half dozen or so support personnel like secretaries and phone answerers. He said they could all be used for this, unless there was some breaking crime they needed to respond to. Since there wasn't a whole lot of breaking crime in Eckersville, I figured we had them working with us for the duration.

"I'm familiar with many of the people from our high school that stayed in Eckersville after graduation," Parkman said. "Why don't I focus on reaching out to them? You two—and everyone else—can try to track down all the ones who've moved away. Does that sound like a plan?"

"Still going to be a helluva job talking to 700 men," Manning grunted.

"Actually, only 699." Parkman smiled. "I went to Eckersville High, too, back then, remember? And you're already talking to me. That's one less person we have to find."

"I like a glass-half-full kind of guy," I told him.

"Did you know Dale Blanchard at all?" Manning asked.

I'd already asked Parkman that question. But Manning, like the good FBI agent he was, asked it again in hopes of jogging something from Parkman's memory that he might have forgotten over the years.

"Like I told Ms. Carlson, I was just a freshman. All of them—Blanchard, Becky Bluso, the Lofton woman—were older. They had no time for me. I saw them in the hall sometimes, but I don't believe I ever said a word to any of them. I do remember Blanchard being with Teresa Lofton a few times. They were a very attractive couple."

"But you never saw Blanchard with Becky Bluso?" I asked.

"Not that I remember."

"And Blanchard wasn't ever a suspect in the Bluso murder investigation back in 1990?" Manning wanted to know.

"I can only go by the reports I've seen from back then. They might have looked at him as a potential suspect, but they were looking at a lot of people as potential suspects. None of it ever led to anything. Until now. But, at least with this confession on his deathbed that you've got now, we can pretty much close the book on the Becky Bluso murder. That's a big deal for this town. It was the only unsolved murder case in our history."

"Now all we have to do is solve nineteen more murders," I pointed out.

"Let's get started," Parkman said.

*   *   *

It was late that evening by the time Manning and I left the Eckersville Police Station. We'd been going through hundreds of names, sending emails, and reaching out by phone and even sending police officers to knock on doors of addresses in Eckersville. We'd found a few people who remembered Dale Blanchard, but nothing that really helped.

Manning and I agreed we should get some rest—then start fresh in the morning.

We'd both rented separate cars at the airport. I started walking toward mine now.

"Do you want to get dinner before we go back to the hotel?" Manning asked.

"No, I'm fine. I'll get room service there."

"I saw a steak place down the road before."

"Steak?"

"Probably better food there than you'll get from room service."

"I have trouble saying no to a good steak."

"Cool. Let's take my car. You can leave your car here. Then I'll drive you back to the hotel afterward."

"How will I get back here in the morning?"

"We're staying at the same hotel, Clare. I'll give you a ride."

"Thanks."

"Hey, we're a team, right?"

CHAPTER 55

THE RESTAURANT TURNED out to be one of those chain steak places you see a lot throughout the country once you leave New York City. That was fine with me. The steak was good, the portions big, the prices reasonable—and they served alcohol. All I needed to make me happy right now. Plus, I had Scott Manning with me.

I tried my best to keep the conversation about business while we ate and drank beer.

"What do you think?" I asked him about the long-ago Eckersville High student who Blanchard might have confessed his murder to.

"It's like looking for a needle in a haystack, Clare. No, worse than a needle in a haystack. With a needle in a haystack, you've at least got a chance of getting lucky. This seems hopeless."

"So why are you even here looking for him with me?"

"You know the answer. It's what we do in law enforcement on a cold case like this where there's not many fresh leads. We check out everything no matter how much of a waste of time it might seem. Then we eliminate that possibility and move on to something else until we find the answers we're looking for."

I nodded. It was the same way I worked as a journalist.

"Even if we do find this guy, it's probably crazy to hope that he turns out to be the one who committed the other murders like Bluso everywhere else," I said.

"I'm not sure that part is so crazy. I've been thinking a lot about this scenario, and it does make a kind of weird sense. The murders all seem the same, except the DNA from the first one is different. But there must be some kind of connection between Becky Bluso and the other women who were victims."

He took a big drink of his beer.

"All we have to do is find this guy, which is probably impossible. Then get him to confess he's a mass murderer. Then we can wrap this all up and go home. Like you said, it should be easy."

He smiled at me. I smiled back.

"And if that ever happens, let's hope the FBI doesn't leak it to another media outlet before I can go on the air with my own story, huh?"

Manning sighed. We hadn't talked about that much. I knew Manning wasn't responsible for the leak, it had been Wharton or someone else at the FBI. But I was still furious at the FBI because of it. And Manning was the only FBI guy here with me right now to complain to.

I asked him if he knew any more about what had happened.

"I don't think it was Wharton who did it," Manning said. "Oh, he didn't want you as part of the investigation. And I know he didn't like you. At least not at first. But I've talked to him and I think he's gotten a certain amount of grudging respect now for the information you've given us."

"Are you saying Wharton likes me?"

"I wouldn't go that far. Let's just say he's not your enemy anymore."

"Damn. I was hoping it was Wharton that was responsible. He's so easy to hate."

"My guess is it was one of the other people on the task force. Someone you met at one of those meetings. You didn't make many friends in that room. A lot of people there didn't like you."

"I tend to have that effect on some people."

We both had had quite a bit to drink. At one point, the conversation began moving away from pure business.

"Kind of interesting to see a small-town police department up close, huh?" Manning said. "I know Parkman probably envies my job as a big-city FBI agent. But I kind of envy his, too. Being the police chief of a little town can be very comfortable and rewarding. You know everyone, everyone knows you. There's not a lot of crime to worry about. Must be kind of like an Andy Griffith of Mayberry life. Maybe even get to go fishing with your family like Andy did. I never had any time for fishing with my family. I've always been too consumed with my job."

"Do you really think you could be happy in a small town like Eckersville?" I asked.

"I don't know. Maybe. My wife sure would be. She wanted me to get out of the NYPD, and now she wants me out of the FBI. She likes the quiet life where we live in Staten Island. I'm sure she'd love a town like this."

His wife. There it was again.

I finished off the beer in front of me. "I think we should probably head back to the hotel now and get some rest. We've got a big day ahead of us tomorrow."

Our rooms were on the same floor, several doors apart. He walked me to my door and waited while I used the key on it.

"Well, good night, Clare."

"Good night."

"I . . . I . . . well, I just want to say I'm glad we're working together again like this. I know I was a bit difficult with you when you first came to me with the serial killer information, but I realize now that we're both professionals. We've been able to move past all the personal things that went down between us and do our jobs. I'm happy about that."

"Me, too, Scott."

Then he began walking toward his own room. And I let myself into mine.

All very professional.

*   *   *

I got undressed, lay down on the bed, and tried to go to sleep. I couldn't. I turned on the TV to a newscast, which showed a reporter talking about traffic jams on some bridge I'd never heard of. I thought about ordering something from room service, but I'd already eaten a big steak dinner and drank too much.

There was a knock at the door. I pulled my clothes on and walked over to it.

"Who's there?"

"Scott."

I opened the door.

I'm not really sure what happened next. All I remember is there was a lot of kissing, hugging, and taking off of clothes. I'm not sure which one of us started it, or if we both did it simultaneously. Then we were on the bed, making love. Mad, passionate love. The kind of love I'd remembered having with him the last time we were together.

So much for the Walls of Jericho.

When it was over, we both lay there in the hotel bed for a long time without saying anything.

He finally spoke first.

"About my wife and us . . . I want you to know . . ."

"Shh," I said, putting my finger on his lips. "Don't say it."

"What?"

"Don't tell me how you're thinking about leaving her again. How you really want to be with me instead. How you feel guilty about doing this to her again, but you're more attracted to me. Let's not go there, Scott. Let's accept this for what it is. A wonderful moment. You're not going to leave her for me. You know that, and I know it, too. And, even if you did, you'd be so guilt ridden about it that you and I probably wouldn't last any longer than any of my marriages did. We've got tonight, and this is a pretty good night. Let's leave it like that."

He fell asleep a while after that. I looked over at him and wondered if we'd ever be together like this again. I reached over, kissed him gently, put my arms around him, and hugged him. He stirred slightly in his sleep and moved closer to me. I held onto him as tightly as I could until the first rays of morning sunlight began coming through the window.

CHAPTER 56

THE NEXT MORNING, Manning went back to his own room to shower and get dressed. Then we met at a coffee shop in the hotel for breakfast. After that, he drove me back to my car that I'd left in the parking lot of the police station. Neither of us said anything about the night before. It was as if nothing ever happened. I wanted it that way, and I think he did, too.

The plan for the day was he'd go back to the station to work with Chief Parkman and his people to try to identify more Eckersville High students from 1990 who might still be in the area. At the same time, Manning was working with the task force at FBI headquarters to locate students who had moved to other places throughout the country.

I had a different lead to check out. I'd gone on my computer that morning and discovered that one of the students from back then now operated a hardware store right here in town. I called and got a phone answering message saying the store opened at nine a.m. I drove there to wait for the store to open and interview the owner in person.

The name of the store was Elliott's Hardware, and it looked like the kind of place you'd expect in a small town like Eckersville. You don't run into a lot of hardware stores in New York City.

People there buy their hardware tools in big chain stores or else ask the super to fix stuff, I guess.

Elliott Hardware—like a lot of the rest of Eckersville—was a throwback to a part of America that was rapidly disappearing.

I introduced myself to Larry Elliott, the owner, as soon as he showed up to open the front door. He was a pleasant enough looking man, but noticeably overweight and had thinning hair. I'd found a picture of him from the Eckersville High yearbook online back at the hotel. He looked a lot better at eighteen than he did now. But I suppose that's true of all of us.

The good news is that he was happy to talk to me. He told me how his father had owned this store for many years before him. How he had left Eckersville to go to college, but then returned to take over the business when his father retired. How successful the business had been since then. He proudly took me around the store, showing me a lot of tools and gadgets I didn't really understand, but pretended I did.

There is a pace to every interview. A good journalist knows this, and I'd figured out a long time ago not to rush to ask my questions. You let the person you want to interview talk for a while, make them feel comfortable—and then switch to the questions you really want the answers to.

When it came time to ask about Dale Blanchard, I used the same approach I'd been doing with other former Eckersville High students. I didn't tell him the real reason for my interest in Blanchard. I said I was a journalist working on a story about forgotten war heroes. And I wanted to find out more about the brave young man who had given his own life to save a fellow soldier.

He said he remembered Blanchard very well.

"Dale was a bit of an unforgettable character to me," Elliott said. "He was kind of like a Fonzie character . . . you know, from the *Happy Days* show. Super-cool. The girls loved him; they always flocked around him. But he was weird. He had a really bad temper, and an ugly side that scared people. He could be friendly one minute, then explode in a tirade the next minute.

"I used to try to hang around him. Mostly because he was so popular with the girls, I guess. It wasn't just that he was so good-looking, as I recall now. There was also this sense of danger about him that made him even more intriguing to people. Especially the women. A lot of girls seemed to really get off on that with Dale."

"Was one of those girls Teresa Lofton?"

"Sure, I remember that. He and Teresa were an item. I used to run into them together, her hanging on his arm. But then Dale joined the Army after he graduated. Never saw much of him after that. Until I heard he had died."

I tried to ask the next question as casually as I could.

"Did Blanchard ever tell you anything—give you any kind of information—about anything he might have done wrong here in Eckersville before the Army?"

"Like what?"

"Just asking."

"No, I can't think of anything like that. But I wasn't that close to him. I wanted to be, but a few of the other guys spent more time with him back then in high school."

"Do you remember any of their names?"

"Sure, give me a minute. Oh, let me show you something, too. If you're writing about Dale and what he did during that war, you might be interested in this."

He opened up a drawer in a filing cabinet and took out an old newspaper. It was yellow and tattered, but you could still read it. The headline said: "Memorial Service for Slain Eckersville War Hero."

The story detailed the facts of how Blanchard died in Iraq. Plus, more about him attending Eckersville High School. And there was also a description of the memorial service that had been held to honor him in death.

There was a picture, too. It showed Dale Blanchard's casket draped in an American flag. There were several young men standing next to it. The caption didn't identify the men, just said they were pallbearers. I looked at the faces. I recognized one of them.

"Isn't that Jeff Parkman, the police chief?" I asked Elliott.

"Yep, that's Jeff."

"Why was he part of the honorary pallbearers at the service?"

"Remember I told you about the young guys who used to follow Blanchard around and wanted to be like him? Jeff Parkman was one of them. God, he used to be around Blanchard all the time back then. Everything Blanchard did, Jeff would try to do it, too. He worshipped Blanchard. Always wanted to be like him."

Elliott chuckled at the memory. "Who would have ever thought that Jeff would grow up to be the police chief here now?" he said.

*   *   *

I called Manning on his cell phone and told him everything I'd found out.

"Parkman said he hardly remembered Blanchard, that he never really knew him. Elliott says they were very close. That Parkman always wanted to be like Blanchard. Tried to do everything Blanchard did. Why would Parkman lie to us about that?"

"Are you thinking . . . ?"

"Maybe one of those things Jeff Parkman did like Blanchard was murder."

"Jesus."

"Let's see what more we can find out about Parkman. See if it links him up in any way with The Wanderer murders. You can check with your FBI people back in New York and in Washington. I'll ask around town here. Send a picture of Parkman to the Miami bureau, too. They can run it past the victim that survived, Dianna Colson. See if she recognizes him as the person who attacked her."

"Don't forget she thought she recognized Danziger, too."

"She 'sort of' recognized him. I think we pushed her to make her identify Danziger as the killer. It won't hurt to see what she says about Parkman. He could be the guy we're looking for."

"Let's not get ahead of ourselves, Clare. That's what happened with Danziger. We still don't have any real evidence . . ."

There was a muffled sound on the phone, and I realized it was Manning talking to someone else. Then he came back on the line.

"I'm here with Chief Parkman now," he said. "We're going through all those files looking for something helpful."

"You can't talk anymore?"

"That's right."

"I'll be in touch later."

*   *   *

A few hours later—after a trip to the library where I read old stories written in local media about Eckersville's police chief and conversations with city officials and other people in town—I had a better take on him.

Jeffery Alan Parkman had graduated from Eckersville High three years after the Becky Bluso murder. He'd come from a broken home. His father disappeared even before he was born.

His mother worked as a waitress in several local restaurants before losing the jobs because of a drinking problem. Drugs, too.

Guess things weren't that idyllic in Eckersville then, after all.

She was living with her own parents, and eventually, it was Parkman's grandmother who raised him. The mother died of a drug overdose when Jeff was fourteen. A traumatic ordeal for a teenager to endure, but he managed good grades in high school, went to college, and got a degree in law enforcement and criminal justice.

He loved to travel and he loved to fly, one of the articles about him said in a profile after his appointment to police chief. He originally thought about being a pilot. But then he applied for—and was accepted—for U.S. Air Marshal training after college. He spent a number of years as a federal air marshal, flying around the country to all sorts of locations, including during the terrible days after the 9/11 terror attack.

A few years later, when the government closed some of the U.S. Air Marshal units, Parkman decided to return to his hometown and joined the Eckersville Police Department. He had a good record as a police officer and—with his impressive background as a federal air marshal, along with a college degree in criminal justice—quickly moved up the ranks of the handful of officers until he was named chief.

Parkman was well liked, well respected, and well thought of in general as a good police chief by the people of the town that I had talked to.

Along the way, he'd gotten married. His wife, Doris, was a flight attendant Parkman met while flying as an air marshal. She continued in her flight attendant job even after Parkman left the air marshal job for the Eckersville Police Department, commuting back and forth to the Indianapolis and Fort Wayne airports for flights.

She got a lot of free air miles, so Parkman would sometimes fly to whatever city she was going to on his days off from the police department, one person told me. That's how much in love they were, the person said.

She'd left the job several years ago to raise their children, the children Parkman proudly displayed pictures of on his desk at the station house. But, because of her background with the airline, she got special access to tickets that allowed her to fly around the country on trips even after she was no longer working as a flight attendant. People said the couple took several trips a year, using Parkman's vacation days to visit all sorts of spots throughout America. "They love to travel," one Eckersville resident told me. "Me, I've barely even been out of Indiana. But Chief Parkman and his wife . . . well, you should hear some of their stories about all those trips."

Parkman definitely checked off a lot of the boxes in the profile that the FBI had developed for who The Wanderer might really be.

Most importantly, obviously, was the travel. The Wanderer moved around the country to find his victims. Parkman was a U.S. Air Marshal. That meant he could well have traveled to many of the places where the women died. Investigators at the FBI would be able to do a more detailed check of his long-ago flight records as a marshal and compare them to the murder locations. I was also intrigued by the fact that his wife continued to work on flights after he joined the police force, and that he sometimes accompanied her on these trips. Also, they'd continued traveling around the country recently. That might answer a big part of the puzzle.

Then there was the background of him coming from a broken home, without a real mother. That raised the possibility of a boy who had a resentment against women at a young age because of the one that abandoned him before he even had a chance to know her. It was a scenario that had been found in a number of other serial killers of women in the past.

And then there was his life now. A seemingly happy family man, husband and father. Liked and respected by everyone who knew him. Good-looking, charming, the perfect image for a chief of police in a town. The last person in the world you'd suspect of being a brutal serial killer of women. Except that fit the scenario of many serial killers. It was eerily similar to the most notorious American serial killer of all time: Ted Bundy. Bundy was good-looking, charming, and didn't look like a serial killer, either. Until he preyed on his victims. If Parkman was a Ted Bundy–like serial killer masquerading as a good guy and model citizen, that made him even scarier. Because he carried a badge.

I tried to call Manning again, but his phone went to voicemail. Maybe he was still with Parkman and didn't want to answer a call from me in front of him. Or maybe he was somewhere else where he couldn't take a call. I left a message telling him what I'd found out and said I'd meet him back at the hotel to figure out what our next move should be.

CHAPTER 57

THE HOTEL WE were staying at was about three miles away. I was driving the Toyota Corolla that I'd rented at the airport. Not a great car, and a few times, I made a sudden stop or swerved to stay in my lane as I struggled to figure out the gears and unfamiliar dashboard items.

That happened again now as I was about to pull into the hotel parking lot. I wound up switching lanes in a hurry without using my turn indicator light. Mostly because I couldn't find it. Another driver behind me honked and gave me the finger as he passed. I smiled and waved politely at him, which seemed to make him even madder. Midwestern hospitality and friendliness weren't all it was cracked up to be.

I stepped on the accelerator and speeded up into the right lane, but as I did, I heard something behind me.

A police siren.

I looked in my rearview mirror and saw the police car coming up behind me with a flashing red light on top.

I stopped and pulled over to let the police car go wherever it was going. But it pulled up right behind me. I realized the cop was stopping me.

Damn.

Maybe he'd seen that weird traffic incident and thought I was drunk.

I didn't have time for this now.

But I had no choice except to sit in my car and wait for him to come to the driver's window to ask for my driver's license and rental registration and all the rest. Hopefully, that and my media ID, plus me talking about working for his boss Chief Parkman, would be enough to get me off without a ticket.

But the cop didn't appear by my window. Instead, I heard a voice coming over a loudspeaker that said: "Step out of the car. Keep your hands up and in plain sight. Do not make any sudden moves or gestures."

All this for a minor traffic infraction?

I did what the cop said. I got out of the car, put my hands in the air, and waited. Finally, the cop got out of his squad car. He had a gun out and pointed at me. That's when I recognized who it was.

Parkman.

"Chief Parkman, it's me. Clare Carlson. What's going on here? You know who I am . . ."

"I do," Parkman said, moving closer to me with the gun still pointed. "And now, I'm afraid you know who I am, too."

CHAPTER 58

PARKMAN HANDCUFFED ME, led me to his squad car, and pushed me into the back seat. There was a plexiglass divider between the front seat and me, and the doors were locked. I was trapped there, even if I did somehow manage to get at the door handle. He got into the front seat, pulled away from the curb where he was parked—and began driving. I could see we weren't headed in the direction of the police station. I didn't think we would be.

"What's going on here?" I asked, still trying to maintain the illusion that I didn't know the truth about him. "I was headed over to the station to work with you on tracking down more of those names. Is this about something I did wrong in my car? I'll pay the fine if you want to give me a ticket."

Parkman didn't say anything until we were far enough out of town that there were no other cars close to us on the highway. Then he pulled over to the side of the road, got out and unlocked the back door, grabbed me by my hair, and delivered a vicious blow across my face. I fell back onto the seat, stunned and feeling blood trickling down my face. He grabbed me again and hit me a second time. "Now you know what's going on," he sneered. Then he locked the back door again, got back in the front seat, and kept driving.

"I was there when you called your pal Manning," he said. "Manning doesn't have a very good poker face. I could tell something was wrong. Then I found you were asking questions about me around town. Yes, I have friends who tell me things like that. It didn't take much for me to figure out you knew about me."

Manning. He was my only hope now. He knew about Parkman. If I didn't show up at the hotel, he'd go looking for me. And he'd be even more suspicious when he couldn't find Parkman either. Maybe he would put out an FBI arrest warrant on Parkman, and they'd track him down before he did whatever he was going to do to me. But that would take time. I didn't know how much time I had. I had to keep Parkman talking until Manning could find me.

"Why did you lie about knowing Dale Blanchard?" I asked him. "I stumbled across your relationship with Blanchard when I interviewed someone this morning. But, if you'd told the truth about that at the beginning, maybe it wouldn't have seemed so important. It was the lie that made me think you had something to hide."

Parkman shrugged. Like it didn't matter one way or another. I wasn't sure what that meant, but I kept talking.

"The biggest thing though was all your traveling over the years. Moving around the country as a federal air marshal. Did you stop off in some city between flights, murder someone, and get back on the plane to fly home? You kept traveling with your wife, too, even after you stopped being a marshal and joined the police force. What did she think you were doing? Did you tell her you were stepping out of the hotel to go buy cigarettes or something, then murder another innocent woman?"

Still nothing from him. I kept going anyway.

"I don't understand," I said. "You have a loving wife. A beautiful family. Why couldn't you be happy with them?"

"That's different."

"Different how?"

"That's all good, but it has nothing to do with why I've killed all those other women. It might surprise you to know that I have an extremely healthy sexual relationship with my wife. I didn't have sex with any of my victims. You always wondered about that, you told me. Well, sex isn't what this is about."

"What other reason is there?"

"Fun," he said.

Parkman laughed. A scary laugh.

"What about Becky Bluso? Did you kill her, too?"

"Oh no, that was really Dale Blanchard. I was the one he got drunk with and confessed it all to. We met when he was home on leave from the Army before going to Iraq. I guess it had been weighing on his conscience and he needed to tell someone. He talked about how he used to play this sex game with girls, tie them up and pretend to threaten them with a big knife. He said he didn't know why he did it, it just got him excited. But he'd never actually hurt anyone. Until that last time with Becky Bluso. The next day after our drunken conversation he called me in a panic. Tried to claim he'd never really killed her. That he made up the whole story, and I shouldn't ever tell anyone. But I knew it was true.

"I never did tell anyone, but not to protect him. I liked having the secret. It excited me in the same way it did him. Thinking about how he'd tied up women and then murdered one of them. I used to fantasize I was him plunging that knife into that goddamned snotty bitch Bluso who wouldn't even give me the time of day.

"I thought about it a long time. I fantasized all the time about murdering a woman like that. Holding her helpless, having her completely under my control—and at my mercy—until I decided it was the right moment to end it. I used to plan out every minute of how I would do it. Subdue the girl. Tie her up. Stand over her with the knife or the rope I was going to use. Or sometimes I thought about using my hands to kill her. That was so much more personal.

"It got to the point where I couldn't think about anything else. I'd sit in my room after school and fantasize about doing what Blanchard had done to Becky Bluso. Blanchard felt guilty about murdering her. The guilt was eating him up, he told me that night. But I knew I would never feel guilty if I did it. I would feel . . . well, exhilarated. And now Blanchard was dead, so it was my turn to carry on with what he'd started that day on Oak Park Drive.

"One day I did it. I got up the nerve to do it for real. And you know what? The actual deed was even more exciting than the fantasy. God, I loved it! I started to read about all the serial killers and the things they'd said about how it felt to murder a woman. Especially remembered a quote from Ted Bundy. About how it made him feel like God when he looked into a woman's eyes before he killed her. That's how I felt. I felt like God. I was in complete control of when this person died.

"Sometimes I played out the scene for hours. I'd hold the knife over her, make her think I was about to stab her and then stop. Then I'd do it again. Or I'd start to strangle her, then let her breathe again just as she was gasping for air. I loved to see the hope in their eyes when I did that. The hope that this was all a game, that I wasn't really going to kill them. Then, when I did, it was even more satisfying for me.

"After that first time, I did it again. And again. Never enough so that anyone could ever put together a pattern between the murders. And never in the same location. The best part was when I joined the police force, then became the police chief. I was on the inside of criminal law enforcement.

"I even went to an FBI seminar for local police in Washington once that was all about how to identify and capture serial killers. How great was that? I was getting firsthand advice from law enforcement on how to avoid getting caught by them. Not that anyone ever came close to figuring out what I was doing. Until you. I mean, I was the police chief. Who would ever suspect me? I was incredibly successful when you think about it. I murdered all those women in a period of thirty years, and no one ever suspected a thing. I became one of the most prolific serial killers in history. Only no one knew that except me."

We were several miles out of town, on a lonely road with no other cars in sight. I wondered what Scott Manning was doing now. Had he figured out that I was missing?

"And then Marty Barlow came to see you," I said.

"Yes, that old man wanted to talk about the Becky Bluso murder. Said he'd covered it back when he worked here at the newspaper. Now he wanted to find out some answers—closure, he called it."

"But how did he find out about the other murders?"

"I told him."

"What?"

"Oh, I didn't tell him directly. He never knew it came from me. I just anonymously sent him enough information after he visited here that led him to suspect there was a silent serial killer at work responsible for all of the murders, including Becky Bluso."

"Why would you do that?"

"Not because I wanted to get caught. But I decided it was time for people to be impressed by what I had done. I mean everyone knew about other famous serial killers. Like Ted Bundy and Son of Sam and the Zodiac Killer. Now it was time my work got recognized for my achievements. Even if no one could ever find out that

I was the one responsible for it all. I still want people to know about my accomplishments. I want them to know that there's someone out there who is the greatest serial killer ever. Better than Bundy, better than Son of Sam, better than Zodiac or any of the others."

"Did you murder Barlow because he found out too much about you?"

"Of course not. He never suspected me. Hell, I showed him that plaque from Russell Danziger, like I showed it to you. And he took the bait, too. I kept feeding him anonymous stuff that pointed him in the direction of Danziger. He thought Danziger was The Wanderer, not me. Why would I kill Martin Barlow? And I don't even know where he lived in New York. What happened to that old man had nothing to do with me. I was simply hoping he'd write about the murders. He was going to, too. Even gave me a nickname, right? The Wanderer. I kind of liked that. But he died before he could write his story."

"Then I came along?"

"Same thing with you. I wanted you to write about The Wanderer. Let everyone know about my exploits. Without anyone ever finding out who The Wanderer really was. Except you did your job too well."

He pulled the car into a secluded area of the road now. No one could see us.

"You won't get away with this," I said. "I'm a journalist. People know I'm working on this story. If you kill me, they're going to figure out there's a connection between my death and the story I'm working on here."

"Maybe they will. But they won't suspect me."

"Why not?"

"Because I'm the police chief. I'm going to be in charge of the investigation into your death."

"You're forgetting one thing. I'm here with the FBI. Agent Manning knows the truth about you. He's going to know you're responsible for my death, too. Think about that before you do anything stupid. Maybe we could work out some kind of plea bargain for you . . ."

He laughed.

"A plea bargain? God, you're desperate, aren't you? I don't think anyone's going to give me a plea bargain for nineteen murders. So why not make it an even twenty, huh?"

He smiled at that—a scary smile.

"Manning knows," I repeated, hoping that might somehow make him hesitate. "I called him on the phone before you grabbed me. I left a message telling him everything."

Parkman reached into his pocket and took out a cell phone. I recognized it right away. It was Manning's cell phone. He played the last message on it for me.

"Scott, I'm headed back to the hotel," I heard my own voice saying. "Let's meet there and figure out what to do about moving on Parkman . . ."

Parkman shut off the phone.

"If you're waiting for help from Scott Manning, well . . . I don't think Agent Manning will be helping anyone anymore."

CHAPTER 59

I COULDN'T HANDLE the idea of Scott Manning being dead.

I tried to stop thinking about Manning—to focus on my own dire situation—but I couldn't. Not completely. I mean I'd just had sex with Scott Manning less than twelve hours earlier in my hotel room. And now he was dead? I refused to accept that. I kept hoping that, somehow, he would still show up and rescue me, even though I realized that wasn't going to happen.

If Manning was dead, the man who killed him was here with me.

And he was planning to kill me next.

But I'd made up my mind about one thing: I wasn't going to go easy.

Sure, I was handcuffed in his police car. But I didn't think he would kill me inside the car. It would be too easy to trace back to him if I died there. That meant he would have to take me somewhere else—probably into the woods—to finish me off.

And that would be my only—my last—chance to survive.

I tried desperately to remember everything I'd ever written or read in stories about how a woman managed to get away from a deadly attacker. The one that popped into my head was about one of Ted Bundy's targeted victims. I'd been reading a lot about Bundy and his killing spree since I started working on The Wanderer story.

There had been a lot of women victims for Bundy, but only one was different. Carol DaRonch. She got away from him.

The facts of that long-ago crime raced through my mind as I waited in Parkman's police car.

DaRonch was walking back to her car in a mall shopping lot when Bundy, posing as a police officer, approached her and said he'd caught someone trying to break into her vehicle. He asked her to ride with him to the station to file an official police report. Once she was in his car, however, she realized something was terribly wrong. Then he attacked her and tried to put handcuffs on her. But she did what none of his victims had ever been able to do successfully. She fought back. She punched him, she kicked him, she even bit him. "I knew he was going to kill me," she said afterward. Eventually, he'd gotten a handcuff on one of her wrists, but her other hand was still free. She finally was able to push him away from her enough to open the car door and flee the killer Bundy.

Could I do the same thing with my killer?

I was pretty sure I had one thing in my favor Parkman's other victims never did. He wasn't prepared this time. In all his other killings, he'd clearly spent time stalking the women and then murdering them in a plan he'd thought out very well. This was all improvised. I was hoping that might make him slip up.

He confirmed that this wasn't his normal modus operandi when he came back to get me from the car.

"This is your lucky day," Parkman said. "I told you before how I normally spend a long time working on my victims. I like to see them suffer. I enjoy the way they plead for their lives and beg me to stop hurting them and promise me anything I want. That's the best part of it for me. I kept one of them alive like that for forty-eight hours once. That's a good memory for me, although

I'm sure it wasn't for her. But with you . . . we're going to do this fast. I want to get you out of the picture. Once you and that FBI guy are both gone, then I can get back to work again. My work. There's a lot of women out there for me to kill yet. So many choices, so little time."

He had a crowbar in his hand. When he unlocked me from the car, he whacked me in the head with the crowbar.

"Just a little reminder to you not to try anything," he said. "We can make this an easy death for you, or a hard one. Up to you, TV lady."

The blow from the crowbar was a glancing one, and it didn't hurt me too badly. But I pretended it did. I went limp and made him drag me out of the car, then behind him as he walked toward the woods. Once I disappeared in there, I knew I was done. I had to make my move, whatever it was, before then. I continued to play dead as he pulled me behind him, hoping against hope that I wouldn't be experiencing the real thing in a few minutes.

When we finally stopped next to a big tree, he stood over me and slapped my face. "Wakey-wakey!" he said. "I want you awake for this. It's more fun that way."

I saw he'd dropped the crowbar on the ground and now held a big knife in his hand. The weapon he'd used on so many victims.

He reached down to my handcuffed hands, unlocked one of them, and started to pull the other one up to a lower tree branch next to us. I realized what he was doing. He was going to handcuff me to the tree, which would leave me unable to move or resist in any way while he did whatever he planned to do to me next.

This was my last chance.

I pulled my suddenly free hand away from him as hard as I could before he had a chance to lock me onto the tree branch. I might not have had the strength to do it if he'd expected it. But he'd bought into the idea that I was so out of it that I was no threat to him. He was wrong about that. I was going to be a helluva threat.

I fought back with everything I had. Just like Carol DaRonch had all those years ago against Ted Bundy. I punched Parkman. I kicked him. I swung the metal handcuffs at his head, opening up a gash there that left blood streaming down his face. But it was the next thing I did that really saved me. I bit him. I bit the sonofabitch as hard as I could on his hand as he tried to grab me. He howled in pain, then shoved me away from him.

I landed on the ground.

Next to where he'd left the crowbar.

I picked it up.

Parkman was still looking down at his hand, cursing in anger and frustration as it was bleeding now, too. He was so upset, he wasn't paying enough attention to me. Holding the crowbar, I walked up and smashed him across the back of the head with it as hard as I could. It worked. I knocked him unconscious.

While he lay there not moving from the blow, I had to make a decision. I could run before he woke up or do something else. I did something else.

I reached for the gun he had in the holster at his side. When Parkman woke up, I was waiting there with the gun pointed at him.

"What are you going to do with that?" he asked, anxious now.

He was scared; the arrogance was gone.

I liked that.

"I'm going to shoot you with it."

His eyes opened wide in fear.

"You're going to kill me?"

"Nah, although I would like to do that. It would be a benefit to society to have you no longer on this planet. But I'll leave that to the courts."

He relaxed a little now.

"Be careful with that gun . . . it could go off."

"That's the idea."

"You said you weren't going to kill me."

"No, but I have to make sure you don't make a run for it. So . . ."

I walked a little closer so I wouldn't miss, pulled the trigger, and shot Parkman in the right foot.

"Jesus, you bitch!" he screamed out in pain.

But he wasn't going anywhere now.

"Now we wait," I said.

"Wait for what?"

"I used Manning's phone to call for help. They should be here soon."

Sure enough, a few minutes later, the sound of sirens came closer to us.

"You're in a lot of trouble," Parkman said.

"You think?"

"I'm a police officer. You shot me."

"After you tried to kill me."

"No one's going to believe you. I'm the police chief. It's my word against yours. And you stole my gun."

The sirens were almost to us now.

"You're going to have a lot of explaining to do," Parkman told me.

"So are you," I said.

CHAPTER 60

I HADN'T CALLED the Eckersville police. Not first. No, first I called the FBI. Then I called Jack Faron at Channel 10. Then I called Janet, my friend—and, if needed—my lawyer. I wanted a record of my story with all of them in case things went wrong when the local police showed up and found me standing with a gun over their police chief.

I wound up talking to Gregory Wharton at the FBI. I thought that might be a problem, but it wasn't at all.

"Where are you?" he asked when I told him what had happened.

"I'm not sure. It's on a highway heading north out of Eckersville. About five miles or so. That's all I can tell you."

"You're calling on Manning's phone, right?"

"Yes."

"Leave it on, and we'll track you from that."

"How long will it take you to get people here? I'm a little worried about dealing with the Eckersville police department at the moment."

"I've got a team of agents that should be there in fifteen minutes."

I didn't understand.

"How can you get here so fast?"

"We're already in Eckersville. Sent a team there earlier. Because of Manning."

"Oh, right," I said, thinking about Scott Manning and how Parkman had killed him, too, like he'd killed all those women.

"They just left him in the hospital."

"Hospital?"

"Looks like Scott is going to make it."

It turned out that Parkman had attacked Manning with the same crowbar he used on me, beaten him badly, and left him for dead in a parking lot. But Manning survived and was able to contact the FBI from his hospital bed and tell them what happened.

"He was very worried about you," Wharton said.

"I thought he was dead."

"Manning thought the same about you."

"My God!"

"Hang on, Carlson. This is almost over. The cavalry is on the way."

*   *   *

It took a while to sort everything out.

Parkman, as he said he would, denied it all at first. Denied being The Wanderer. Denied taking part in any of the murders. Denied abducting me or threatening my life. He said I'd grabbed his gun, forced him to drive there, and claimed I'd made up the rest of it because I wanted a sensational story.

He didn't know at first Scott Manning was still alive.

And that Manning was talking and backing up everything I said.

But, even after Parkman found that out, he continued to maintain he was the chief of police, a man with an honorable record— not a murderer. He stuck to that story even as they were leading him away to jail.

No one believed him anymore though.

Not even the members of his own police force.

Faron sent a freelance video crew from Indianapolis to shoot a live broadcast with me from the scene. He said that he, Maggie, Brett, and Dani would also fly there and they planned to do the Channel 10 evening newscasts remotely from Eckersville, too. But, before that, I'd do a big "The News Never Stops" segment about everything that would break into regular programming.

And so, once the FBI and other authorities took Parkman away, I started to do my real job.

To be a journalist.

We shot video at the spot in the woods where Parkman had taken me. Then more in the town of Eckersville, at the police station and other places. And, finally, at Becky Bluso's old house.

That's where I was standing when they gave me the cue in my earpiece from New York that we were ready to go live.

And then I was on the air:

> ME: Three decades ago, seventeen-year-old Becky Bluso was murdered here in this small town of Eckersville, Indiana. That brutal crime—unsolved all these years—eventually led to a series of 19 other murders of women around the country since that time. Today the man who committed these 19 murders was finally apprehended, and I was there. He tried to kill me, too. But now he's in jail and can't hurt anyone else.
>
> Law enforcement and we in the media had called him The Wanderer.
>
> But his name is Jeff Parkman, and shockingly, he was the chief of the Eckersville Police Department in this quiet town.
>
> Here's everything that has happened . . .

I then told the whole story. Parkman's murders. His travels around the country to find female victims. His kidnapping of me when I got too close to the truth. His attack on FBI agent Scott Manning. His attempt to kill me. And how I turned the tables on him and was able to help the FBI finally catch the man we'd known as The Wanderer.

While I talked, the station ran pictures of his victims on the screen below me.

All nineteen of them.

Innocent women who Parkman had killed.

Like he almost killed me.

A newsbreak like this generally only ran a minute or two. But this one went on for much longer. It was quickly picked up by the cable news channels and the TV network news shows and went viral on a lot of social media and websites.

At the end of my live broadcast, I said:

> Again, one of the worst serial killers of all time—the man who was known as The Wanderer—has been apprehended. More details about this sensational breaking story will be coming on the Channel 10 evening newscasts tonight at 6 and 11. For now, this is Clare Carlson reporting to you live from Eckersville, Indiana . . . and glad to be alive to do it.

CHAPTER 60

THE EVIDENCE AGAINST Jeff Parkman built quickly in the days afterward.

FBI investigators put together details of his trips that matched up with the locations of many of the murders. A search of Parkman's home and office turned up evidence like pieces of clothing and strands of hair—believed to be "souvenirs" he'd kept from the murders. No one had any doubt that Parkman was The Wanderer, despite his continued denials.

But the biggest thing was the DNA results. Now that they had a suspect in custody, the FBI was able to compare his DNA with the DNA found at the various crime scenes. It was a match.

When he was confronted with this, Parkman finally broke down and confessed. To all nineteen of the murders. And more, too. There were some dead women out there he was responsible for that we didn't know about. Parkman seemed almost eager to boast about the murders once he knew there was no way out for him.

I remembered him telling me that's why he'd first put Marty Barlow on the trail of The Wanderer. "I want people to know about my accomplishments—I want them to know that there's someone out there who is the greatest serial killer ever. Better than Bundy, better than Son of Sam, better than Zodiac or any of the others."

Jeff Parkman had carried out his murderous spree anonymously for three decades. Now he was finally getting a chance to tell the world about it. During hours of questioning, he described in terrifying detail how he stalked, tortured, and then murdered his victims.

The final death toll was still unclear.

But there was no doubt he would achieve his goal: to go down in history as one of the worst serial killers of all time.

*   *   *

Scott Manning made a full recovery from his injuries.

I went to see him in the hospital in Eckersville several times before I went back to New York. The last time his wife was there at his bedside. She knew who I was from the news accounts of everything that happened. I'm not sure if she knew the rest of the story about me and her husband. She was pretty and pleasant and she thanked me profusely for helping to save Scott's life. She squeezed his hand when she said that, then leaned over and kissed him.

I nodded numbly and hoped I didn't give anything away with the expression on my face when she did that. Damn, I had a big problem. My problem was I liked her. I wanted to hate Susan Manning, but I didn't. That made this all so much harder for me. I finally told Manning I'd talk to him when he was out of the hospital and back at FBI headquarters in New York.

I never have though.

I'm not with Gary Weddle anymore either. I told Weddle the truth about what happened between Manning and me in Eckersville. I realize that probably wasn't the smartest thing to do, but I needed to. I couldn't start a whole relationship with him with this on my conscience. He was hurt, but I think he would have continued seeing me anyway. Except I knew I couldn't do that. Not now. I'd realized that ever since I slept with Manning. I was still in love with Scott Manning. I knew that for a fact, even though I was also pretty sure nothing would ever come of it. I wasn't in love with Gary Weddle. I liked Weddle. I liked him a lot. But I wasn't in love with him. He finished up his consulting job with the station and then disappeared from my life, too.

What the hell was wrong with me anyway? Why could I never settle down in a healthy relationship with a good guy like Gary Weddle? Why did I always have to go after the one I couldn't have? Why couldn't I be satisfied with a good guy who I liked? Well, maybe for the same reason none of my marriages ever lasted either.

*   *   *

Terri Hartwell made one last try to get me to join her campaign team for mayor.

Her connection with the long-ago murder of Becky Bluso—albeit an innocent one—didn't hurt her popularity. In fact, her poll numbers went up. Like they did after her involvement in exposing the payoff scam between her top aide, Chad Enright, and Morelli. She was widely expected to be the next mayor of New York City.

"Remember what I told you that first day we met in my office?" Hartwell said to me. "You're a tough lady. I'm a tough lady. We're a couple of tough ladies, you and me, Clare. Let's work together. We'd make a helluva team. Look what we've accomplished so far. Imagine what we could do if we were running this city."

I thanked her again for the offer, but I told her I already had a job.

The only job I ever wanted.

I was a journalist.

* * *

At Channel 10, we worked The Wanderer story and all the follow-ups for days after Parkman's arrest.

I did most of the initial on-air coverage. In addition to an inside look at the investigation as it proceeded, I went back and interviewed family members and loved ones of the nineteen women who had had their lives snuffed out by Parkman. I've always had mixed feelings about doing stories like that. On the one hand, it's usually good television and delivers ratings. And, I suppose, it's a way to remember the dead. But it also opens up a lot of wounds and terrible memories for the people I was interviewing. Wounds and memories that they thought they'd put behind them a long time ago.

I told the definitive story on the Becky Bluso murder, too. About the troubled young man named Dale Blanchard who had killed her in a fit of rage. About how Blanchard had heroically saved another man's life in Iraq months later. And about Blanchard's deathbed confession of the murder to that same man.

Believe it or not, Russell Danziger thanked me later for telling the secret he had held onto for so long. He also thanked me for everything I had done for Terri Hartwell. And Danziger even said I should reach out to him if I ever needed his help on anything. I think Russell Danziger actually liked me. Go figure.

But soon I began ceding the story over to the rest of the news team to do the reporting and broadcasts.

I had plenty of other things to do. Brett and Dani were back to screaming at each other off camera about their sex lives; Jack

Faron kept telling me to be a news director again and stop playing reporter on the big stories; and everyone was uptight about the big ratings sweeps week coming up for our newscasts.

In other words, everything was back to normal.

*   *   *

There was still one loose end though.

Who killed Marty Barlow?

Morelli had insisted he didn't do it, and the authorities believed him. Parkman, who admitted to everything else, also said he knew nothing about it. So there was no obvious connection to either the corruption scandal or The Wanderer killings. In the end, the murder of Barlow seemed to be what it always appeared to be for police at the beginning. A senseless, random crime in New York City. Marty had simply been in the wrong place at the wrong time. And it cost him his life. As everyone always said, a lot of the murders in this city never make any sense. And, after a while, we stopped caring.

But I still cared.

I still wanted some answers about Marty.

And, so, one day—just for the hell of it—I went back to the eight buildings he had gone to investigate that started all of this.

Things were sure different at all the locations now. The elevator had been fixed at the Lower East Side, and the building's new owner was dealing with many of the other tenant problems that had been neglected for so long, people there told me. The pizza parlor was still in business, but under new management—and the long lines of double-parked cars were nowhere to be seen. The gambling operation and other illegal activities were gone from the other spots that I visited—replaced by hair salons, coffee shops, and other familiar-looking stores. The last place I went back to was the kinky sex dungeon on East 23rd Street. It was now a childcare center.

This was all nice, but I knew the mob influence in New York City was not gone. It had simply moved to other locations because of what I'd done. That was confirmed when I asked someone at the day care center if they knew the business that used to be run out of their building. They told me they did, and they'd heard the woman there then—Rebecca Crawley—had moved her operation to a warehouse building on East 36th Street, north of Herald Square.

I decided to go there and visit Rebecca Crawley again. Mostly because I couldn't think of anything else to do. But this was the story Marty had started working on before he died, even before The Wanderer. Maybe there was something there that could give me some answers about his death.

So that's exactly what I did.

And when I got to Rebecca Crawley's place, I found out what I'd been missing all along.

Michelle Wincott was there.

Marty's granddaughter.

I almost didn't recognize Michelle at first. She was wearing a wig, lots of makeup, and dressed in leather from head to toe. She was as shocked to see me as I was to see her in that place.

"You work here?" I asked.

"Yes."

"What about being an actress?"

"I lied. I couldn't make a living doing that. I didn't want to admit that to anyone. Certainly not my father."

Suddenly, it all made sense. Marty had gone back to the sex dungeon that last night looking for more information on the corruption story. He'd accidentally run into his granddaughter, just as I did. And then something had happened between them. Something totally senseless. Like so many murders turn out to be.

"He just started laughing," Michelle Wincott would say later in her confession, sobbing as she did so. "Laughing about what my father would say if he knew I was working as a hooker. All I ever wanted was for my father to love me. Now I knew that could never happen if he found out the truth. Afterward, I waited outside the house for my grandfather to come home. I was going to beg him not to say anything, to keep this a secret. But when he got there . . . I don't know what happened. I guess I went crazy for a few seconds. I picked up a heavy tree branch that had fallen onto the street and I hit him over the head with it. I didn't want him to die. I loved him. I just didn't want my father to know. I didn't want to disappoint him again."

No, it wasn't me who turned Michelle Wincott into the police. I didn't want to do that. I didn't want to ruin her life. I knew Marty had loved her, and she loved him, too. But she insisted on confessing to the authorities. She'd been living with the guilt and said she needed to try to make things right. Sort of like Dale Blanchard needed to do a long time ago.

I was never exactly sure why Marty went back to the BDSM dungeon that last night after he'd seemingly stopped working on the corruption story to focus on the hunt for The Wanderer. But Marty had gone to that community board meeting earlier in the day where the topic of building corruption had come up. I think he probably got curious about it again and went back to check out those buildings where he'd been before. That was Marty. He could never stop working on a story until it was finished. This time it cost him his life.

*   *   *

One day, not long afterward, I went to the Sunrise Coffee Shop on Madison Avenue, Marty's favorite place in the city. It was the spot where I'd promised to meet up with him when I could find time. Except I never did.

I sat now in a booth by the window where I knew Marty used to like to sit and people watch on the street outside. I ordered two cups of coffee. One of them I pushed to the other side of the table, the spot Marty would have sat in if he were with me. It was a silly ritual, I knew that. But somehow it made me feel better.

Marty used to say no story ever works out exactly the way you expect. "You pull on a thread at the beginning, and you see where it takes you," he told me once back when I was a young reporter at that newspaper in New Jersey. "Sometimes it takes you places you don't want to go," Marty said. "But that's what being a journalist is all about. Following the facts, no matter what. And then you report the story, you report the facts, whatever they turn out to be. That's the job of a journalist."

I drank my coffee and thought about everything that had happened since that last meeting in the Channel 10 offices when Marty accused me of only being interested in "fake news" these days instead of being a real journalist. He'd given me a chance that day to work on a real news story again with him. I didn't take it. Not then. But, in the end, I'd done my job as a journalist. The kind of a journalist that Marty had taught me to be.

I like to think that Marty would have been proud of me.

CHAPTER 61

I DEAL IN lies for a living. Big lies. Little lies. My job at Channel 10 News is to catch people in their lies and reveal these lies to the world.

I have wrapped myself in the cloak of truth for a long time. As a journalist and as a person. Proclaiming loudly that I believe in the truth. I tell the truth at all times. I expose anyone who doesn't tell the truth.

But everyone lies.

Including me.

The thing about lying is it gets easier the more you do it. And a lie—any lie, no matter how small it starts out—becomes a bigger and bigger one the more a person repeats the lie. Eventually, before we even realize it, we find ourselves caught up in an endless cycle of dishonesty and discretion.

I've been living a lie for most of my adult life.

A big lie.

It was finally time for me to tell the truth.

*   *   *

I drove to Linda Nesbitt's house in Westchester, Virginia, and knocked on the front door. I hadn't told her I was coming, but she answered on the first knock. I had a feeling she had been waiting for me to show up again. I didn't want to waste any time with what I had to say to her; I'd wasted too much time already. I put the lead right in the first paragraph as any good newswoman would.

"I'm not just a reporter," I blurted out to her. "I'm your biological mother. I gave you up for adoption when you were born."

"I know," she said.

I stared at her.

"How did you figure that out?"

"Hey, my mother is a hotshot investigative reporter. I guess I inherited some of those genes. Maybe I could be a reporter, too, huh?"

"Why didn't you say anything before this?"

"I figured you'd tell me when you were ready."

Then she hugged me.

"Hello, Mom, glad I finally met you," she whispered into my ear.

I hugged her back as tightly as I could.

And I cried.

I cried all those tears I'd been holding back for so long.

Now there was just one more thing I needed to do.

I told her all about it—and she agreed.

* * *

At 6 p.m., the pulsating theme music signaled the beginning of another Channel 10 newscast. Brett and Dani at the anchor desk went through the top headlines of the day. "But first, we have a special report from our news director, Clare Carlson," Brett said. And then I was on screen.

"I won a Pulitzer Prize as a newspaper reporter for my coverage of the Lucy Devlin disappearance story," I told the viewers. "And then here at Channel 10, I reported two years ago on what authorities said was the discovery of Lucy's body and the confirmation of her death.

"But I have never told you the whole truth about me and about Lucy Devlin.

"That's what I'm going to do tonight.

"Twenty-eight years ago, I gave birth to a baby girl . . ."

AUTHOR'S NOTE

Like my earlier Clare Carlson books, *The Last Scoop* is a "ripped from the headlines" mystery inspired by sensational crime stories that I covered as a journalist.

I've spent a lot of years working in the New York City media. I was metropolitan editor of the *New York Post*; managing editor of the *New York Daily News*; news editor of *Star* magazine; and a managing editor at NBC News. I wound up covering most of the big news stories of recent years: crimes like Son of Sam, O.J., Etan Patz, Casey Anthony, and Jodi Arias; political sex scandals like Bill Clinton, Gary Hart, John Edwards, and, of course, Donald Trump; and celebrity deaths like John Lennon, Michael Jackson, and even Elvis.

No way some of this real-life news isn't going to find its way into my fiction!

And so when people ask me where I get the ideas for writing crime novels, I tell them, "Hey, I just go to work in the newsroom every day."

In *The Last Scoop*, I drew upon two of the most popular types of tabloid stories I covered—serial killers and unsolved cold cases.

The serial killer in the book—the man I call The Wanderer—comes in part from the Son of Sam case, which happened when I was a young journalist. I still remember the day in our newsroom at the *Post* back in 1977 when news broke that police had linked a series of unsolved murders to one killer—the man later known as Son of Sam. It would become the most sensational crime story in New York City history.

But I also have always wondered what would have happened if the police hadn't connected those murders so quickly. Would Son of Sam have continued to murder people without anyone realizing there was a serial killer out there? And would there have come a time when he went public himself because he wanted media attention for his deadly work?

Those were the kind of questions I tried to deal with when I created The Wanderer for *The Last Scoop*.

The first murder in the book, Becky Bluso in Indiana, is also based on memories of a notorious murder case from my youth. The shocking murder of a teenage girl in her home that never made sense and never was solved. In real life, police will probably never get the answers to the crime after so many years. But that's the great thing about writing mystery novels. You get to make up your own answers as I did with Becky Bluso.

And I draw on my journalistic expertise to write about two other tabloid staples here, too: government corruption and the mob. Especially the mob stuff. I've seen so many sensational mob stories—from Crazy Joe Gallo to John Gotti and all the rest. You can't make up stuff any wilder than some of those real-life mob stories I've covered working in New York City.

But the biggest "ripped from the headlines" element I wanted to convey to you in this book is about the people who work in big-city newsrooms.

People like Clare.

And to show you the adrenalin, the insanity, and the pressure these people have to deal with every day on their jobs.

People always ask me if Clare is based on any journalist I worked with in a newsroom. The answer is yes, she is. Plenty of them. Believe me, I've known a lot of Clare Carlsons in my life.

I suppose there's a lot of me in Clare Carlson, too.

Especially the part about how seriously she takes the job of being a journalist and the responsibility that goes with that. She looks upon it as a noble calling, like being a priest or a doctor. And I love the quote from Humphrey Bogart's old movie *Deadline USA* that she uses about being a reporter: "It may not be the oldest profession, but it's the best."

Yep, that's the way Clare Carlson feels about going to work every day in a newsroom.

Me, too.